Praise for

Everlost

"Marvelously inventive . . . and magically beautiful."
—Orson Scott Card, author of *Ender's Game*

"A rip-roaring adventure complete with monsters, blimps, and high-diving horses."
—*SLJ*

"Shusterman elegantly reveals the complexities of his parallel world . . . a funny, irreverent, and memorable adventure."
—*The Bulletin of the Center for Children's Books*

"A unique exploration of life after death."
—*Booklist*

Also by Neal Shusterman

Novels
Bruiser
Challenger Deep
Chasing Forgiveness
The Dark Side of Nowhere
Dry (with Jarrod Shusterman)

Dissidents
Downsiders
The Eyes of Kid Midas
Full Tilt
The Shadow Club
The Shadow Club Rising
Speeding Bullet

The Accelerati Series
(with Eric Elfman)
Tesla's Attic
Edison's Alley

The Antsy Bonano Series
The Schwa Was Here
Antsy Does Time
Ship Out of Luck

The Unwind Dystology
Unwind
UnWholly
UnSouled
UnDivided
UnStrung (an eBook original)

The Skinjacker Trilogy
Everlost
Everwild
Everfound

The Star Shards Chronicles
Scorpion Shards
Thief of Souls
Shattered Sky

The Dark Fusion Series
Dreadlocks
Red Rider's Hood
Duckling Ugly

Story Collections
Darkness Creeping
Kid Heroes
MindQuakes
MindStorms
MindTwisters
MindBenders

Arc of a Scythe
Scythe
Thunderhead
The Toll

Visit the author at storyman.com
and Facebook.com/NealShusterman

EVERLOST

BOOK 1 OF THE SKINJACKER TRILOGY

NEAL SHUSTERMAN

SIMON & SCHUSTER BFYR

NEW YORK LONDON TORONTO SYDNEY NEW DELHI

For my aunt, Mildred Altman, who taught me a love of books and reading

SIMON & SCHUSTER BFYR

An imprint of Simon & Schuster Children's Publishing Division
1230 Avenue of the Americas, New York, New York 10020

Cover design by Lucy Ruth Cummins

Also available in a SIMON & SCHUSTER BFYR hardcover edition
Interior design by Daniel Roode
The text for this book was set in Cochin.
Manufactured in the United States of America
This SIMON & SCHUSTER BFYR paperback edition September 2020
10 9 8 7 6 5 4 3 2 1
The Library of Congress has cataloged the hardcover edition as follows:
Shusterman, Neal.
Everlost/Shusterman, Neal.—1st ed. p. cm.
Summary: When Nick and Allie are killed in a car crash, they end up in Everlost, or limbo for lost souls, where although Nick is satisfied, Allie will stop at nothing—even skinjacking—to break free.
ISBN 978-1-5344-8329-3 (hc)
ISBN 978-1-5344-8328-6 (pbk)
ISBN 978-1-4391-10725-6 (eBook)
[1. Traffic accidents—Fiction. 2. Death—Fiction. 3. Future life—Fiction. 4. Spirit possession—Fiction.] 1. Title.
PZ7.S55987Eve 2006
2005032244

PART ONE

Afterlights

CHAPTER 1

On the Way to the Light . . .

On a hairpin turn, above the dead forest, on no day in particular, a white Toyota crashed into a black Mercedes, for a moment blending into a blur of gray.

In the front passenger seat of the Toyota sat Alexandra, Allie to her friends. She was arguing with her father about how loud the radio should be playing. She had just taken off her seat belt to adjust her blouse.

In the center backseat of the Mercedes, dressed for his cousin's wedding, sat Nick, trying to eat a chocolate bar that had been sitting in his pocket for most of the day. His brother and sister, who sandwiched him on either side, kept intentionally jostling his elbows, which caused the molten chocolate to smear all over his face. As it was a car meant for four, and there were five passengers, there was no seat belt for Nick.

Also on the road was a small piece of sharp steel, dropped by a scrap metal truck that had been loaded to the brim. About a dozen cars had avoided it, but the Mercedes wasn't so lucky. It ran over the metal, the front left tire blew, and Nick's father lost control of the car.

As the Mercedes careened over the double yellow line, into oncoming traffic, both Allie and Nick looked up and saw the other's car moving closer very quickly. Their lives didn't quite flash before them; there was no time. It all happened so fast that neither of them thought or felt much of anything. The impact launched them forward, they both felt the punch of inflating air bags—but at such a high speed, and with no seat belts, the air bags did little to slow their momentum. They felt the windshields against their foreheads, then in an instant, they had each passed through.

The crash of splintering glass became the sound of a rushing wind, and the world went very dark.

Allie didn't know what to make of all this quite yet. As the windshield fell behind her, she felt herself moving through a tunnel, picking up speed, accelerating as the wind grew stronger. There was a point of light at the end of the tunnel, getting larger and brighter as she got closer, and there came a feeling in her heart of calm amazement she could not describe.

But on the way to the light, she hit something that sent her flying off course. She grabbed at it, it grunted, and for an instant she was aware that it was someone else she had bumped—someone about her size, and who smelled distinctly of chocolate.

Both Allie and Nick went spinning wildly, crashing out of the blacker-than-black walls of the tunnel, and as they flew off course, the light before them disappeared. They hit the ground hard, and the exhaustion of their flight overcame them.

Their sleep was dreamless, as it would be for a long, long time.

CHAPTER 2

Arrival in Everlost

The boy had not been up to the road since forever. What was the point? The cars just came and went, came and went, never stopping, never even slowing. He didn't care who passed by his forest on their way to other places. They didn't care about him, so why should he?

When he heard the accident he was playing a favorite game; leaping from branch to branch, tree to tree as high from the ground as he could get. The sudden crunch of steel was so unexpected, it made him misjudge the next branch, and lose his grip. In an instant he was falling. He bounced off one limb, then another and then another, like a pinball hitting pegs. It didn't hurt, all this banging and crashing. In fact he laughed, until he had passed through all the branches, and all that remained was a long drop to the ground.

He hit the earth hard—it was a fall that would have certainly ended his life, had circumstances been different, but instead the fall was nothing more than a quicker way to reach the forest floor.

He picked himself up and got his bearings, already hearing the echoes of commotion up on the road. Cars were screeching to a halt, people were yelling. He hurried off in the direction of the sounds, climbing the steep granite slope that led up to the road. This wasn't the first accident on this treacherous strip of highway; there were many—a few every year. Long ago a car had even left the road, flown like a bird, and landed smack on the forest floor. Nobody came with it, though. Oh, sure there had been people in the car when it had crashed, but they got where they were going even before the boy came to inspect the wreck.

This new wreck was bad. Very bad. Very messy. Ambulances. Fire trucks. Tow trucks. It was dark by the time all the trucks were gone. Soon there was nothing but broken glass and bits of metal where the accident had been. He frowned. The people got where they were going.

Resigned, and a little bit mad, the boy climbed back down to his forest.

Who cared anyway? So what if no one else came? This was *his* place. He would go back to his games, and he'd play them tomorrow and the next day and the next, until the road itself was gone.

It was as he reached the bottom of the cliff that he saw them: two kids who had been thrown from the crashing cars, over the edge of the cliff. Now they lay at the base of the cliff, in the dirt of the forest. At first he thought the ambulances might not have known they were here—but no; ambulances always know these things. As he got closer, he could see that neither their clothes, nor their faces bore any sign of the accident. No rips, no scratches. This was a very good sign! The two seemed to be about fourteen years old—a few years older than he was—and they lay a few feet apart from one another, both curled up like babies. One was a girl with pretty blond hair, the other a boy who looked somewhat Asian, except for his nose, and his light reddish-brown hair. Their chests rose and fell with a memory of breathing. The boy smiled as he watched them, and made his own chest rise and fall in the same way.

As the wind passed through the trees of the forest, not rustling them in the least, he waited patiently for his playmates to awake.

Allie knew she was not in her bed even before she opened her eyes. Had she fallen onto the floor in the middle of the night again? She was such a thrasher when she slept. Half the time she woke up with the sheets tugged off the mattress and wrapped around her like a python.

Her eyes opened to clear sunlight streaming through the trees, which was not unusual except for the fact that there was no window for the light to shine through. There was no bedroom either; only the trees.

She closed her eyes again, and tried to reboot. Human brains, she knew, could be like computers, especially in the time that hung between sleep and wakefulness. Sometimes you said strange things, did even stranger things, and once in a while you couldn't figure out exactly how you got where you got.

She wasn't bothered by this. Not yet. She simply concentrated, searching her memory for a rational explanation. Had they gone camping? Was that it? In a moment the memory of falling asleep beneath the stars with her family would come exploding back into her mind. She was sure of it.

Exploding.

Something about that word made her uneasy.

She opened her eyes again, sitting up this time. There were no sleeping bags, no campsite, and Allie felt strange, like someone had filled her head with helium.

There was someone else a few feet away, sleeping on the ground, knees to chest. A boy with a bit of an Asian look about him. He seemed both familiar and unfamiliar at the same time, as if they had once met, but only in passing.

Then an icy wave of memory flowed over her.

Flying through a tunnel. He was there. He had bumped her, the clumsy oaf!

"Hello!" said a voice behind her, making her jump. She turned sharply and saw another, younger boy sitting cross-legged on the ground. Behind him was a granite cliff that extended high out of sight.

This boy's hair was unkempt, and his clothes were weird—sort of too heavy, too tight, and buttoned way too high. He also had more freckles than she had ever seen on a human being.

"It's about time you woke up," he said.

"Who are you?" Allie asked.

Instead of answering, he pointed to the other kid, who was starting to stir. "Your friend is waking up, too."

"He's not my friend."

The other kid sat up, blinking in the light. He had brown stuff on his face. *Dried blood?* thought Allie. No. *Chocolate.* She could smell it.

"This is freaky," the chocolate boy said. "Where am I?"

Allie stood up and took a good look around. This

wasn't just a grove of trees, it was an entire forest.

"I was in the car, with my dad," Allie said aloud, forcing the scrap of memory to her lips, hoping that would help to drag the rest of it all the way back. "We were on a mountain road, above a forest. . . ." Only this wasn't the forest they had driven past. *That* forest was full of tall dead tree trunks, with stubby, rotting limbs. "A dead forest," Dad had said from the driver's seat, pointing it out. "It happens like that sometimes. A fungus, or some other kind of blight—it can kill acres at a time."

Then Allie remembered the squealing of tires, and a crunch, and then nothing.

She began to get just a little bit worried.

"Okay, what's going on here," she demanded of the freckled kid, because she knew Chocolate Boy was as clueless as she was.

"This is a great place!" Freckle-face said. "It's my place. Now it's your place, too!"

"I've got a place," said Allie. "I don't need this one."

Then Chocolate Boy pointed at her. "I know you! You bumped into me!"

"No—*you* bumped into *me*."

The freckled kid came between them. "C'mon, stop talking about that." He started bouncing excitedly on the balls of his feet. "We got stuff to do!"

Allie crossed her arms. "I'm not doing anything until I know what's going on—" and then it all came crashing back to her with the fury of—

"—A head-on collision!"

"Yes!" said Chocolate Boy. "I thought I dreamed it!"

"It must have knocked us out!" Allie felt all over her body. No broken bones, no bruises—not even a scratch. How could that be? "We might have a concussion."

"I don't feel concussed."

"Concussions are unpredictable, Chocolate Boy!"

"My name's Nick."

"Fine. I'm Allie." Nick tried to wipe the chocolate from his face, but without soap and water it was a lost cause. They both turned to the freckled kid. "You got a name?" Allie asked.

"Yeah," he said, looking down. "But I don't have to tell you."

Allie ignored him, since he was starting to become a nuisance, and turned to Nick. "We must have been thrown clear of the accident, and over the cliff. The branches broke our fall. We have to get back up to the road!"

"What would you want to go up there for?" the freckled kid asked.

"They'll be worried about us," Nick said. "My parents are probably searching for me right now."

And then suddenly Allie realized something. Something she wished she hadn't.

"Maybe they won't," she said. "If the accident was bad enough . . ."

She couldn't say it aloud, so instead, Nick did.

"We could be the only survivors?"

Allie closed her eyes, trying to chase the very idea away. The accident had been bad, there was no question about it, but if *they* came through it without a scratch, then her father must have as well, right? The way they made cars nowadays, with crumple zones, and air bags everywhere. They were safer than ever.

Nick began to pace, losing himself in morbid thoughts of doom. "This is bad. This is really, really bad."

"I'm sure they're all okay," Allie said, and repeated it, as if that would make it so. "I'm sure they are."

And the freckled boy laughed at them. "The only survivors!" he said. "That's a good one!" This was no laughing matter. It made both Nick and Allie furious.

"Who are you?" Allie demanded. "Why are you here?"

"Did you see the accident?" Nick added.

"No," he said, choosing to answer Nick's question only. "But I heard it. I went up to look."

"What did you see?"

The kid shrugged. "Lots of stuff."

"Were the other people in the cars all right?"

The kid turned and kicked a stone, angrily. "Why does it matter? Either they got better, or they got where they were going, and anyway there's nothing you can do about it, so just forget about it, okay?"

Nick threw his hands up. "This is nuts! Why are we even talking to this kid? We have to get up there and find out what happened!"

"Can you just calm down for a second?"

"I am calm!" Nick screamed.

Allie knew there was something . . . off . . . about the whole situation. Whatever it was, it all seemed centered on this oddly dressed, freckle-faced boy.

"Can you take us to your home? We can call the police from there."

"I don't got a telly-phone."

"Oh, that's just great!" said Nick.

Allie turned on him. "Will you just shut up—you're not helping." Allie took a good long look at the freckled boy again. His clothes. The way he held himself. She thought about the things he had said—not so much *what* he said, but the way he had said it. *This is my place . . . now it's your place, too.* If her suspicions were correct, this situation was even weirder than she had thought.

"Where do you live?" Allie asked him.

"Here," was all he said.

"How long have you been 'here'?"

The Freckle-boy's ears went red. "I don't remember."

By now Nick had come over, his frustration defused by what he was hearing.

"And your name?" Allie asked.

He couldn't even look her in the eye. He looked down, shaking his head. "I haven't needed one for a long time. So I lost it."

"Whoa . . . ," said Nick.

"Yeah," said Allie. "Major whoa."

"It's okay," said the boy. "I got used to it. You will, too. You'll see. It's not so bad."

There were so many emotions for Allie to grapple with now—from fear to anger to misery—but for this boy, Allie could only feel pity. What must it have been like to be lost alone in the woods for years, afraid to leave?

"Do you remember how old you were when you got here?" she asked.

"Eleven," he told them.

"Hmm," said Nick. "You still look eleven to me."

"I am," said the boy.

Allie decided to call him Lief, since they had found him in the forest, and he blushed at the name as if she had kissed him. Then Lief led them up the steep stone slope to the road, climbing with a recklessness that not even the most skilled rock climbers would dare show. Allie refused to admit how terrified she was by the climb, but Nick complained enough for both of them.

"I can't even climb a jungle gym without getting hurt!" he complained. "What's the point of surviving an accident, if you're going to fall off a mountain and die?"

They reached the road, but found very little evidence of the accident. Just a few tiny bits of glass and metal. Was that a good sign or bad? Neither Allie nor Nick was sure.

"Things are different up here," Lief said. "Different from the forest, I mean. You better come back down with me."

Allie ignored him and stepped onto the shoulder of the road. It felt funny beneath her feet. Kind of soft and spongy. She had seen road signs before that said SOFT SHOULDER, so she figured that's what it meant.

"Better not stand in one place too long," Lief said. "Bad things happen when you do."

Cars and trucks flew by, one every five or six seconds. Nick was the first one to put up his hands and start waving to flag down help, and Allie joined him a second later.

Not a single car stopped. They didn't even slow down. A wake of wind followed each passing car. It tickled Allie's skin, and her insides as well. Lief waited just by the edge of the cliff, pacing back and forth. "You're not gonna like it up here! You'll see!"

They tried to get the attention of passing drivers, but nobody stopped for hitchhikers nowadays. Standing at the edge of the road simply wasn't enough. When there was a lull in the traffic, Allie stepped over the line separating the shoulder from the road.

"Don't!" warned Nick.

"I know what I'm doing."

Lief said nothing.

Allie ventured out into the middle of the northbound lane. Anyone heading north would have to swerve around her. They couldn't possibly miss seeing her now.

Nick was looking more and more nervous. "Allie . . ."

"Don't worry. If they don't stop, I'll have plenty of time to jump out of the way." After all, she was in gymnastics, and pretty good at it, too. Jumping was not a problem.

A harmonica hum that could only be a bus engine began to grow louder, and in a few seconds a northbound Greyhound ripped around the bend. She tried to lock eyes with the driver, but he was looking straight ahead. *In a second he'll see me,* she thought. *Just one second more.* But if he saw her, he was ignoring her.

"Allie!" shouted Nick.

"Okay, okay." With plenty of time to spare, Allie tried to hop out of the way . . . only she couldn't hop. She lost her balance, but didn't fall. Her feet wouldn't let her. She looked down, and at first it looked like she had no feet. It was a moment before she realized that she had sunk six inches into the asphalt, clear past her ankles, like the road was made of mud.

Now she was scared. She pulled one foot out, then the other, but when she looked up, she knew it was too late; the bus was bearing down on her, and she was about to become roadkill. She screamed as the grill of the bus hit—

—Then she was moving past the driver, through seats and legs and luggage, and finally through a loud grinding engine in the back, and then she was in the open air again. The bus was gone, and her feet were still sinking into the roadway. A trail of leaves and dust swept past her, dragged in the bus's wake.

Did I . . . Did I just pass through a bus?

"Surprise," said Lief with a funny little smile. "You should see the look on your face!"

Mary Hightower, also known as Mary Queen of Snots, writes in her book *Sorta Dead* that there's no easy way to tell new arrivals to Everlost that, technically, they are no longer alive. "If you come across a 'Greensoul,'" as new arrivals are called, it's best to just be honest and hit them with the truth quickly," Mary writes. "If necessary, you have to confront them with something they can't deny, otherwise they just keep on refusing to believe it, and they make themselves miserable. Waking up in Everlost is like jumping into a cold pool. It's a shock at first, but once you're in, the water is fine."

CHAPTER 3

Dreamless

Lief, having been so long in his special forest, never had the chance to read any of Mary Hightower's brilliantly instructional books. Most everything he knew about Everlost, he had learned from experience. For instance, he had quickly learned that dead-spots—that is, places that only the dead can see—are the only places that feel solid to the touch. He could swing from the branches of his dead forest, but once he got past its borders to where the living trees were, he would pass through them as if they weren't there—or, more accurately—like *he* wasn't there.

He didn't need to read Mary Hightower's *Tips for Taps* to know that you only need to breathe when you're talking, or that the only pain you can still feel is pain of the heart, or that memories you don't hold tightly on to are soon lost. He knew all too well about the memory part. The worst part about it was that no matter how much time passed, you always remembered how many things you'd forgotten.

Today, however, he had learned something new. Today, Lief learned how long Greensouls slept before awaking to their new afterlife. He had started a count on the day they arrived, and as of this morning, it was 272 days. Nine months.

"Nine months!" Allie yelled. "Are you kidding me?"

"I don't think he's the kidding type," said Nick, who appeared to be actually shivering from the chilliness of the news.

"I was surprised, too," Lief told them. "I thought you'd never wake up." He didn't tell them how every day for nine months he kicked and prodded them, and hit them with sticks hoping it would jar them awake. That was best kept to himself. "Think of it this way," he said. "It took nine months to get you born, so doesn't it figure it would take nine months to get you dead?"

"I don't even remember dreaming," Nick said, trying hopelessly to loosen his tie.

Now Allie was shaking a bit, too, at this news of her own death.

"We don't dream," Lief informed them. "So you never have to worry about nightmares."

"Why have nightmares," said Allie, "when you're in one?" Could all this be true? Could she really be dead? No. She wasn't. If she was dead she would have made it to the light at the end of the tunnel. Both of them would have. They were only half-dead.

Nick kept rubbing his face. "This chocolate—I can't get it off my face. It's like it's tattooed there."

"It is," Lief said. "It's how you died."

"What?"

"It's just like your clothes," Lief explained. "It's a part of you now."

Nick looked at him like he had just pronounced a life

sentence. "You mean to tell me that I'm stuck with a chocolate face, and my father's ugly necktie until the end of time?"

Lief nodded, but Nick wasn't ready to believe him. He reached for his tie, and tried to undo it with all his strength. Of course, the knot didn't give at all. Then he tried to undo the buttons on his shirt. No luck there, either. Lief laughed, and Nick threw him an unamused gaze.

The more frustrated Nick and Allie became, the harder Lief worked to please them. He brought them to his tree house, hoping it might bring them out their sour mood. Lief had built it himself out of the ghost branches that littered the ground of the dead forest. He showed them how to climb up to the highest platform, and when they got there, he pushed them both off, laughing as they bounced off tree limbs and hit the ground. Then he jumped and did the same, thinking they'd both be laughing hysterically when he got there, but they were not.

For Allie the fall was the most terrifying moment she ever had to endure. It was worse than the crash, for that had been over so quickly, she had no time to react. It was worse than the Greyhound bus passing through her, because that, too, had come and gone in a flash. The fall from the tree, however, seemed to last forever. Each branch she hit jarred her to the core. Jarred her, but didn't hurt her. Still, the lack of pain made it no less terrifying. She screamed all the way down, and when at last she smashed upon the hard earth of the dead forest with a hearty thump, she felt the wind knocked out of her, only to realize there was never actually any wind in her to knock out. Nick landed beside her, disoriented, with eyes spinning like he just came off a carnival ride. Lief landed beside them, whooping and laughing.

"What's wrong with you?" Allie shouted at Lief, and the fact that he still laughed when she grabbed him and shook him made her even angrier.

Allie put her hand to her forehead as if all this was giving her a killer headache, but she couldn't have a headache now, could she, and that just made her all the more aggravated. The rational part of her mind kept wanting to lash out, telling her that this was all a dream, or a misunderstanding, or an elaborate practical joke. Unfortunately her rational mind had no supporting evidence. She had fallen from a treetop and had not been hurt. She had passed through a Greyhound bus. No, her rational mind had to accept the irrational truth.

There are rules here, she thought. Rules, just like the physical world. She would just have to learn them. After all, the rules of the living world must have seemed strange when she was very little. Heavy airplanes flew; the sky turned red at sunset; clouds could hold an ocean full of water, then rain it down on the ground below. Absurd! The living world was no less bizarre than this afterworld. She tried to take some comfort in that, but instead found herself bursting into tears.

Lief saw her tears and backed away. He had little experience with girls crying—or if he did, his experience was, at best, a hundred years old. He found it highly unexpected and disturbing. "What are you crying for?" he asked her. "It's not like you got hurt when you fell from the tree! That's why I pushed you—to show you it wouldn't hurt."

"I want my parents," Allie said. Lief could see that Nick was fighting his own tears, too. This was not at all how Lief had imagined their first waking day would be, but maybe he should have. Maybe he should have realized that leaving one's life behind is not an easy thing to do. Lief supposed he would have missed his parents, too, if he could still remember them. He did remember that he used to miss them, though. It wasn't a good feeling. He watched Nick and Allie, waiting for their tears to subside, and that's when the unthinkable occurred to him.

"You're not going to stay here, are you?"

Nick and Allie didn't answer right away, but that silence was enough of an answer.

"You're just like the others!" he shouted out, before he even realized what he was going to say.

Allie took a step closer to him. "The others?"

Lief silently cursed himself for having said it. He hadn't meant to tell them. He wanted them to think it was just the three of them. That way maybe they would have stayed. Now all his plans were ruined.

"What do you mean others?" Allie said again.

"Fine, leave!" Lief shouted. "I don't care anyway. Go out there and sink to the center of the Earth for all I care. That's what happens, you know. If you're not careful, you sink and sink and sink all the way to the center of the Earth!"

Nick wiped away the last of his tears. "How would you know? All you know is how to swing from trees. You haven't been anywhere. You don't know anything."

Lief bolted away from them. He climbed his tree to

the highest perch, up in the slimmest branches.

They won't leave, he told himself. *They won't leave because they need me. They need me to teach them to climb, and to swing. They need me to show them how to live without being alive.*

Here on his high perch, Lief kept his special things: the handful of precious items that had made the journey with him, crossing from the living world into Everlost. These were the things he had found when he woke up after the flood that had taken his life—ghost things that he could touch and feel. They kept him connected to his fading memories. There was a shoe that had been his father's. He often put his own foot in it, wishing that someday he would grow into it, but knowing that he never would. There was a water-damaged tin picture of himself—the only thing he had to remember what he looked like. It was pocked with so many spots, he couldn't tell which spots were dirt, and which were freckles. In the end, he just assumed they were all freckles. Finally there was a rabbit's foot that was apparently no more lucky for him than it had been for the rabbit. There had once been a nickel, but it had been stolen by the first kid he came across in Everlost—as if money had any value to them anymore. He had found all these items marooned on the small dead-spot he had awoken on, and when he had stepped off the little spot of dried mud, onto living-land, his feet had begun to sink in. The sinking was the first lesson he had learned. You had to keep moving or down you went. He had kept moving, afraid to stop, afraid to sleep. Crossing from towns to woods, and back to towns, he had come to understand his ghostly nature, and although it terrified him, he endured it, for what else could he do?

Why was he a ghost and not an angel? Why did he not go to heaven? That's what the preacher always said: Heaven or hell—those were the only choices. So then why was he still here on Earth?

He had asked himself these questions over and over until he tired of asking, and just accepted. Then he had found the forest; a huge dead-spot large enough to make his home. It was a place where he could actually feel the trees—a place where he did not sink—and he knew in his heart that the good lord had provided him with this forest. It was his personal share of eternity.

As for these new kids, they would spend forever with him. It was the design of things. They might leave now, but once they saw what the rest of the world was like, they would come back to him, and he would build them their own platforms in the tree, and they would laugh together, and they would talk and talk and talk to make up for all the years Lief had existed in silence.

Down below, Nick had watched Lief climb up the tree until he disappeared into the lush canopy. Nick found himself trying to balance his feelings of sympathy for the boy with his own confused feelings about being dead. He felt queasy, and wondered how that could be if, technically, he didn't actually have a stomach anymore. The thought just made him even more queasy.

"Well," said Allie. "This sucks."

Nick let loose an unexpected guffaw, which made Allie giggle. How could they be laughing at a time like this?

"We have some decisions to make," said Allie.

Nick didn't exactly feel in a decision-making frame of mind. "You think it's possible to have post-traumatic stress disorder if you're dead?" he asked. Allie had no answer.

Nick looked at his hands, which were smudged with everlasting chocolate, like his face. He rubbed his arm. If he had no fleshly body, why could he still feel his skin? Or maybe it was just a memory of skin. And what about all the things people told him in life, about what happened to you when you died? Not that he was certain about any of it. His father had been an alcoholic who found God, and it changed his life. His mother was into new age stuff, and believed in reincarnation and crystals. Nick always found himself caught in some uncomfortable in-between. He had faith in faith, though—that is to say, he deeply believed that someday he'd find something to deeply believe. That "someday" never came for Nick. Instead, he wound up here—and this place didn't fit with either of his parents' versions of the afterlife. And then, of course, there was his friend, Ralphy Sherman, who claimed to have had a near-death experience. (According to Ralphy, we're all briefly reincarnated as insects, and the light at the end of the tunnel is actually a bug-zapper.) Well, this place was not purgatory, Nirvana, or any sort of rebirth, and it occurred to Nick that regardless of what people believed, the universe had its own ideas.

"At least now we know there's an afterlife," Allie said, but Nick shook his head.

"This isn't the afterlife," he said. "We never made it to the afterlife. This is kind of an *interlife*. A space between life and death." Nick thought back to that light he had seen at the end of the tunnel, before he had crashed into Allie on the way. That light had been his destination. He still didn't know what was in that light—Jesus, or Buddha, or the light of a hospital delivery room where he would be reborn. Would he ever know?

"What if we're lost here forever?" he asked.

Allie scowled at him. "Are you always so full of gloom and doom?"

"Usually."

Nick looked at the forest around them. Was this such a bad place to spend eternity? It wasn't exactly paradise, but it was kind of pretty. The trees were full and lush. They'd never lose their leaves. He wondered if the weather of the living world could still affect him. If not, then it wouldn't be so bad staying here. Certainly the boy they called Lief had adjusted, so couldn't they? But then, that wasn't the real question. The question was, did they want to?

Lief waited in his tree house, and soon they climbed up to him, as he knew they would. He quickly hid his special things as Nick and Allie reached the platform, both of them huffing and puffing, as if they were out of breath.

"Stop that," he told them. "You're not out of breath, you just think you are, so stop it."

"Lief, please, this is important," Allie said. "We need you to tell us about the 'others' you were talking about before."

There was no sense trying to hide it now, so he told them what he knew. "They come through my forest every once in a while. Other kids on their way places. They never stay long—and none have come through here for years."

"Where do they go?"

"Anywhere. They're always running. They're always running from the McGill."

"The what?"

"The McGill."

"Is that a grown-up?"

Lief shook his head. "No grown-ups here. Only kids. Kids and monsters."

"Monsters!" said Nick. "That's great. That's wonderful. I'm so glad I asked."

But Allie wasn't shaken. "There are no such things as monsters," she told Lief.

He looked to Allie, then to Nick, then back to Allie again.

"There are here."

On the absence of adults in Everlost, Mary Hightower writes: "To date no grown-up has ever been documented to cross into Everlost. The reason is quite obvious when you stop to think about it. You see, adults, being the way they are, never get lost on the way to the light no matter how hard they get bumped, simply because adults always think they know exactly where they're going, even if they don't, and so they all wind up going somewhere. If you don't believe me, ask yourself this: Have you ever seen a grown-up get into a car so they could go 'nowhere in particular'?"

On the presence of monsters, Mary Hightower is curiously silent.

CHAPTER 4

A Coin on its Edge

Night had fallen over the woods, and the three dead kids sat on the highest platform of the tree house bathed in an unnaturally bright moonlight that truly made them look like ghosts. It took a while for Nick and Allie to realize that the moon wasn't out that night.

"Great," said Nick, not thinking it was great at all. "Just what I always wanted—to be a glow-in-the-dark ghost."

"Don't call us ghosts," Allie said.

Nick simply didn't have the patience for Allie's issues with word choice. "Face it, that's what we are."

"'Ghost' implies a whole lot of things that I am NOT. Do I look like Casper to you?"

"Fine," said Nick. "We're not ghosts, we're Undefined Spectral Doohickies. USDs. Are you happy now?"

"Well that's just stupid."

"We're *Afterlights*," said Lief. They both turned to him. "The others who pass through—that's what they call us, on account of how we glow in the dark—in the daytime, too, if you look close enough."

"Afterlights," repeated Allie. "See, I told you we weren't ghosts."

Allie and Lief began to talk about monsters again, and, as far as Nick was concerned, this was a conversation he would just as well stay out of. Instead, Nick decided to hold his breath, to see if it were true that oxygen was no longer a requirement. Still, he listened.

"If nothing can hurt you here," asked Allie, "why be afraid of the McGill?"

"The McGill knows how to hurt you in other ways. It knows how to make you suffer till the end of time, and it'll do it too, if it gets the chance." Lief's eyes were wide, and he made sweeping gestures with his hands like he was telling a campfire story. "The McGill hates kids that get stuck here—hates the sounds we make. It'll tear out your tongue if it hears you talk, and rip out your lungs if it hears you pretending to breathe. They say the McGill is the devil's own pet hound that chewed through its leash, and escaped. It couldn't make it all the way to the living world, but it made it to here. That's why we have to stay in the forest. It doesn't know about the forest. We're safe here."

Nick could tell that Allie wasn't convinced. He wasn't convinced himself, but in light of their current predicament, suddenly anything seemed possible.

"How do you know all this?" Allie asked.

"The other kids who come through the forest. They tell stories."

"Did these kids actually see the McGill?" Allie asked.

"No one who's ever seen it has escaped."

"How convenient."

Nick released his breath, having held it for ten minutes with no ill effects. "Technically speaking," Nick said, "there have always been monsters, or at least they were called that until people knew something better to call them. The giant squid. The megamouth shark. The anaconda."

"See!" said Lief.

Allie threw Nick a withering look. "Thank you Mr. Google. The next time I need some crucial information, I'll type in some choice keywords."

"Yeah," said Nick. "I'm sure your keywords will all have four letters."

Allie turned back to Lief. "So, is this McGill a giant squid?"

"I don't know," said Lief, "but whatever it is, it's terrible."

"It's made-up," insisted Allie.

"You don't know everything!"

"No," said Allie, "but now I've got all the time in the world, so I eventually will."

Nick had to admit that both Lief and Allie had their points. Lief's stories reeked of exaggeration, but every story had some basis in truth. On the other hand, Allie had a practical view of things.

"Lief," Nick asked, "has anyone who's passed through here ever come back?"

"No," Lief said. "They were all eaten by the McGill."

"Or they found a better place to be," suggested Nick.

"Either we stay here, or we get eaten by the McGill," said Lief. "That's why I'm staying here."

"What if there's another choice?" said Nick. "If we're not alive, but we're not quite dead, then maybe . . ." He pulled a coin out of his pocket—one of the few things that had come with him, along with those overly formal clothes he wore. "Maybe we're like coins standing on their edge?"

Allie considered this. "Meaning?"

"Meaning, we might be able to shake things up a little, and find a way to come up heads."

"Or tails," suggested Allie.

"What are you *talking* about?" said Lief.

"Life and death." Nick flipped the coin, and slapped it down on the back of his palm, keeping it covered with his other hand, so none of them could see how it had landed. "Maybe—just maybe—we can find a way out of here. A way into the light at the end of the tunnel . . . or maybe even a path back to life."

It seemed the trees themselves held the thought, sifting it through their boughs, giving it resonance.

"Could that be possible?" Allie asked, and looked to Lief.

"I don't know," he told them.

"So the question is," said Nick, "where do we go to find out?"

"There's only one place I want to go," said Allie. "Home."

Nick instinctively sensed that going home wouldn't be a good idea—but just like Allie, he wanted to go home. He had to find out if his family had survived, or if they "got where they were going." They were in Upstate New York, though; it was far from home.

"I'm from Baltimore," Nick said. "How about you?"

"New Jersey," Allie said. "The southern tip."

"Okay. Then we head south from here, and keep an eye

out for others who can help us. Someone has got to know how to get out of this place . . . one way, or another."

Nick put his coin away, and they all began to talk about life, death, and a way out of this place in-between. None of them had noticed on which side the coin had landed.

Allie had always been a goal-oriented girl. It was both her strength and her weakness. She had a drive to completion that always got things done, but it also made her inflexible, and stubborn. Even though she adamantly denied being stubborn, she knew deep down it was true.

The coin-on-its-edge business might have been fine for Nick, but Allie was not at ease with all this metaphysical talk. Going home, however—*that* was a goal she could buy into. Whether she was dead or half-dead, whether she was spirit or wraith, didn't matter. It was too unpleasant to think about. Better to put on the blinders, and keep her thoughts fully focused on the house where she had spent her life. She would go back there. And once she was there, all things would sort themselves out. She had to believe that, or she would lose her mind.

Lief had his own unique way of seeing things, too—and his vision began and ended with the forest. He wouldn't be going with them, because for Lief, being alone in his safe haven was better than having company in the big bad world of the living.

As for the snowshoes, they were Nick's idea, although Allie was the one who figured out how to make them, and Lief was the one with the practical know-how to actually do it with twigs and strips of bark. Allie thought they looked kind of goofy, but after all it wasn't like they'd be posing for a fashion show any time soon.

"What's the point," Lief had said when Nick first mentioned the idea of snowshoes. "It's not going to snow for months, and we move right through snow anyway."

"They're not for snow," Nick had told him. "It's so we can walk on living-world roads without sinking in. We'll be able to move faster if we don't have to pluck our feet out of the asphalt after every step."

"So then they're road-shoes, not snowshoes," Lief said, then went about tying twigs together with strips of bark. When he had finished the shoes, he handed them to Nick and Allie. "Aren't you afraid at all?" he asked. "Aren't you afraid of what's out there? All the things you couldn't see when you were alive? Evil spirits? Monsters? I've been waiting forever for you to come. I prayed for you, did you know that? God hears our prayers here. Maybe even better than before, because we're closer to him here." Lief looked at them with big, mournful eyes. "Please don't go."

It tugged at Allie's heart, and brought a tear to her eyes, but she couldn't let her emotions influence this decision. She had to remind herself that Lief wasn't really a little kid. He was an Afterlight who was more than a hundred years old. He had done fine in his forest alone, and there was no reason to think he wouldn't be fine once they left.

"I'm sorry," Allie told him. "But we can't stay. Maybe once we learn more, we'll come back for you."

Lief put his hands in his pockets and sullenly looked at the ground. "Good luck, then," he said. "And watch out for the McGill."

"We will."

He stood there for a moment more, then said, "Thank you for giving me a name. I'll try to remember it." Then he climbed away, disappearing high in his tree house again.

"South," said Nick.

"Home," said Allie, and they climbed out of the forest to face the treacherous unknowns of the living world.

Whether or not careless children actually sink down to the center of the Earth, no one can say for sure. Certainly many do disappear, but as it always seems to happen when no one else is looking, it confounds all attempts to discover where they actually go. The official term for sinking, coined by none other than Mary Hightower herself, is "Gravity Fatigue."

In her groundbreaking book *The Gravity of Gravity*, Mary writes: "Do not believe rumors that children leave Everlost. We are here to stay. Those who can no longer be seen have simply fallen victim to Gravity Fatigue, and are either at, or on their way to the center of the Earth. I imagine the center of the Earth must be a crowded place by now, but perhaps it is the spirits of those of us residing there that keep the Earth alive and green."

CHAPTER 5

Friends in High Places

Mary Hightower was not born with that name. She could no longer remember what her true name was, although she was relatively certain her first name started with an *M*. She took the name Mary because it seemed a proper, motherly name. True, she was only fifteen, but had she lived, she would most certainly have become a mother. And anyway, she was a mother to those who needed one—and there were many.

The name Hightower came because she was the very first who dared to ascend.

That singular bold act of climbing the stairs and staking a claim had earned her a level of respect from others she could not have imagined. They were in awe of her, and many other Everlost children followed her lead. Realizing her position was now high in more ways than one, she decided it was time to share what she knew about Everlost with all Afterlights. Although she had been writing for more than a hundred years, she had only shared it with the small group of younger children she had taken under her wing. But the moment she became Mary Hightower, all that changed.

Now her writings were read by everyone—and what had once been a small group of children in her care had grown into hundreds. She had no doubt she would eventually be a mother to thousands.

Some people thought of her as a god. She had no desire to be a god, but she did like the respect and honor with which she was now treated. Of course, she did have her enemies, and they called her less flattering things, but always from a safe distance.

Today her view from the top floor was magnificent, and sometimes she swore she could see the whole world from here. Yet she knew it was a world that had gone on without her. Far below the traffic of the living world passed, dots of buses and taxis in constant congestion. *Let them go about their business,* she thought. *It means nothing to me. My concern is this world, not theirs.*

A knock at the door drew her attention away from the view. In a moment Stradivarius stepped in, a mousy boy with tufts of tightly curled blond hair.

"What is it, Vari?"

"A Finder's here to see you, Miss Mary. He says he's got something really good."

Mary sighed. Everyone called themselves "Finders" these days. Usually they had never actually found anything of importance. A scrap of paper, a piece of driftwood, maybe. The true Finders had far better goods. They were masters at what they did, and knew all the circumstances that could cause an object to cross over into Everlost. The *true* Finders were few.

"Is this someone we've seen before?"

"I think so," said Stradivarius. "And I think he's got real food!"

This news caught Mary's attention, although she tried not to show Vari how much. She was good at keeping her emotions to herself, but if the Finder truly had food that had crossed over from the living world, it would be hard to contain herself.

"Show him in."

Vari slipped out, and returned with a young man, about thirteen years old, wearing nothing but a bathing suit, its waistband hidden by a pasty root-beer belly. *Well,* thought Mary, *we can't choose the moment and manner of our crossing.* Just as this boy was condemned to travel eternity in a wet bathing suit, she was consigned to the most uncomfortable school dress she owned. The only good thing about it was that it was green and matched her eyes.

"Hi, Miss Mary," the Finder said, respectfully. "You remember me, right?" He smiled, but his mouth stretched much too wide, and he had far too many teeth, giving the impression that she could tip back the top of his head like a boy-shaped cookie jar.

"Yes, I remember you. You're Speedo, from New Jersey. The last time you came, you brought an orange, wasn't it?"

"Grapefruit!" he said, thrilled to be remembered.

It had been a long time since she had last seen this particular Finder, but how could she forget that bathing suit? "What did you bring today?"

His smile stretched even wider. Now he was teeth all the way to his ears. "I brought something fantastic! . . . How would you like a little . . . dessert?"

"Dessert?" said Mary. "Please don't tell me you've brought some of those horrid fortune cookies!"

Clearly Speedo was offended by the suggestion. "I'm a *Finder*, Miss Mary. I know better than to waste your time with fortune cookies. I won't even touch them."

"That's very wise," Mary told him. "And I'm sorry, I didn't mean to insult you. Please—show me what you've got."

He hurried out, and returned with a box that he set on the table. "You may want to sit down," he told her. When she didn't, he removed the lid to reveal something Mary thought she'd never have the good fortune to see again.

"A birthday cake!" There was no sense trying to hide her astonishment—and yes, perhaps she should have sat down, because the sight of it made her feel faint. This wasn't just a slice of bread, or a gnawed chicken bone, as many of the Food-Finders brought; this was an entire birthday cake, round and white, completely unmarred. It said "Happy 5th Birthday Suzie." She had no idea who Suzie was, and she didn't care, because if she was having a birthday, she was one of the living, and the living were not her concern. Mary lifted her finger, then turned to the Finder. "May I?"

"Of course!"

Slowly, carefully she dipped her finger down and touched it to the cake, dragging it over the tiniest edge, feeling the frosting stick to her fingertip. She pulled her finger back and put it to her mouth to taste. The explosion of flavor was almost too much to bear. It took over all her senses, and she had to close her eyes. Vanilla buttercream! So perfectly sweet!

"It's good stuff, huh?" said Speedo. "I was gonna eat it myself, but then I thought my favorite customer might want it." And he added, "That's you," just in case there was any doubt.

Mary grinned and clapped her hands together, as she realized how the Finder had come across the cake. "You wait at birthday parties! How very clever!" Everyone knew the only food that ever crossed over was food lovingly prepared—and it only happened when that lovingly prepared food met an untimely, unlikely end. Where better to find such food than a birthday party, where mothers baked their love right into the batter? "That's brilliant!" Mary said. "Absolutely brilliant."

Speedo looked nervous, and hitched up his bathing suit—a nervous habit, since it was in no danger of falling down. "You're not going to tell anyone, are you? I mean, it's a trade secret. If people knew where I go to find food, everyone else'll do the same, and I'll be out of business."

"I won't tell a soul," Mary said, "but you have to tell me one thing. How many birthday parties did you have to sit through until a cake crossed over?"

He puffed up proudly. "Three hundred and seventy-eight!"

Mary shook her head. "You must be sick of birthdays!"

"Hey, you do what you've gotta do, right?" Then he walked around, talking about the cake like it was a used car he was trying to sell. "It was something to watch, though. That little kid reached up and pulled the whole cake right off the table before they could even put the candles in! It smashed in a heap on the floor, but as you can see, it left a lasting impression on the table where it sat: The ghost of a birthday cake, just waiting for me to take."

Mary looked at the cake and thought about dipping her finger in again, but stopped herself. It would be too easy to keep on eating it and not stop until the last crumb was gone.

"So," said Speedo, "what do you think it's worth?"

"What are you asking?"

"How am I supposed to know what I want, when I don't know what ya got to give?"

Mary considered this. The cake was worth ten times anything she had ever traded for. This, she knew, was this Finder's gold mine, and he might never find another one. He deserved a fair and honest trade.

Mary crossed the large room to a chest of drawers, and pulled out a set of keys. She tossed them to Speedo, and he caught it.

"Keys?" he said. "I've found lots of keys. They ain't no good unless the thing they unlock also crossed into Everlost—and that never happens."

"Something very strange happened in the living world a few weeks ago," Mary told him. "A man sent his car into one end of a carwash, and it never came out the other end. No one has any idea what happened to it."

He looked at her, his face a mix of hope and distrust. "And what *did* happen to it?"

"Sunspots."

"Huh?"

Mary sighed. "If you had read my book, *Everything You Ever Wanted to Know About Vortexes but Were Afraid to Ask*, then you would know that sunspot activity tends to create vortexes from the living world to ours, through which living-world objects sometimes fall."

"Oh," said Speedo. "Sunspots, yeah."

Mary grinned. "In a parking stall at the north side of old Penn Station, you'll find a silver Jaguar. I don't travel much, so I doubt I'd have much use for it. It's yours, if you promise to bring me all of your best food finds."

She could tell that the Finder was excited about the car, but he was a good negotiator. "Well," he said, "I already do have a pretty sweet ride. . . ."

"Yes," said Mary, "you talked about it last time you were here. As I recall, it's more trouble than it's worth, because you can never find a place to park it."

"Yeah," he said, "I guess I could do with something smaller. Okay—it's a deal!" He shook her hand a little too forcefully, finally letting his true excitement show. "A Jag. Wow!" His smile stretched right into the middle of his ears, and Mary simply had to say something about it. Someone had to.

"You should try to remember that the living only have thirty-two teeth."

He looked at her, stunned by her directness.

"Eight incisors," Mary continued, "four canine, eight bicuspids, and twelve molars, if you've got wisdom teeth."

"Oh," he said, getting red in the face.

"It's clear you put a lot of importance on your smile, but when you think about it *too* much, it starts to take over."

Even before he turned to leave, Mary could see the information taking effect; his mouth was shrinking back to sensible proportions.

In her book *Spectral Visions: An Afterlight's Guide to Looking One's Best,* Mary Hightower writes, "If, at times, you find others looking at you strangely, and you don't know why, chances are you're losing touch with your own self-image. That is to say, your body, or your face, is beginning to distort. Remember, we look the way we look only because we remember looking like that. If you forget that your eyes are blue, they may just turn purple. If you forget that human beings have ten fingers, you may suddenly end up with twelve.

"A simple remedy to image-loss is to find a picture that you think resembles you—and if you happened to have crossed over with an actual picture of yourself, all the better. Study the picture. Take in as much detail as you can. Once the image is firmly in your mind, you'll start looking like your old self in no time. Never underestimate the importance of remembering how you looked in life. Unless, of course, you'd rather forget."

CHAPTER 6

Scavengers

Nick remembered everything about his life in perfect detail. How he looked, how his parents looked, what he had for lunch before the miserable accident that landed him here. It troubled him, though, that Lief had become such a blank slate over the years he had been in his forest. If memories aged badly, fading like an old newspaper, how long until Nick suffered the same loss? He didn't want to forget anything.

Having been used to travel at sixty-five miles per hour, Nick's southbound trek with Allie was a slow one. Hiking was not one of Nick's favorite activities. In life it would make his joints ache, and he would invariably stumble on some rude protrusion of nature, and skin a knee. This hike-after-death was no more pleasant. True, the bruises and body aches were gone, but he could not deny how thirsty it made him. Thirsty and hungry. Lief had told them that they no longer needed to eat or drink, anymore than they needed to breathe, but it still didn't stop the craving. "You get used to it," Lief had told them, back in the forest. Nick wasn't sure he ever wanted to get used to an eternity of longing.

They also discovered their spectral bodies didn't actually require sleep, but, as with food, it didn't change the craving for it. Nick and Allie had agreed that they would take time to sleep, as they would have if they were still alive. It was a connection to the world of the living that they did not want to lose. The simple act of resting, however, couldn't be done just anywhere.

"How can we sleep if we sink?" Nick had asked on the first evening. The road-shoes they wore did their job while Nick and Allie walked, keeping them mostly on the surface of the road, but if they stood still for too long, the ground began its slow swallow. They couldn't find a way to keep from sinking that first night, and so they kept walking.

It was on the second day of their journey that the solution came. When the mountain road became treacherous, they began to find odd little patches of asphalt that weren't like the rest of the road. They were solid! The patches were never more than a few feet wide. It was Allie who figured it out when they came across one that was marked with a small white wooden cross.

"I know what this is!" Allie said. "I saw them when we visited Mexico. They put little crosses by the side of the road where people died in car accidents. I never thought to look for it here in the States, but I'll bet there are people who do it here, too."

"So the passing of a spirit must leave a permanent mark on the spot where it happened, turning it into a dead-spot!" Nick had to admit it was an exciting, if somewhat morbid discovery.

They rested on one of the so-called dead-spots, close

together, because the spot was so small, and as they basked in the light of their own glows, they allowed themselves the luxury of small talk. They discussed all those subjects that didn't matter much in the larger scheme of things, like what music they liked, and who they thought won the World Series during their nine-month transition. Their conversation took a sober turn, as late night conversations often do.

"When I get home," Allie said, "I'm going to find a way to make them all see me."

"But what if they never see you?" Nick said. "What if they just keep on living their lives like you're not even there?"

"That's not gonna happen."

"Why not?" said Nick. "Because you say so? That's not how the world works."

"How do you know? You don't know how this world works any more than I do."

"Exactly. That's why I say we learn more about it before we go home. We've got to find other ghosts with more experience."

"Other *Afterlights*," Allie corrected, still refusing to admit she was a ghost.

The thought made Nick look at his hands and arms, studying his own peculiar incandescence; his gentle Afterlight glow. The lines that ran across his palms were still there. He could see his fingerprints—but perhaps that was just because fingerprints are what he expected to see. He wondered if he would still look the same if he had made it all the way to the light at the end of the tunnel, or if the memory of flesh would completely dissolve into the glow once he reached his final destination—a destination where his family might already be.

"We have to accept that there may be nobody to go home to," Nick reminded Allie.

Allie pursed her lips. "Maybe for you, but it was just my dad and me in our car. Mom stayed home because my sister was sick."

"Doesn't it even bother you that your dad might not have made it?"

"He made it somewhere," Allie said, "which is more than I can say for us. It's like Lief said—everyone else in the accident either survived or they got where they were going—which means that either way they're sort of okay."

Allie did have a point; it was some comfort to know that there truly was some place they were all ultimately going—that the end wasn't the end. Even so, the thought of his whole family making that mysterious journey all at the same terrible time . . . Then something occurred to Nick. "I didn't see any dead-spots where the accident happened. We got thrown into the forest, but there were no dead-spots on the road!"

"We weren't looking for dead-spots then," Allie pointed out, but Nick chose to believe there were none. It was better than the alternative.

"Where were you going that day?" Nick asked.

Allie took her time before she answered him. "I can't remember. Isn't that funny?"

"I'm starting to forget things, too," Nick admitted. "I don't want to forget their faces."

"You won't," she said—and although there was no evidence to back it up, Nick chose to believe that, too.

* * *

By the third day, they had passed out of the mountains, and the highway became wider and straighter. They were still in Upstate New York, many miles away from their respective destinations. At this rate it would take weeks, maybe months to get there.

They passed town after town, and soon learned how to easily identify dead-spots. They were different from the living places. First of all, there was a clarity to them—they were in sharper focus, and the colors were far more vibrant. Secondly, when you stood in one of those spots, there was a certain sense of well-being—a sense of belonging—as if the ghost places were the true living places, and not the other way around.

It was that fundamental grayness of the living world that struck more deeply than any chill. Although they wouldn't speak it aloud, it made both Nick and Allie long for the lush and comforting beauty of Lief's forest.

At dusk, on the fifth day, they found a nice patch of solid ground, beneath a big sign that said, WELCOME TO ROCKLAND COUNTY! Leaves poked through the pavement, lush and green to their eyes, eternally unaffected by the changing of seasons. The spot was large enough for both of them to stretch out and sleep.

"I'm tired of sleeping every night," Nick said. "We don't need it. We don't get tired," and then he said the real reason why he didn't want to sleep. "I don't like not dreaming."

Allie felt the same way, but didn't want to say anything about it. Once, many years ago, her appendix had burst, and she had gone under general anesthesia. It was a strange sensation. She started to breathe in the anesthetic, and boom, she was out. Then suddenly she was awake again, and it was all over. There was just a hiccup of time, some groggy confusion, and she was back, with an ache in her side and some stitches. It was like . . . not existing. Sleep here was the same way.

"We sleep because we can," she told Nick. "Because it reminds us of what it's like to be alive."

"How can eight hours of death remind us of being alive?"

Allie had no answer for him, only that it felt right. It felt natural, and in their unnatural state, anything that felt natural was a good thing. In the end Nick stopped his grumbling, and lay down. "I'll lie here, but I'm not going to sleep. I'll stay awake and watch the stars."

The stars, however, were not sufficiently exciting to keep him awake. In fact, they were sedating. He fell asleep before Allie did, leaving her to ponder their predicament. What if she got home, and her parents weren't there? What if her father had died in the accident, and her mother had moved away? She wouldn't be able to ask anyone about it, she'd have no way of finding out. She was thankful when the anesthetic sleep of Everlost finally overtook her.

The ambush came without warning in the middle of the night.

Nick and Allie opened their eyes to four stern, glowing faces looking down on them. In an instant they were grabbed and hauled to their feet, roughed up and manhandled. Allie tried to scream, but a large hand covered her mouth. A hand like that of a monster. Only these weren't monsters; these were boys no older than she.

"Nick!" she called. But Nick was too busy fighting off two boys who were struggling to hold him as well.

"What's your problem?" Nick shouted. "Who are you? What do you want?"

"We ask the questions," said the boy who was apparently in charge. He was smaller than the rest, but clearly the toughest of the lot. He wore baggy knickerbockers, not much different from Lief's, and from his lip dangled a cigarette that never got smaller and never went out. But by far the strangest thing about him was his hands. They were the size of a man's hands, big and knobby, and when he curled them into fists, they seemed as large as boxing gloves.

"I think they're *Greensouls*, Johnnie-O," said one kid with a weird mop of candy-apple-red hair that made him look like a Raggedy Andy doll. "A week old, maybe less."

"I can see that," Johnnie-O said. "I'm not stupid, I know a Greensoul when I see one."

"We're Afterlights," Nick shouted out, "just like you, so leave us alone."

Johnnie-O laughed. "Of course you're Afterlights, idiot. What we're saying is that you're new arrivals. Greensouls. Get it?"

"They might still got stuff," said Raggedy Andy. "Greensouls always got stuff."

"Welcome to Everlost," Johnnie-O said in a voice that wasn't welcoming at all. "This here's my territory, and you gots to pay me for passage."

Allie gave the boy holding her a punch in the face to

get him to let go. "Is this how you always greet visitors?" Allie said.

Johnnie-O took a suck on his cig. "Visitors ain't always friendly."

Nick shrugged off the two boys who were holding him. "We don't have anything to pay you with."

"Yeah, so I guess you'll just have to kill us," Allie said snidely, and added, "Oh, sorry, guess you can't."

"Turn their pockets," Johnnie-O ordered, and his goons reached into Nick and Allie's pants pockets and turned them inside out. Mostly they got lint, but Nick had a couple of things he had forgotten were in there. There was that old coin, which must have been a nickel, although the face had worn off. The tough kids weren't interested in it, and flicked it back at him. He caught it and returned it to his pocket.

It was the other object in Nick's pocket that got their attention.

"Look at this," said a funny-looking kid with dark purple lips, like he had died while sucking on a grape jawbreaker. He held up a hard little object that had fallen out of Nick's pocket, which Nick quickly recognized as a piece of what is commonly referred to as "ABC" gum, wrapped up in its original wrapper. His mother always complained that he left his chewed gum in his pockets and it got all over the clothes in the wash.

The purple-mouthed kid held the hard, cold wad of gum and looked over at Johnnie-O, hesitating.

"Hand it over," said Johnnie-O. His voice was commanding for a boy of his size. He opened up his huge, beefy hand.

Still Purple-puss hesitated. "We can cut it into pieces," he suggested.

"I said hand it over." Johnnie-O held his upturned palm right before the boy. You didn't say no to a palm that big. Purple-puss gingerly put the small, round wad into Johnnie-O's hand.

"Next time I have to ask you twice," Johnnie-O said, "you're going down."

Purple-puss's Adam's apple bobbed nervously, like a walnut in his throat. Or a jawbreaker.

Then Allie and Nick watched in utter disbelief as Johnnie-O peeled the paper from the sticky piece of gum and popped it in his mouth.

"Oh, gross," said Nick.

In response, Raggedy Andy punched him in the stomach. Nick doubled over out of reflex, only realizing a second later that it didn't hurt. *How annoying it must be for bullies*, he thought, *to not be able to inflict pain*. This place must be a bully's version of hell.

Johnnie-O worked the gum until it was soft again. He closed his eyes for a moment as he chewed. "A lot of flavor still left in this one," he said. "Cinnamon." Then he looked at Nick. "You always waste your gum like that?" he said. "I mean, when you were living?"

Nick only shrugged. "I chew until I can't taste it anymore."

Johnnie-O just kept on chewing. "You ain't got no tastebuds."

"Can I have it next?" said Purple-puss.

"Don't be gross," Johnnie-O said.

Allie laughed at that, and Johnnie-O threw her a sharp

gaze, followed by a second gaze that was more calculated.

"You're not the prettiest thing, are you?" he said.

Her lips pulled tightly together in anger, and she knew that made her less attractive, which only made her angrier. "I'm pretty enough," she said. "I'm pretty in my own way." Which was true. No one had ever called Allie a ravishing beauty, but she knew very well that she wasn't unattractive, either. What made her madder still was that she had to justify herself and the way she looked to this big-handed creep, who chewed other people's used gum. "On a scale of one to ten," Allie said, "I suppose I'm a seven. But you, on the other hand, I estimate you to be about a three." She could tell that it stung, mainly because it was true.

"Seven's not worth lookin' at," he said. "And the way I see it, we're not going to have to look at each other much longer, are we?"

"What's that supposed to mean?" said Nick, who did not like the sound of it any more than Allie did.

Johnnie-O crossed his arms, making his oversized hands seem even larger compared to his small chest. "A single piece of gum don't buy you passage over my territory," he said. He turned to Nick. "Which means you gots to be my servant now."

"We'll do no such thing," said Allie.

"I wasn't talkin' to you. We don't need the likes of you around here."

"Well," said Allie, "I'm not going without him."

And the others laughed.

"Oh," said Raggedy Andy, "I don't think he'll want to go where you're going."

Allie didn't quite know what that meant, but even so, she started to panic.

"Grab her," Johnnie-O ordered his comrades.

Allie knew she had to think of something quick, and so she said the first thing that came to mind. "Stay away from me or I'll call the McGill!"

That stopped them dead in their tracks.

"What are you talkin' about?" said Johnnie-O, not as sure of himself as he was a second ago.

"You heard me!" Allie yelled. "The McGill and I have a special arrangement. It comes when I call it. And I feed it bad little thieves whose hands are bigger than their brains."

"She's lying," said another kid, who hadn't spoken until now, probably because he had such a nasty, squeaky voice.

Johnnie-O looked all irritated. "Of course she's lying." He looked at Allie and then back at the quiet kid. "So how do you know she's lying?"

"She's a Greensoul—probably just crossed over," the squeaky kid said, "which means she hasn't even seen the McGill."

"Besides," said Purple-puss, "no one sees the McGill and lives."

"Except for her," said Nick, figuring out his own angle on the situation. "That's why I stay with her. As long as I'm with her, the McGill protects me, too."

"So, what's it look like?" Johnnie-O said, looking closely at Allie, trying to read the bluff in her face.

"Well, I could tell you," she said, using one of her father's favorite lines. "But then I'd have to kill you."

The others laughed at that, and so Johnnie-O curled his

heavy hand into a fist and smashed the closest kid for laughing. He flew back about five feet. Then Johnnie-O got closer to Allie again.

"I think you're lying," he said.

"Guess you'll just have to find out," Allie taunted back. "Touch me and I call the McGill."

Johnnie-O hesitated. He looked at Allie, looked at Nick, then looked at the boys around him. His authority had been challenged, and Allie realized too late that she should have figured another bluff—one that would allow this little creep to keep his dignity, because a kid like this would rather risk getting eaten by a monster than be disrespected by a girl.

He looked her square in the eye and said, "You're going down." With that, he snapped his fingers, a dry, brittle sound, like a cracking plate. Then three kids grabbed her, pulled her off the dead-spot, put her down on the living-world roadway, and began to lean heavily on her shoulders.

In an instant she had sunk into the asphalt up to her knees, and an instant later up to her waist.

"No!" she screamed. "McGill, McGill!" she called.

It only gave them a brief moment's pause, and when the beast did not materialize out of thin air, they kept on pushing. Now it was easier for them, with Allie in up to her waist.

Nick struggled and kicked against the hands holding him, but it was no use. All he could do was watch as the others leaned and pressed on Allie's shoulders, pushing her deeper and deeper into the ground. Soon her shoulders disappeared and she was up to her neck and still she was screaming, hysterically now, and Johnnie-O just laughed.

"Let me do the honors," he said. And with that, he came over, grabbed her on the top of the head and began to push down. "Enjoy the trip," he said. "Don't bother writing."

And then another voice entered the fray. A high-pitched scream came out of nowhere, and a figure burst onto the scene, arms flailing wildly.

"The McGill!" shouted one of the other boys, "the McGill!"

Again that squealing war cry, and then Allie heard no more of it, for her ears and her eyes and the top of her head had sunk into the asphalt. Johnnie-O had stopped pushing, but gravity was doing the rest. The earth had her like quicksand and she was going down. She tried to scream, but no sound came out, it was completely muffled by the earth filling it. The Earth had swallowed her, and the feeling of it in her chest—in that place where her lungs should have been—was more awful than anything she could remember, and it dawned on her that this could very well be her eternity. She was on her way to the center of the Earth. How deep was she beneath the surface of the road now? Six inches? Six feet? She forced her arms to move, using every ounce of strength she had. It was like swimming in molasses. She forced one hand up high, and tried to haul herself upward, but it did no good. Then, just before all hope left her, someone reached down out of nowhere, grabbed her hand, and pulled. She felt herself sliding upward inch by inch. She forced her other hand up through the asphalt until her fingertips brushed the cool air, and someone grasped on to that hand as well. She moved up, and could feel the top of her head and her eyes and ears clearing, and finally her mouth, and she released the scream that had been held back by the dirt and the rocks, like a gag in her mouth.

Had Johnnie-O and his gang changed their minds? Or was this the monster that she had summoned out of the woods, pulling her out of the Earth, only to devour her? But with her eyes clear, she could now see into the face of her savior.

"Lief?"

"Are you okay?" Lief said. "I thought you were lost for sure."

Nick was there too, and together the both of them pulled until Allie came out and landed on the solid ground of the dead-spot. She collapsed in a heap, breathing heavily, and Lief looked at her strangely.

"I know, I know," said Allie. "I don't have to be out of breath, but I want to be. It feels right to be."

"It's okay," said Lief. "Maybe someday you can teach me to feel that way again."

"Where's Johnnie-O and his cast of morons?" Allie asked.

"Gone," Nick told her. "They were so freaked when Lief came charging out at them, they took off."

Lief laughed. "They really thought I was the McGill. Ain't that a hoot and a half?"

Lief began to pull ghost weeds from beneath the WELCOME TO ROCKLAND COUNTY! sign, and used their stalks to repair his road-shoes, which must have broken when he charged Johnnie-O. "Have you been following us all this time?" Allie asked.

Lief shrugged. "Well, yeah. I had to make sure you didn't get eaten by no monsters, didn't I?"

"Great," said Nick. "We've got our own guardian angel."

"If I were an angel, I wouldn't be here, would I?"

Allie smiled. After all these years Lief had left his forest for them. It could not have been a choice he made lightly, and so she vowed to herself that from this moment on, she would look out for him in any way she could.

They didn't wait until dawn, figuring Johnnie-O and his gang might come back. Rather than being troubled by the encounter, Allie found herself heartened by it. Nick was his usual gloom and doom, talking about *Lord of the Flies* and the dangers of rogue bands of parentless kids—but even in his worry, there was a new energy—because running into Johnnie-O proved that there were lots of Afterlights around. Not all of them would be as unpleasant as Johnnie-O's gang.

They came to the Hudson River, and stayed on the highway that ran along the Palisades: sheer cliffs, carved by the relentless glaciers of the last Ice Age, which lined the western shore of the river. Traffic became denser, but they bore it no mind, not caring if the occasional car passed through them. In fact, for a while they tried to make a game of it, trying to figure out what song was playing on the radio during the brief instant each car sped through.

"The things we dead folk do to amuse ourselves," Allie said, heaving a heavy sigh. The game didn't last long, mainly because Lief, who had never heard a car radio, much less rock 'n' roll, felt increasingly left out.

By sunset of the next day, the cheese-grater gridwork of the George Washington Bridge appeared downriver, heralding their arrival in New York City.

Lief was overwhelmed by the sight of the great city looming before him. It was a clear day, and the whole skyline could be seen from across the river. Lief had been to New York before. Twice. Once for the Fourth of July, and once for Mr. P. T. Barnum's circus. There were tall buildings to be sure, but none like these.

Nick and Allie stared as well. Lief assumed they were also in awe of the spectacular view. In truth, they were awed, but for an entirely different reason.

"I think I know where we should go," Nick said, a strange hollowness to his voice. Allie didn't answer him for a while.

"Manhattan is out of our way," Allie finally said. "We should stay on this side of the river, and keep heading south."

Nick looked to the city again. "I don't care what you say. I'm taking a detour."

This time Allie didn't argue.

Night had fallen by the time they reached the Manhattan side of the bridge. It took the whole night without rest to make it to the heart of the city.

The towers of midtown Manhattan would have taken Lief's breath away, if he indeed had breath to be stolen. But the most wondrous sights of all were the two silver towers he saw glimmering in the light of dawn as they neared the southern tip of the city. The two towers were identical monoliths, steel and glass twins reflecting a silvery light of daybreak.

"I never knew buildings like that existed," Lief said.

Allie sighed. "They don't exist," she said. "At least . . . not anymore."

Lief could tell the sadness in her voice went straight down to the center of the Earth.

PART TWO

Mary, Queen of Snots

CHAPTER 7

The Forever Places

In the course of time and history there are certain places that can never truly be lost. The living world by its very nature moves on, but some places are forever. The boy now called Lief had the good fortune to stumble upon such a place many years before: a lush mountain forest that had once been the inspiration for poets. The place brimmed with such warmth and good feeling, it inspired countless young men to propose marriage beneath its canopy, and countless young women to accept. The woods caused stiff-collared people to lose their inhibitions and dance among the leaves, wild with joy, even though they knew such dancing could have them condemned as witches.

The forest was a fulcrum of life, and so when it grew old, and a beetle infestation routed bark and bough, the forest did not die. Instead it crossed. Its life persisted—not in the living world, but in Everlost. Here it would be eternally green, and on the verge of turning, just as the poets themselves would have liked to see it, had they not gotten where they were going.

It can be said, then, that Everlost is heaven. Perhaps not

for people, but for the places that deserve a share of forever.

Such places are few and far between, these grand islands of eternity in the soupy, ever-changing world of the living. New York had its share of forever-places. The greatest of these stood near Manhattan's southern-most tip: the two gray brothers to the green statue in the bay. The towers had found their heaven. They were a part of Everlost now, held fast, and held forever by the memories of a mourning world, and by the dignity of the souls who got where they were going on that dark September day.

The three kids approached the great twin towers in silence. What they saw as they neared them was not at all what they expected.

There were children there. Dozens of Afterlight kids playing on the grand marble plaza: hopscotch, tag, hide-and-seek. Some were dressed like Allie, in jeans and a T-shirt. Others were more formal. Still more had clothes that seemed more from Lief's time, all coarse and heavy. A few kids wore the gaudy bright colors of the seventies, with big hair to match.

They hadn't been noticed yet, as they stood just beyond the edge of the plaza. Allie and Nick were almost afraid to step onto it, as if doing so would cross them into yet another world. They stood there so long they sank to their ankles, even with their road-shoes on.

As Lief's sense of awe did not have history nor context for this place, he had no problem moving forward. "C'mon," he said, "what are you waiting for?"

Nick and Allie looked at one another, then took that

first step forward, onto the very solid marble of the plaza that no longer existed. After the first step it became easier. It felt strange beneath their feet, so much solid ground. A team of girls playing double-dutch jump rope noticed them first.

"Hi!" said an African-American girl in drab clothes and tight cornrowed hair. "You're Greensouls, aren't you?" All the time, she never stopped spinning her two ropes. Neither did the girl on the other end, who seemed entirely out of place there in the plaza, dressed in teddy-bear pajamas. Other girls skillfully jumped in and out of the arc of their spinning ropes. One girl took enough time away from the game, though, to size them up. She wore a sparkling silver halter top, and jeans that were so tight, she looked like a sausage bursting out of its skin. She looked Allie over, clearly unimpressed by Allie's nonglittering wardrobe. "Is that what they wear now?"

"Yeah, pretty much."

Then the girl in tight jeans looked at Lief, examining his clothes as well. "You're not a Greensoul."

"Says who?" said Lief, insulted.

"He's new to the city," Allie said. "He might have crossed a long time ago, but he's still kind of like a 'Greensoul.'"

A big red handball came flying past, chased by a group of younger kids. The ball flew out of the plaza and into the street, crowded with the living. "Hurry," one little boy yelled, "before it sinks!"

Another boy raced out into traffic, grabbed the ball that was already beginning to sink into the pavement, and disappeared beneath a city bus and two taxis. He paid them no mind, passing through the trunk of the last taxi as he stood up with the ball, and happily ran back to the plaza.

"You remember all those things your momma told you not to do?" said the girl with the cornrows. "Like not running out into traffic? Well, you can do them here."

"Who's in charge?" asked Nick.

"Mary," she said. "You oughta go and see her. She loves Greensouls." Then she added, "We were all Greensouls once."

Nick tapped Allie on the shoulder. "Look," he said.

By now their presence had been noticed by most of the kids around the plaza. Many of the games had stopped, and the kids stared, not sure what to do. Out of the crowd a girl stepped forward. She had long blond hair that nearly touched the floor, wore a tie-dyed shirt, and bell-bottoms so big, the cuffs practically trailed behind her like a bridal train. A '60s hippie girl, if ever there was one.

"Don't tell me," said Allie, "your name is Summer, and you want to know if we're groovy."

"My name's Meadow, and I don't say groovy anymore, because I got tired of people making fun of me."

"Do you have to insult everybody you meet?" Nick whispered to Allie, then turned back to Meadow. "I'm Nick, and this is Lief. The rude one is Allie."

"I wasn't being rude," Allie insisted. "I was being facetious. There's a difference."

"No sweat," said Meadow, which was almost as bad as groovy. "C'mon, I'll take you to Mary." Then she looked down. "What are those on your feet?"

They looked down to the bundles of sticks extending

from the soles of their shoes. "Road-shoes," said Nick. "Kind of like snowshoes, so we don't sink, you know?"

"Hmm. Clever," said Meadow. "But you won't need them anymore."

They took off their road-shoes, and followed Meadow across the plaza toward Tower One. Behind them, the rest of the kids returned to their games.

They passed a fountain in the center of the plaza, and Meadow turned to them.

"Would you like to make a wish?" Meadow asked. A closer look revealed the fountain to be full of coins beneath the shimmering water.

"Not really," Allie said.

"Mary says every Greensoul who comes here has to make a wish."

Nick was already reaching into his pocket.

"I don't have a coin," Allie said.

Meadow just smiled. "Sure you do."

And so to prove it Allie reached into her pockets, and turned them out. "See?"

"What about your back pockets?"

Allie sighed and checked her back pockets, knowing full well they were empty—she never used her back pockets. So it surprised her when she found the coin. Not even Johnnie-O's goons had found it. But then, she had given them such a nasty look when they had reached for her rear, they never actually checked her back pockets.

"Weird," Allie said, as she looked at the coin.

"Not really." Meadow gave her a hippie love-fest smile. "With all the money living people spend, everyone has at least one coin in their pocket when they cross."

"I once had a coin," Lief said, dejectedly, "but it got stolen."

"Make a wish anyway," said Meadow. "Mary says all wishes have a chance of coming true, except one."

Nick threw his coin in, then Allie threw hers. She made the wish every Greensoul made. The wish to be alive again. The one wish that didn't come true.

Once their wishes had joined the others in the fountain, Meadow led them toward Tower One. Lief was the ultimate tourist, staring heavenward to where the towers touched the sky. He bumped into other kids again and again, for he refused to look down. "How do they stay up?" Lief asked. "Wouldn't something so tall fall down?"

Allie was not a girl quickly given to tears, but she had found herself crying at least once a day since her arrival. Sometimes it was the revelation of just how drastically her existence had changed that would draw tears to her eyes. Other times it was the depth of how much she missed her family. Today the tears were sudden and unexpected.

"What's the matter?" Lief asked. But there really was no way to explain to him. She wasn't even sure of the reason. Was she crying with joy that this place had left a permanent impression on the world, and that it was still here in Everlost? Or was being here a reminder of how much was truly lost on that awful day when the towers crossed so violently from the world of the living? So many souls got where they were going that day, when they shouldn't have been going at all.

"This is wrong," Allie said. "Children shouldn't be playing here. It's . . . it's like dancing on a grave."

"No," said Meadow, "it's like putting flowers on a grave. Mary says the more happiness we bring back to this place, the more we honor it."

"So, exactly who is this Mary?" Nick asked.

Meadow scrunched up her lips, trying to think of how to explain. "Mary's kind of like, a shaman, you know? A spiritual leader. Anyway, she knows lots of stuff, and so she pretty much runs things around here."

The elevator stopped abruptly and the door slid open, to reveal that they had come all the way up to the observation level. They could tell because of all of the coin-operated binocular machines lined up by the narrow windows that stretched from ceiling to floor. But everything else here had changed. It must have been remodeled into a makeshift orphanage. Just as in the square below, young Afterlights from various time periods lingered, playing games or just sitting, waiting for something to happen to them. Allie still wasn't sure whether this was like some desecration of hallowed ground, or if having children here was somehow healing.

As they walked around the floor to the north side, they passed a food court with a pizza place and a hot dog stand. The counters were closed. It looked like they hadn't served any food in a long time—but at each table sat kids, eating what appeared to be very, very small pieces of cake.

"That can't be," said Lief. "They're eating. How can they be eating?"

Meadow smiled. "Mary traded something for a birthday cake. She shared it with all of the younger children."

"But, we don't eat," said Lief, confused.

"Just because we *don't*, doesn't mean we *can't* when there's ghost food around."

"Ghost food?" said Lief. "There's ghost food?"

Nick looked at him and shook his head. "You've been around a hundred years, and you didn't know there was ghost food?"

Lief looked like a kid who had missed the bus to Disneyland. "No one ever told me."

Seeing the smaller children eating the birthday cake reminded Allie how hungry she was. Just like her craving for sleep, she knew her hunger would eventually pass, but there was no telling when. If it had been she who had gotten the birthday cake, she would not have been so generous as to share it with anyone. Maybe with Nick and Lief, but certainly not a hoard of little kids.

"You'll really dig Mary," said Meadow. Allie had to admit there was something comforting when Meadow's lingo matched her clothes.

A makeshift wall had been built, blocking off the north half of the floor. Mary's personal residence. A scrawny little kid with curly blond hair stood at the door like a pint-size guard.

"Some Greensouls to see Mary," Meadow announced.

"Greensouls!" said the curly-haired boy excitedly. "I'm sure Miss Mary will want to see them right away."

"Okay then. Ciao." Meadow waved a quick good-bye, and sauntered away.

"She's funny, isn't she?" said the curly-headed boy. "Meadow's always good for a laugh." He put out his hand to shake. "I'm Stradivarius," he said, "but everyone just calls me Vari. Come on, I'll introduce you to Miss Mary."

Miss Mary's private residence was full of mismatched furniture. Just like the kids here, everything seemed to come from different times and different places. It was all furniture that had crossed into Everlost: bright to the eye and hard to the touch. Apparently Mary was good at collecting things that had crossed over.

When Mary saw them, she came gliding toward them, graceful on her feet. Allie wasn't one to judge a person by her wardrobe—after all, the snobs from her school judged her often enough—but you couldn't help but notice Mary's dress: rich emerald velvet, with white lace cuffs and a lace collar so tight it seemed about ready to strangle her.

"It looks like you must have died on the way to a wedding," Allie said. Nick didn't settle for rolling his eyes this time. Instead he elbowed Allie in the ribs. "No," Nick said. "That was me."

Mary never broke eye contact with Allie. "It's impolite to comment on how someone crosses."

Allie felt heat rise to her cheeks, surprised to know that she could still blush from embarrassment, but Mary took her hand warmly. "Don't feel bad," she said. "I was just pointing it out. You couldn't possibly be expected to know—you're new to all of this." She turned to Lief and Nick. "There are many things you'll be learning about your new lives and until you do, you mustn't feel bad if you make mistakes."

"I'm not new," said Lief, unable to meet her eye.

"You're new here," Mary said with a warm smile, "and so you have permission to *feel* just as new as you want."

Nick couldn't look away from Mary. He was captivated

from the moment he saw her. It wasn't just that she was beautiful—she was also elegant, and her manner was as velvety smooth as her dress. Everyone introduced themselves, and when Nick took Mary's hand, she smiled at him. He was convinced that her smile was just for him, and although his rational mind told him otherwise, he refused to believe she smiled at everyone that way.

"You must be tired from your journey," Mary said, turning and leading them deeper into her apartment.

"We can't get tired," Allie said.

"Actually," said Mary, "that's a common misconception. We do get tired, exhausted even—but it isn't sleep that refreshes us. We're refreshed by the company of others."

Allie crossed her arms. "Oh, please."

"No," said Vari, "it's true. We gain strength from each other."

"So what about Lief?" Allie asked. By now, Lief had gravitated to the window, more interested in the view than anything else. "He's been alone for a hundred years, and he's got plenty of energy."

Mary didn't miss a beat. "Then he must have found a marvelous place, full of love and life."

She was, of course, right. Lief's forest had been a sustaining place for him. Allie didn't know how to feel about this "Miss Mary." Allie hated know-it-alls, but in this case, Mary actually did appear to know it all.

"We've turned the top floors of this tower into living quarters—but most of them are still empty. You're free to choose where you'd like to stay."

"Who said we were staying?" said Allie.

Nick nudged her with his elbow, harder this time. "Allie . . . ," he said between his teeth, "it's impolite to turn down an invitation in this world. Or in any world for that matter."

But if Mary was offended, she didn't show it. "Consider this a rest stop, if you like," Mary said cordially. "A way station on to wherever it is you're going."

"We weren't going anywhere," Nick said with a smile. He was trying to sound charming, but instead wound up sounding heavily sedated.

Allie was fully prepared to smack that starry gaze clear out of Nick's eyes, but she restrained herself. "We *were* going home," she reminded him.

"Of course that would be your first instinct," Mary said with supreme patience. "You couldn't be expected to know the consequences."

"Please stop talking to me like I'm ignorant," said Allie.

"You *are* ignorant," said Vari. "All Greensouls are."

It infuriated Allie that it was true. She, Nick, and even Lief were at a disadvantage.

Vari went over to a cabinet, and pulled out three books. "Here; a crash course in Everlost." He handed them each a book. "You have to forget what you know about the living world, and get used to the way things are here."

"What if I don't want to forget the living world?" Allie asked.

Mary smiled politely. "I understand how you feel," she said. "Letting go is hard."

"*Tips for Taps*," Nick said, reading from the cover of the book. "'By Mary Hightower.' That's you?"

Mary smiled. "We all must do something with our afterlife," she said. "I write."

Allie looked at her own volume, impressed in spite of herself. She leafed through the book. Three hundred pages at least, and each page handwritten, with painstakingly perfect penmanship.

Well, thought Allie, *we came here looking for answers—and now we're in the company of the Authority of Everlost.* What could be better? Yet for some reason Allie didn't feel all that comforted.

In her book *Death Be Not Dull,* Mary Hightower writes, "Afterlight Greensouls are precious. They are fragile. There are so many hazards for them here in Everlost, for they are like babies with no knowledge of the way things are—and like babies they must be nurtured and guided with a loving, but firm hand. Their eternity rests on how well they adjust to life in Everlost. A poorly adjusted Afterlight can warp and distort in horrifying ways. Therefore Greensouls must be treated with patience, kindness, and charity. It's the only way to properly mold them."

CHAPTER 8

Dominant Reality

Mary Hightower detested being called Mary Queen of Snots, although there was some truth to it. Most of the Afterlights in her care were much younger than her. At fifteen, she was among the oldest residents of Everlost. So when kids closer to her age arrived in her towering domain, she paid extra-special attention to them.

She sensed, however, that Allie was going to be a problem. To say that Mary didn't like Allie would be a stretch. Mary, quite simply, liked everyone. It was her *job* to like everyone, and she took it very seriously. Allie, however, was dangerously willful, and could spell disaster. Mary hoped she was wrong, but had to admit that she seldom was. Even her worst predictions came true—not because she had any glimpse into the future—but because her many years in Everlost had made her a keen judge of character.

"The Greensouls are taken care of," Vari announced after he returned. "The boys chose a room together facing south, the girl chose a room alone facing north. All on the ninety-third floor."

"Thank you, Vari." She gave him a kiss on the top of his curly head, as she often did. "We'll give them a few hours to settle in, and I'll pay them a visit."

"Would you like me to play for you?" Vari asked. "Mozart, maybe."

Although Mary didn't feel like listening to music, she told him yes. It gave him pleasure to bring her happiness, and she didn't want to deny him that. He had been her right-hand man since before she could remember, and she often forgot that he was only nine years old, forever trapped at that age where he wanted to please. It was wonderful. It was sad. Mary chose to focus on the wonderful. She closed her eyes and listened as Vari raised his violin, and played a concerto she had heard a thousand times, and would probably hear a thousand times more.

When the sun sank low, she went to visit the three Greensouls. The boys first.

Their "apartment" was sparsely furnished with flotsam and jetsam furniture that had crossed over. A chair here, a desk there, a mattress, and a sofa that would have to suffice as a second bed.

Lief sat on the floor trying to make sense of a Nintendo DS. It was an old device by living-world standards, but certainly new to him. He didn't even look up when Mary entered. Nick, on the other hand, stood, took her hand, and kissed it. She laughed in spite of herself, and he blushed bright red. "I saw that in a movie once. You seemed so . . . royal, or something, it just seemed like the thing to do. Sorry."

"No, that's fine. I just wasn't expecting it. It was very . . . gallant."

"Hey, at least I didn't leave behind chocolate on your hand," he said. She took a long look at him. He had a good face. Soulful brown eyes. The more Mary looked, the deeper his blush. As Mary recalled, a blush was caused by blood rushing to the capillaries of one's face. They no longer had blood or capillaries—but Greensouls were still close enough to the living world to mimic such physiological reactions. He may have been embarrassed, but for Mary, that crimson tinge in his face was a treat.

"You know," she told him, gently touching the chocolate on the side of his lip, "some people are able to change the way they appear. If you don't like the chocolate on your face, you can work on getting rid of it."

"I'd like that," he said.

Mary could sense that he was having another physiological reaction to her touching his face, so she took her hand back. She might have blushed herself, if she was still capable of it. "Of course, that sort of thing takes a long time. Like a Zen master learning to walk on hot coals, or levitate. It takes years of meditation and concentration."

"Or I can just forget," offered Nick. "You said in *Tips for Taps* that people sometimes forget how they look, and their faces change. So maybe I can forget the chocolate on purpose."

"A good idea," she answered. "But we can't choose what we forget. The more we try to forget something, the more we end up remembering it. Careful, or your whole face will get covered in chocolate."

Nick chuckled nervously, as if she were kidding, and he stopped when he realized she wasn't.

"Don't worry," she told him. "As long as you're with us,

you're among friends, and we will always remind you who you were when you arrived."

In the corner, Lief grunted in frustration. "My fingers don't work fast enough to play this." He banged his Game Boy against the wall in anger, but didn't stop playing.

"Mary . . . can I ask you a question?" Nick said.

Mary sat with him on the sofa. "Of course."

"So . . . what happens now?"

Mary waited for more, but there was no more. "I'm sorry . . . I'm not sure I understand the question."

"We're dead, right."

"Well, yes, technically."

"And like your book says, we're stuck in this Everlost place, right?"

"Forever and always."

"So . . . what do we do now?"

Mary stood up, not at all comfortable with the question. "Well, what do you *like* to do? Whatever you like to do, that's what you get to do."

"And when I get tired of it?"

"I'm sure you'll find something to keep you content."

"I'm not too good at contentment," he said. "Maybe you can help me."

She turned to Nick, and found herself locked in his gaze. This time he wasn't blushing. "I'd really like it if you could."

Mary held eye contact with Nick much longer than she expected to. She began to feel flustered, and she never felt flustered. Flustered was not in Mary Hightower's emotional dictionary.

"This game's stupid," said Lief. "Who the heck is Zelda, anyway?"

Mary tore herself away from Nick's gaze, angry at herself for allowing a slip of her emotions. She was a mentor. She was a guardian. She needed to keep an emotional distance from the kids under her wing. She could care about them—but only the way a mother loves her children. As long as she remembered that, things would be fine.

"I have an idea for you, Nick." Mary went to a dresser, and opened the top drawer, getting her errant feelings under control. She pulled out paper and a pen. Mary made sure all arriving Greensouls always had paper and pens. Crayons for the younger ones. "Why don't you make a list of all the things you ever wanted to do, and then we can talk about it."

Mary left quickly, with a bit less grace than when she arrived.

Allie found the paper and pens long before Mary showed up in her "apartment," or "hotel room," or "cell." She wasn't quite sure what to call it yet. By the time Mary arrived, Allie had filled three pages with questions.

When Mary came, she stood at the threshold until Allie invited her in. *Like a vampire,* Allie thought. Vampires can't come in unless invited. "You've been busy," Mary said when she saw how much Allie had written.

"I've been reading your books," Allie said. "Not just the one you gave us, but other ones I found lying around."

"Good—they will be very helpful for you."

"—and I have some questions. Like, in one book, you

say haunting is forbidden, but then somewhere else you say that we're free spirits, and can do anything we want."

"Well, we can," said Mary, "but we really shouldn't."

"Why?"

"It's complicated."

"And anyway—you say that we can have no effect on the living world—they can't see us, they can't hear us . . . so if that's true, how could we 'haunt,' even if we wanted to?"

Mary's smile spoke of infinite patience among imbeciles. It made Allie furious, and so she returned the same "you're-an-idiot-and-I'm-oh-so-smart" smile right back at her.

"As I said, it's complicated, and it's nothing you need to worry about on your first day here."

"Right," said Allie. "So I haven't read all the books yet, I mean you've written so *many* of them—but I haven't been able to find anything about going home."

Allie could see Mary bristle. Allie imagined if she had been a porcupine all her quills would be standing on end.

"You can't go home," Mary said. "We've already discussed that."

"Sure I can," Allie said. "I can walk up to my house, walk in my front door. Well, okay, I mean walk *through* my front door, but either way, I'll be home. Why don't any of your books talk about that?"

"You don't want to do that," Mary said, her voice quiet, almost threatening.

"But I do."

"No you don't." Mary walked to the window, and looked out over the city. Allie had chosen a view uptown: the Empire State building, Central Park, and beyond. "The world of the living doesn't look the way you remembered, does it? It looks washed out. Less vibrant than it should."

What Mary said was true. The living world had a fundamentally faded look about it. Even the new One World Trade Center, rising just beside their towers, seemed like they were seeing it through fog. It was so clearly a part of a different world. A world where time moves forward, instead of just standing still, keeping everything the way it is. Or, more accurately, the way it once was.

"Look out over the city," Mary said. "Do some buildings look more . . . *real* . . . to you?"

Now that Mary had mentioned it, there were buildings that stood out in clearer focus. Brighter. Allie didn't need to be told that these were buildings that had crossed into Everlost when they were torn down.

"Sometimes they build living-world things in places where Everlost buildings stand," Mary said. "Do you know what happens when you step into those places?"

Allie shook her head.

"You don't see the living world. You see Everlost. It takes a great effort to see both places at the same time. I call it 'dominant reality.'"

"Why don't you write a book about it," snapped Allie.

"Actually, I have," said Mary with a big old smirk that made it clear Mary's was the dominant reality around here.

"So the living world isn't that clear to us anymore. That doesn't mean anything."

"It means that Everlost is the more important of the two worlds."

"That's one opinion."

She thought that Mary might lose her cool, and they'd get into a nice fight about it, but Mary's patience was as eternal as Everlost itself. Keeping her tone gentle and kindly as it always was, Mary gestured at the city beyond the window, and said "You see all of this? A hundred years from now, all those people will be gone, and many of the buildings torn down to make room for something else—but we will still be here. This place will still be here." She turned to Allie. "Only the things and places that are worthy of eternity cross into Everlost. We're blessed to be here—don't taint it by thoughts of going home. This will be your home far longer than the so-called 'living world.'"

Allie looked to the furniture around the room. "Exactly what makes this folding table 'worthy of eternity'?"

"It must have been special to someone."

"Or," said Allie, "it just fell through a random vortex." She held up one of Mary's books. "You said that happens yourself."

Mary sighed. "So I did."

"Correct me if I'm wrong, but didn't you just contradict yourself?"

Still, Mary lost none of her poise. In fact, she rose to the challenge better than Allie expected.

"I see you're smart enough to know there are no simple answers," Mary said. "It's true that things sometimes do cross over by accident."

"Right! And it's not a blessing that *we're* here, it's an accident."

"Even accidents have a divine purpose."

"Then they wouldn't be accidents, would they?"

"Believe what you want," said Mary. "Eternity is what

it is—you can't change it. You're here, and so you must make the best of it. I'd like to help you, if you'll let me."

"All right—but just answer me one question. Is there a way out of Everlost?"

Mary didn't answer right away. For a moment Allie thought she might tell her something she had never written in any of her books. But instead, all she said was, "No. And in time you'll know the truth of it for yourself."

In just a few days, Allie, Nick, and Lief came to know all there was to know about life in Mary's world. The daily routine was simple. The little kids played ball, tag, and jumped rope all day long in the plaza, and when it got dark, everyone gathered on the seventy-eighth floor to listen to stories the older kids told, or to play video games, or to watch the single TV that Mary had acquired. According to Meadow, there were kids out there who traveled the world searching for items that had crossed over, and they would trade them to Mary. These kids were called "Finders." One Finder had brought a TV, but it only played TV shows that had aired on the day it crossed over. The same ancient episodes of *The Love Boat* and *Happy Days* played every single day during prime time, and presumably would continue to play until the end of time. Strangely, there were some kids who watched it. Every day. Like clockwork.

Nick watched the TV for a few days, amazed at the old commercials and the news more than anything. Watching it was like stepping into a time machine, but even time travel gets dull when you're constantly traveling to April 8, 1978.

Allie chose not to watch the TV. She was already sensing

something profoundly wrong with Mary's little Queendom, although she couldn't put her finger on it yet. It had to do with the way the little girls jumped rope, and the way the same kids would watch that awful TV every single day.

If Nick felt that anything was wrong, it was lost beneath everything that was right about Mary. The way she always thought of others before herself, the way she made the little kids all feel loved. The way she took an interest in him. Mary always made a point of coming over to Nick and asking what he was up to, how he was feeling, what new things he was thinking about. She spoke with him about a book she was working on, all about theories on why there were no seventeen-year-olds in Everlost, when everyone knew eighteen was the official age of adulthood.

"That's not actually true," Nick offered. "That's voting age, but drinking age is twenty-one. In the Jewish religion, adulthood is thirteen, and I know for a fact there are fourteen-year-old Jewish kids here."

"That still doesn't explain why kids older than us aren't admitted into Everlost."

Admitted to Everlost, thought Nick. That sounded a lot better than *Lost on the way to heaven*. Her way of thinking was such a welcome relief from his own propensity toward gloom and doom. "Maybe," suggested Nick, "it's a very personal thing. Maybe it's the moment you stop thinking of yourself as a kid."

Vari, who was lingering at the door, snickered. He had snickered at every single comment Nick made.

"Vari, please," Mary told him. "We value a free flow of ideas here."

"Even the stupid ones?" Vari said.

Nick couldn't really see why she kept Vari around. Sure, he had musical talent, but it didn't make up for his attitude.

Mary took Nick to show him how her books were made. The sixty-seventh floor was the publishing room. There were thirty kids there, all sitting at school desks. It looked like a classroom with kids practicing their penmanship.

"We've yet to find a printing press that's crossed over," she told him. "But that's all right. They enjoy copying by hand."

And sure enough, the kids in the publishing room seemed thrilled to do their work, like ancient scribes copying scriptures on parchment.

"They find comfort in the routine," Mary said, and Nick accepted it, without giving it much thought.

Allie, on the other hand, had begun to understand the nature of the "routines" these children found comfort in. She grabbed Nick one day, during one of the times when he wasn't following Mary around.

"I want you to watch this kid," she told Nick. "Follow him with me."

"What for?"

"You'll see."

Nick was reluctant, but it wasn't like he had anything pressing to do, so he played along at whatever game Allie had up her sleeve. For Allie, it wasn't a game, though. It was very serious business.

The boy, who was about seven, was on the plaza playing kickball with a dozen other kids.

"So what are we looking for?" Nick asked, growing impatient.

"Watch," said Allie. "His team is going to lose. Nine to seven."

Sure enough, the game ended when the score reached nine to seven.

"What are you telling me? You can tell the future."

"Sort of," Allie said. "I can when there is no future."

"What's that supposed to mean?"

"Just follow him."

Nick was intrigued now. Keeping their distance, they followed the boy into the lobby of Tower Two, where several other kids had gathered with a deck of cards to play go-fish.

Allie and Nick hid behind a pillar, but it didn't seem to matter—these kids didn't notice, or care that they were being watched.

"He's going to ask for threes," Allie said.

"Got any threes?" the kid asked the girl next to him.

"Go fish," Allie whispered to Nick. "Got any sevens?"

"Go fish," said the girl. "Got any sevens?"

Now Nick was a little bit freaked. "How do you know this?"

"Because it's the same. Every day. The same score in kickball, the same game of cards."

"No way!"

"Watch," said Allie. "In a second the kid we followed here is going to throw down his cards and accuse the little girl of cheating. Then he's going to run out the third revolving door from the left."

It happened just as Allie said.

It was the first time since arriving in Mary's world that Nick felt uneasy. "It's like . . . it's like . . ."

Allie finished the thought for him. "It's like they're ghosts." Which, of course, they were. "You know how there are those ghost sightings—people say they see a ghost doing the same thing, in the same place, every day?"

Nick wasn't willing to let it sit at that. He ran toward the boy before he reached the revolving door. "Hey!" Nick said to him. "Why did you leave the card game?"

"They were cheating!" he said.

"I dare you to go back."

The boy looked at him with mild fear in his eyes. "No. I don't want to."

"But didn't you play the same game yesterday?" Nick said. "Didn't they cheat in the same way yesterday?"

"Yeah," said the boy, like it was nothing. "So?"

The boy pushed through the revolving door and hurried off.

Allie came up beside Nick. "I joined their card game a few days ago. It threw them off, but the next day, they were back to the same old routine."

"But it doesn't make sense. . . ."

"Yes it does," said Allie. "I've been thinking about it a lot. You know when you're listening to an old vinyl record, and the music starts to skip? Well it's like our lives are records that started to skip on the very last note. We never got to the end, we're just sort of stuck. And if we're not careful, we start to fall into ruts, doing the same things over and over and over."

". . . Because there's comfort in the routine . . . ," said Nick, echoing Mary's words. "Is that what's going to happen to us?"

"Not if I can help it."

"We are not like the living," Mary writes in her book *The First Hundred Years*. "We are beyond life. We are better than life. We don't need to complicate our existence with a thousand meaningless activities, when one will do fine. Just as the world's great artists learn the value of simplicity, so do we Afterlights learn to simplify. As time goes on, we fall into our perfect routine; our niche in space and time, as consistent as the rising and falling of the sun.

"This is normal and natural. Routine gives us comfort. It gives us purpose. It connects us to the rhythm of all things. One must feel a certain pity for Afterlights who never do find their niche."

CHAPTER 9

Endless Loop

Nick spent the next few days following other Afterlights in Mary's domain, and it confirmed what Allie had shown him. For these kids, each day had become a repetition of the same day—and although he wanted to ask Mary about it, he didn't, because he knew she would find some way of giving it a wonderful, positive spin. He wanted to sit with it for a while and think about it himself without Mary's input.

That didn't stop him from spending as much time as he could with her, though. Mary was not routine. Each day was different for her—the kids she spent time with, the things she did. It eased Nick's mind to know that endless repetition was not an irresistible force. A person had choice in the matter, if they were strong enough.

It was a constant irritation to Nick that he and Mary could never have time alone. Wherever Mary was, Vari was there, too, like her own personal valet. Or like a lap dog. Clinging to Mary kept the boy's life from becoming repetitive, like the others—although Nick wished Vari would just lock himself in a room, and play endless

Beethoven to the walls for a few hundred years.

"Do you always have to hang around her?" Nick asked him. "Don't you ever want to do anything else?"

Vari shrugged. "I like what I do." Then he studied Nick with a certain coldness in his eyes. "You've been spending lots of time with Mary," he said. "Maybe it's time for *you* to do something else."

Nick couldn't quite read Vari's emotions, only that they were unpleasant ones. "It's a free spirit world—I can do what I want," Nick said.

"She'll grow tired of you," said Vari. "She likes you because you're new, but you won't be new forever. Soon you'll be just another Afterlight, and she won't even remember your name. But I'll still be here."

Nick huffed at the suggestion. "She won't forget my name."

"Yes she will. Even you will."

"What are you talking about?"

"Your clothes, and your chocolate-face might cross over with you, but your name doesn't. Not really. It fades just like any other memory. Soon everyone'll just call you Chocolate. Or *Hershey*." Vari grinned, but it wasn't a pleasant grin. "Yeah, that's it. You'll be *Hershey*."

"No I won't. And I won't forget my name."

"Really," said Vari. "Then what *is* your name?"

He was about to answer, when suddenly he drew a blank. It only lasted for a second, but a second was way too long to not remember your own name. It was a profoundly frightening moment. "Uh . . . Uh . . . Nick. My name is Nick."

"Okay," said Vari. And then he asked: "What's your last name?"

Nick opened his mouth, but then closed it again and said nothing. Because he couldn't remember.

When Mary arrived, she noticed the distressed look on Nick's face immediately.

"Vari, have you been teasing our new friend?"

"We were just talking. If he thinks that's teasing, that's his problem."

Mary just shook her head, and gave Vari a kiss on his curly blond hair. Vari threw Nick a gloating grin when she did.

"Will you escort me to the lobby? There's a Finder waiting for me, and I suspect he has some interesting things to sell."

Vari stepped forward.

"No, not you, Vari. You've seen Finders before, but I thought Nick might like to learn how to barter with them."

Now it was Nick's turn to gloat.

Once the elevator door closed, and Vari was out of sight, Nick put him out of mind, dismissing what he had said—not just about his name, but his certainty that Mary would tire of Nick. Vari, after all, was only nine years old. He was a little kid, feeling little-kid jealousy. Nothing more.

What Nick didn't realize was that Vari had been nine for 146 years. Little-kid emotions do not sit well after a century and a half. If Nick had realized that, things might have gone differently.

Lief stood in the arcade, staring at the video-game screen, and didn't dare blink. Move the stick right. Up. Left. Eat the big white ball. The little hairy things turn blue. Eat the hairy things until they start to blink. Then run away from them.

Lief had become a Pac-Man junkie.

There was no telling what caused the old Pac-Man game to cross over all those years ago. Mary had bought it from a Finder who specialized in tracking down electronics that had crossed. Electronics did not cross very often. True, over the years people loved their gramophones, or Victrolas, or 8-track players, or iPods, but in the end, no one "loved" those things with the kind of soulful devotion that would cause the device to cross into Everlost. No love was ever lost on a CD player that broke. It was simply replaced and the old one forgotten. For that reason, Everlost electronics were mostly the result of sunspot activity.

Mary prided herself on keeping current on technology, so that arriving Greensouls would feel somewhat at home. It had taken patience, and work, but over the years, Mary had gotten herself quite a collection of video games, and had turned the sixty-fourth floor into an arcade. There were also countless black vinyl record albums that had crossed, because people did truly love their music, but she had yet to track down a record player on which to play them.

Up. Left. Eat the big white ball. The hairy things turn blue. Eat the hairy things until they start to blink. Run away.

Over and over. The repetition wasn't so much soothing to Lief as it was compulsive. He couldn't stop. He didn't want to stop. Ever.

In the forest he had surely been a creature of habit. He had swung from the trees, playing his games alone—the same games day after day—but that was somehow different. There was no urgency to it. But the endless stimulation from this new-fangled machine demanded his focus in a way the forest never did. Other kids told him it was an old machine—but he didn't care. The games were all new to him.

Up. Down. Left. Right. Eat. Run.

"Lief, what are you doing? How long have you been here?"

He was barely aware of Allie's voice. He didn't even turn to look at her. "A while," he told her. *Up. Left. Down.*

"I think you've been at that machine for five days straight."

"So?"

"This is wrong. I've got to get you out of here! We've *all* got to get out of here!"

But Lief wasn't listening anymore, because the funny little hairy things had turned blue.

It had been a long time since Greensouls had had such an effect on Mary. Lief was not a problem. He simply brought out in Mary the maternal feelings she had for all the children in her care, but Allie, with her incessant questions and her neurosis of hope, brought up feelings in Mary she would much rather have forgotten, and thought she had. Feelings of doubt, frustration, and a sense of remorse as deep as her towers were tall.

And then there was Nick. The feelings he brought out in her were of a different nature, but just as troubling. He was so very much alive. Everything from his anxieties to the flush of his face in her presence. His bodily memory of life was so charming, so enticing, Mary could spend every minute with him. That was dangerous. It was almost as dangerous as being envious of the living. There were whispered tales of Afterlights whose envy of the living had turned them into incubuses—souls helplessly, hopelessly attached to a living host. This was different, but still, it was a weakness, and she was not in a position to be weak. Too many Afterlights relied on her for strength. With all this on her mind, she found herself distracted, and uncharacteristically moody. And so, when no one was watching, not even Vari, she descended to the fifty-eighth floor, the place she went when she needed silence and solitude.

The fifty-eighth floor had no tenants on the day the towers crossed into eternity. For that reason there were no walls or partitions subdividing it, and so, with the exception of the elevator core, the entire floor was nearly an acre of hollow space.

And still Nick found her.

"One of the little kids said you might be here," he said as he approached.

It surprised her that anyone knew where she went. But then, perhaps everyone did, but respected her enough not to disturb her. She watched as he drew nearer, his gentle glow visible in the daylight because the floor was so vast it was mostly in shadows, even with windows on all sides. He was clearly not comfortable with the space. "Why would you come here? It's so . . . empty."

"You see emptiness," she said. "I see possibility."

"Do you think you'll ever need all these floors?"

"There are more Afterlights out there, and more crossing everyday," she told him. "It may take a thousand years until we need the space, but it's nice to know I have it."

Mary looked out at the faded world of the living, hoping Nick would go away, hoping he would stay, and cursing herself for not being able to keep her distance.

"Is something wrong?"

Mary considered how she'd answer, then decided that she wouldn't. "Allie's leaving, isn't she?"

"That doesn't mean *I'm* leaving."

"She's a danger to herself," Mary said. "Which means she's also a danger to you."

Nick wasn't concerned. "She just wants to go home and see if her father survived the accident. Why is that so bad?"

"I know something about going home," Mary told him, and she found that just saying it brought the memory closer, along with all the pain it held.

Nick must have read her emotions, because he said, "If you don't want to talk about it you don't have to." And because he was kind enough not to ask, Mary found herself telling him everything, with the honesty she would have had before a priest. It was a memory Mary had tried desperately to forget, but like the chocolate stains on Nick's face, the harder she tried to forget, the more indelible the memory became.

"I died on a Wednesday, but I didn't die alone," Mary told him. "Like you, I had a companion."

"We weren't exactly companions," Nick told her. "Allie and I were total strangers—until the car accident."

"I had an accident, too, but my companion wasn't a stranger. He was my brother. The accident was entirely our fault. Mikey and I were walking home from school. It was a cool spring day, but sunny. The hills were already turning green. I can still remember the smell of the wildflowers that filled the fields—it's one of the only smells I can still remember from the living world. Isn't that odd?"

"So it happened in a field?" Nick asked.

"No. There were two train tracks side by side that crossed the dirt path that led home. Those tracks were mostly for freight trains. Every once in a while, for no good reason, a freight train would stop on the tracks and sit there for hours on end. It was a terrible nuisance—going around the train sometimes meant a half-mile walk in either direction."

"Oh no," said Nick. "You went under the train?"

"No, we weren't stupid enough to do that, but quite often there was an empty boxcar open on both sides, so we could climb *through* the train. There was one on that day. Mikey and I had been fighting, I don't remember what about, but it must have seemed important at the time because I was just furious and was chasing him. He was laughing and running ahead of me, and there was that boxcar, right in the middle of the dirt path, the doors on both sides pulled open, like a doorway to the other side. Mikey climbed up and into the boxcar. I climbed up right behind him, reaching for the back of his shirt as he ran across. I just missed him. He was still laughing and it just made me even more angry. He leaped out of the boxcar on the opposite side, and turned back to me."

Mary closed her eyes, the image so strong she could just about see it playing on the inside of her eyelids like a cinema show. A *movie,* as the living now called it.

"You don't have to tell me," Nick said gently, but Mary had come too far to stop.

"If I hadn't been so angry, I might have seen the sudden terror in Mikey's eyes, but I didn't see that; I was too dead set on catching him. I jumped down from the box car and slugged him in the arm—but instead of fighting back, he grabbed me and that's when I realized something I had forgotten. *There were two railroad tracks side by side.* One track held the freight car that hadn't moved for hours, and on the second track was another train traveling at full speed. We had both just jumped right into the path of a speeding train that we hadn't been able to see from the other side of the boxcar. When I finally saw it, it was too late. I never felt it hit me. Instead there was the sudden darkness of a tunnel and a light far, far away but moving closer. I was flying down that tunnel, but I wasn't flying alone."

"I remember that tunnel," Nick said.

"Before I got to the light I felt Mikey tugging on me. 'No, no!' he was yelling, and he pulled me and spun me around and I was still so mad at him I started fighting. I hit him and he hit me, he tugged my hair, I pushed him, and before I knew it, I felt myself crashing through the walls of that tunnel and losing consciousness even before I hit the ground."

"That's just like what happened with Allie and me!" Nick said. "We slept for nine months!"

"Nine months," Mary repeated. "Mikey and I woke up in the middle of winter. The trees were bare, the tracks were covered with snow, and of course like so many Greensouls, we couldn't understand what happened. We didn't realize that we were dead, but we knew something was terribly wrong. Not knowing what else to do, we did the worst thing that an Afterlight can do. We went home."

"But didn't you notice yourselves sinking into the ground as you walked?"

"The ground was covered with snow," Mary said. "We simply thought our feet were sinking into the snow. I suppose if we turned around we would have noticed that we left no footprints, but I didn't think to look. It wasn't until we got home that I realized how wrong things were. First of all, the house had been painted, not the light blue it had always been, but a dark shade of green. All our lives, we had lived with our father and our housekeeper since our mom had died giving birth to Mikey. Father never found himself another bride, but all that had changed. Father was there, yes, but with some woman I didn't know and her two kids. They were in *my* house, sitting at *my* table, with *my* father. Mikey and I just stood there, and that's when we first noticed our feet sinking into the ground, and it hit us both at once what had happened. Dad was talking to this woman, she gave him a kiss on the cheek, and Mikey started yelling at them. *'Father, what are you doing? Can't you hear me? I'm right here!'* But he heard nothing—saw nothing. And then gravity—the gravity of the Earth, the gravity of the situation—it all wrapped up into one single force pulling us down. You see, Nick, when you go home, the very weight of your own absence is so unbearably heavy that you start to sink like a stone in water. Nothing can stop you then. Mikey went first. One second he was there, the next second he was up to his neck, and then, the next, he was gone. Gone completely. He sank right through the floor."

"But you didn't?"

"I would have," said Mary, "but I got to the bed. You see, when I started to sink, my reflex was just like anyone else's; to grab on to something. I was already at the doorway to my parents' room. I stumbled in, already up to my waist. Everything I tried to reach for, my hand just passed through and then I grabbed the post of my parents' bed. Solid brass. *Everlost* solid. I held on to it and pulled myself up until I climbed onto the bed and tumbled into it, curled up and began to cry."

"But how—"

"My mother," Mary answered without even letting Nick finish the question. "Remember, she had died giving birth. She died in that bed."

"A dead-spot!"

Mary nodded. "I stayed there for a long time until my father, not even knowing I was there, climbed into the bed with his new wife. I couldn't bear to see them together, so I left. By then I had recovered enough so that the weight of being home wasn't so overwhelming anymore. I raced out of the house and although I sank quickly, I didn't sink entirely, and the farther away from home I got the easier it was to walk."

"What about your brother?" Nick gently asked.

"I never saw him again," Mary answered. "He sank to the center of the Earth."

Mary didn't say anything for a very long time. There was an unpleasant heaviness where her stomach had once been, but everywhere else there was a strange, ethereal sense of weightlessness. Everlost spirits did not float through the air as the living imagined, but right then, she felt like she might. "I've never told anyone that before, not even Vari."

Nick put his hand gently on her shoulder. "I know it must be horrible to lose your brother like that," he said, "but maybe, maybe, I could be like a brother to you." Then he moved a little closer. "Or . . . well . . . what I mean to say is, maybe not like a brother but something else." Then he leaned toward her, and he kissed her.

Mary did not know how to deal with this. In the many years that she had been in Everlost there were boys who would try to force kisses on her. She wasn't interested in those boys, and she always had more than enough strength to fight them off. But here was a boy whose kiss she didn't want to fight off. On the other hand, neither did she want to have her judgment clouded by unfamiliar emotions. So she didn't respond to him at all.

"I'm sorry," he said sheepishly, taking her lack of response as disinterest.

"Don't be," was all Mary said, but kept all of her feelings wrapped up tightly inside, just as she was wrapped up inside her lacy velvet dress.

Rejection was every bit as humiliating in death as it was in life.

It's because of the chocolate, Nick thought. *No, it's because I'm a year younger than her. No, I'm a* hundred *years younger than her.* Nick didn't wait for an elevator, he climbed up the stairs two steps at a time, and returned to his apartment, closing the door. Sure, Nick had been lovesick before. There was that girl in science—or was it history—he wasn't sure anymore—but the point was it had passed. Here in Everlost, though, it would *never* pass, and he wondered if he tried hard enough if he would be able to simply disappear, because how could he ever face Mary again, much less face her for eternity.

Mary, Mary, Mary. Her face and name were locked in his mind. . . . And suddenly he realized that there was no room for the name that truly should have been in his mind. The name that that brat Vari was so sure he would forget. *Hershey* was what the other kids called him now, but that wasn't his name, was it? His name started with an *N*. Nate. Noel. Norman. He was certain that it started with an *N*!

Mary found her moods were always soothed by Vari's masterful playing. He could coax the sweetest sounds from the Stradivarius violin—the same violin from which Vari had taken his Everlost name. Today he played Vivaldi's *Four Seasons*, one of Mary's favorites. It was supposed to be played by a string quartet, but Vari was the only string player among the 320 kids in her care. They had plenty of instruments though. People loved their instruments, so quite a few crossed over. A trumpet that had been run over by a bus, a piano that had fallen sixteen stories. Once in a while Mary tried to put together an orchestra, but not enough kids arrived in Everlost with the talent, or the desire to play.

"What would you like me to play next?"

Mary's mind had been drifting, so she hadn't even realized Vari had stopped playing.

"Whatever pleases you, Vari."

He began to play something mournful and pleading. Mary couldn't identify the composer. She preferred happier music.

"I should bring Nick up," Mary said. "I'm sure he'd enjoy hearing you play, too."

The passion of Vari's playing seemed to fade. "Hershey's a toad."

"You should learn to like him," Mary said.

"He's got a dirty face, and I don't like his eyes."

"He's half-Japanese. You mustn't be prejudiced just because he has an Asian look about his eyes."

Vari said nothing to that. He played a few more brooding stanzas of music, then said, "Why do you always want him around? He can't really *do* anything. Not like some other kids. Not like me."

Mary had to admit that it was true—Nick was not a standout spirit. But then, why did it matter what he could *do*? Why couldn't he just *be*?

She stood, and went to one of the western windows. It was a clear afternoon, and she could see across the Hudson River to New Jersey, but a faint haze hid the horizon from her.

The world had become so small for the living. Airplanes took people across the country in a matter of hours. You could talk with people around the world just by pressing buttons on a telephone, and now those phones weren't even connected to wires. Everlost wasn't like that. It was still an unexplored wilderness of wild children, and gaping unknowns. Mary knew very little of children beyond her sphere of influence. Even after all her years here, her explorations were limited, because safety and security required digging in, and traveling as little as possible. Moving from the Everlost apartment building she had occupied for so many years to the towers had expanded her realm, and drawn many more children to her than she had sheltered before—yet even still, the only information she got from the world beyond her towers came from Finders passing through. Mostly they spoke of rumors. Sometimes she liked what she heard, and sometimes she didn't.

Then a thought occurred to her; a marvelous thought that would give Nick a purpose and a reason to be something more than just one among many in her world.

"Finders have told me they're reading my books as far west as Chicago now," Mary told Vari. "Which means there must be children in other cities in need of care and guidance, don't you think?"

Vari stopped playing. "You're thinking of leaving here?"

Mary shook her head. "No. But that doesn't mean I can't send someone out there. Someone I can train, and teach everything I know. That person can set up an outpost in an unexplored city. Chicago, perhaps."

"Who would you send?"

"I was thinking about Nick. Of course it will take years to train him properly—ten, maybe twenty—but there's no great hurry."

Vari came up beside her, looked toward the hazy horizon, then turned to her.

"I can do it," he said. "And it won't take years to train me, either."

She turned to him and smiled. "That's sweet of you to offer."

"But I *can* do it," he insisted. "I might be little, but the kids respect me, don't they? Even the older ones."

Again she smiled warmly. "Vari, what would this place be without you and your violin? I'd always want you here, playing for us."

"'Us,'" Vari echoed. "I see."

She kissed him on top of the head. "Now, why don't you play something else. Something cheerful."

Vari began to play an upbeat tune, but somehow there seemed to be an edge to the music that was dark and undefinable.

There was no question in Allie's mind that she was getting out. She had no desire to spend eternity caught in an endless loop, no matter how pleasant it might be. But she was also smart enough to know not to leave until she got what she had come for in the first place.

Information.

Not "Miss Mary" information, but the real deal.

"I want to know about all the things Mary won't talk about!"

Allie said it loudly and fearlessly on what was commonly called the "teen floor," since that's where the older kids in Mary's domain liked to congregate. No one seemed to react, but a kid playing Ping-Pong lost his concentration, and sent the ball flying across the room.

"Don't act like you didn't hear me, and don't think that by ignoring me you can make me go away."

Like the younger kids, these kids were also caught in repetition, but it didn't take as much to jostle them out of their stupor. There seemed to be a few fourteen-year-olds here, some thirteen, maybe some twelve-year-olds who eternally wanted to be older. All told, there were maybe thirty of these older kids in Mary's domain—which was only about one-tenth of the population. She wondered if there were simply fewer older kids who got lost on their way to the light, or if most older kids simply didn't stay here with Mary for very long. Nick had said Mary was writing a book on the subject. Allie wondered if there was a subject Mary *wasn't* writing a book on.

"If Mary doesn't talk about something, there's a reason," said the Ping-Pong boy.

But Allie already had her argument well rehearsed. "Mary says there are things we shouldn't think about, and shouldn't do—but she doesn't flatly forbid anything, does she?"

"Because we always have a choice."

"That's right. And Mary respects our choices, right?"

No one said anything.

"Right?" insisted Allie.

The kids halfheartedly agreed.

"Well, I choose to talk about those things we shouldn't. And by her own rules, Mary has to respect my choice."

Several of the kids were suitably confused. That was okay. Shake them up a little, get them to see things in a new way. This was a good thing.

One girl stepped forward. It was Meadow—the girl they had met on their very first day here. "So, like, what do you want to know?"

"I want to know about haunting—and how we can

communicate with the living world. I want to know if there's a way back to life—because no matter what Mary says, we're not entirely dead, or we wouldn't be here. I want to know about the McGill. Is it real, or is it just something made up to scare little kids?"

By now all action had stopped in the room. The routine had been broken. She knew the moment she left, everyone would get right back to it, but for now she had their attention. One kid left a game of pool and approached her—but he still held on to his cue, as if worried he'd need to use it to defend himself.

"No one knows if the McGill is real," he said. "But I think it is, because Mary won't talk about it. If it wasn't real, she'd just tell us so, right?"

A few of the other kids mumbled in agreement.

"How about leaving Everlost? Is it possible to live again?"

Meadow spoke up, blunt, and unsympathetic. "Your body is in a grave, or worse, it's in ashes. I don't think you want it back."

"Yeah, but there are other ways to be alive . . . ," said a kid quietly from the corner. When Allie turned to him, he looked away.

"What do you mean, other ways?" asked Allie.

When he didn't answer, Meadow spoke up. "He doesn't know what he means."

"But you do."

Meadow crossed her arms. "There are . . . *talents* . . . that some people have, and some people don't. They're not nice talents—and they will bring you a world of bad karma. Mary calls them 'The Criminal Arts.'"

By now everyone had begun to gravitate around Allie and Meadow. By the looks on their faces, some kids seemed to know what she was talking about, but most seemed clueless.

"What kind of talents?" asked Allie. "How would I know if I have them?"

"You'd be luckier not to know."

"Excuse me," said a voice from the back. Everyone turned to see Vari standing there. There was no way to know how much he had heard. Meadow instantly put distance between herself and Allie, going back to the game she had been playing. The rest of the kids moved away from Allie as well, as if she was poison.

"Good news," Vari said. "Miss Mary just traded with a Finder for a bucket of fried chicken. She says everyone can have a single bite."

The rush to the elevators nearly swept Allie off her feet. As much as Allie wanted a bite of that chicken as well, she resisted. The fact wasn't lost on Vari, who patiently waited for the last elevator with her.

"What's the matter?" he asked. "Were you a vegetarian when you were alive?" Allie couldn't tell whether he was being sarcastic or sincere.

In her book, *You're Dead—So Now What?*, Mary Hightower offers the following warning for the restless soul: "Wanderlust is a dangerous thing. In Everlost there's safety in staying put. Afterlights who are cursed with a desire to travel don't last for long. They either succumb to Gravity Fatigue, or they are captured by feral packs of unsavory children. The few that escape these fates become Finders, but the existence of a Finder is full of peril. Better to seek a safe haven, and stay there. And if you haven't found a safe haven, by all means, come see me."

CHAPTER 10

An Elevator Down

Allie was alone in an elevator the following morning, when a human skeleton got in on the ninety-eighth floor.

Allie gasped at the sight of him.

"Get over it," the skeleton-boy said as the elevator doors closed.

Allie quickly realized who it was. He wasn't a skeleton at all. He simply had white makeup all over his face, with black around the eyes, and wore a cheap Halloween skeleton costume. His Afterlight glow merely added to the overall effect.

"Sorry," said Allie. "You just caught me off guard."

There were two kids here who had the supreme misfortune of crossing on Halloween: this kid, and another with green face-paint and fake peeling skin. Everyone called them Skully and Molder.

"So," said Skully, after the elevator doors had closed. "I hear you've been asking about the Criminal Arts."

"Yeah," said Allie, "but asking is useless if nobody answers."

"I can tell you stuff, but you can't tell anyone you heard it from me."

The elevator door opened. "Your floor?" asked Skully.

Allie had been going down to the arcade to try to wrestle Lief away from his Pac-Man game, but that could wait. She didn't get out, and the elevator door closed again.

"Tell me what you know. I promise I won't tell anyone you told me."

Skully hit the button for the lobby, and the elevator began its long fall. "There's this place a couple of miles away from here. A building that crossed a long time ago. A pickle factory, I think. There's this kid who lives there. They call him 'The Haunter.' He teaches people how to do things."

"How to do what, exactly?"

"Paranorming, ecto-ripping, skinjacking—you name it."

"I don't know what those things are."

Skully sighed impatiently. "He can show you how to move things in the living world, make yourself heard to the living—and maybe even *seen*. They even say he can reach into the living world, and pull things out of it. He can actually *make* things cross into Everlost."

"And he can teach this?"

"That's what I hear."

"Have you ever met him?" Allie asked.

The kid backed away a little. "I know kids who went there. But they didn't come back."

Allie just shrugged it off. "Maybe after visiting the Haunter, they found something better than this. Maybe they didn't come back because they didn't want to."

"Maybe," said Skully. "If you want, I'll get you the address."

Allie was going to ask him more, but the doors whooshed open, he stepped out, and a gaggle of little kids swept in from the lobby, on their way to higher places.

Nick. Nicky. Nicholas.

It had taken him hours to remember his name, and now that he had captured it, he wasn't letting go. His name was Nick. Nick something-or-other. It was a Japanese last name, because his father was Japanese. His mother was Caucasian, although he couldn't quite remember the details of either of their faces, but that was a battle for another time. Right now, holding on to his first name took all his attention.

Nick. Nicky. Nicholas.

He would remember his last name, too. He *would*. He *had* to. Even if he had to track down his own grave and read it there, he would know his last name again. He would keep them both, and no one would call him Hershey, or Cadbury, or Ghirardelli, or anything other than *Nick, Nicky, Nicholas*.

He took scraps of paper from his room, and wrote it over and over again, shoving a tiny slip into each of his pockets, in every drawer, under his mattress, and even under the cushions of the sofa that Lief slept on. Lief wouldn't care—he hadn't been back to the room for days, anyway.

Nick, Nicky, Nicholas. Maybe even *Nic-o*.

He was interrupted by Allie pounding on the door. He knew it was Allie, because she was the only one who ever pounded. Mary's knock was gentle and refined. Allie knocked like she wanted the door to fall down.

"I'm busy!" Nick said. "Go away."

But she just kept on pounding, so he had to let her in.

When Allie stepped in, she looked around, as if something was wrong. "Nick, what are you doing in here?"

Nick turned around to look at his room, and for the first time he saw what he had done. There were little scraps of paper everywhere—not just in and under things, but all over the room. It looked like the place was covered in a dusting of snow. He hadn't just used the paper in the drawers, he had torn out all the pages of all the books on the shelves. Mary's books. He had torn them to shreds and had written "Nick" on every little shred, both front and back.

Only now did he notice it was daylight. Hadn't he started this at dusk? Had he been doing this all night? Nick was speechless. He had no idea how this had happened. It was as if he were in a trance, broken only by Allie's arrival. The weird thing about it was that a part of him wanted to throw her out, and get back to his work. His important work. *Nick, Nicky, Nicholas.*

Just like the kids playing kickball, or the kids watching *The Love Boat* every day until the end of time, he had found his "niche," and hadn't even realized it.

He looked at Allie, pleadingly, opening his mouth, but unable to say anything. He felt a certain shame about it that he couldn't explain.

"It's all right," Allie said. "We're getting out of here."

"What?"

"You heard me—we're leaving."

Nick resisted. Leave here? Leave Mary? "No! I don't want to leave."

Allie stared at him like he was a mental case. Maybe

he was. "What do you want to do? Stay here writing your name forever?"

"I told Mary I wouldn't leave." But then, thought Nick, that was before she so thoroughly rejected his sorry butt.

Allie scowled, and Nick thought she might start ranting about what a terrible person Mary was, and blah blah blah—but she didn't. Instead she said: "If you really want to impress Mary . . . if you *really* want to be useful to her, then you need to learn a skill."

"What are you talking about?"

"How would you like to be able to talk to the living—or better yet, how would you like to reach into the living world and actually *pull* things out of it?"

Nick shook his head. "But that's Ecto-ripping! Mary hates it!"

"She only hates it because no one here can do it—and just because Mary calls them 'The Criminal Arts,' doesn't mean they really are. They're only criminal if you use them in criminal ways. Think about it, Nick. If you come with me and learn all there is to know, you can come back with food and toys for all her little kids. You can bring her a dozen roses that will never wilt or fade. You can actually *mean* something to her."

Nick found this irresistibly tempting. The more he considered it, the harder it was to refuse. "Who's gonna teach us that?"

"I know a kid who knows a kid," said Allie.

Nick looked at his room, covered in little bits of paper. If an eternity of *that* was the alternative, maybe it was time he trusted Allie, and took a leap of faith.

"Tell me more."

"C'mon," said Allie. "We'll talk on the way to the arcade."

One down, one to go. Allie found Lief exactly where she expected to: practically glued to the Pac-Man machine.

"Lief?"

"Leave me alone, I've got to beat this level."

"Lief, this game is so old, living people don't even play it anymore. 'Retro' is one thing, but this is prehistoric!"

"Stop bothering me!"

Nick leaned his back against the side of the game, with his arms crossed. "He's found his niche," Nick said. "Like I almost did."

"It's not a niche," said Allie, "it's a rut. Mary might think it's a good thing, but it's not." Allie knew now that in the same way water always seeks its lowest point, so do the souls of Everlost—carving a rut that becomes a ditch, that becomes a canyon—and the deeper it gets, the harder it is to escape from. Allie knew it, just as she knew that Lief, if left alone, would play this game until the end of time.

"This is wrong, Lief!"

"Just go."

She went to the back of the machine to pull the plug, only to find out that it wasn't even plugged in, and she cursed the fact that the normal laws of science didn't apply in Everlost. Machines worked not because they had a power source, but because in some strange way, they remembered working.

Allie thought for a moment, then said, "We're going to a place that has even better games!"

"Don't lie to him," said Nick—but she had already caught Lief's attention. He was looking at her instead of at the machine. His eyes were glassy, and his expression vague, like he was surfacing from a deep, deep sleep.

"Better games?"

"Listen," said Allie, "you saved my life before we got here. Now it's my turn to save yours. Don't lose your soul to a Pac-Man machine."

On the screen, his Pac-Man was caught by one of the fuzzy creatures, and died. Game over. But, like everything else in Mary's world, it wasn't over, because it started again. No quarter needed. Lief turned to gaze longingly at the game, but Allie touched his cheek, and turned his head to face her again.

"Nick and I are going to learn about haunting. I want you to come with us. Please."

She could see the moment he pulled himself out of the quicksand of his own mind. "I didn't save your life," he said. "Too late for that. But I did save you from a fate worse than death."

Allie couldn't help but think she had done the same for him.

Deep down, Nick knew that a trip to the Haunter was a betrayal of Mary, but if Allie was right, the skills he'd come back with would be worth it. Mary would forgive him; forgiveness and acceptance were part of who she was. Nick felt a sense of anticipation, like butterflies in his stomach, and he had to admit it was a good feeling. It felt almost like being alive.

Allie had gotten directions from Skully. It wasn't too far away, but there was no safe time to leave. As Everlost was a world of insomniacs, there was always someone there to see every move they made. They decided to leave late at night, during a storm. That way, no kids would be playing outside, and no one on the higher floors would be able to see them, or their Afterlight glow through the sheets of rain when they crossed the plaza. If they timed it right, they wouldn't be seen by the lookouts either. As their elevator descended, Nick turned to Allie. "I oughta have my head examined for agreeing to this."

"It'll be fun," Allie said. "Right, Lief?"

"Yeah." Lief didn't sound too convinced.

While the rain didn't even get the marble plaza wet, lightning and thunder were as real to Everlost as they were to the living. After a bright flash of lightning, they waited for the thunder crash before stepping out, and then they headed uptown, without looking back.

Had they looked back, however, they would have seen Vari peering out from the second floor, watching them as they left. Next to him stood Skully. Once Allie, Nick, and Lief were out of sight, Vari gave Skully a single cherry jelly bean. His reward for a job well done.

"Do not speak of the Criminal Arts," writes Mary Hightower in her pamphlet *The Evils of Paranorming*. "Do not speak of them, do not think of them, and most of all, do not seek to learn them. Attempting to influence the living world can only lead to misery."

CHAPTER 11

The Haunter

Nick and Allie had not been out in the rain since they crossed into Everlost. "Drenched to the bone" took on a whole new meaning when the rain passed through you on its way to the ground.

"Sleet is worse," Lief said.

The old pickle factory was just where Skully said it would be. A white brick building on Washington Street, that, at some point in its life, crossed over into Everlost. A heavy steel door was ominously ajar. Nick didn't like the looks of it.

"Why do I get the feeling this is a really, really bad idea?"

"Because," said Allie, "you're a certified wimp."

And so to prove that he wasn't, Nick was the first to push the door open. Bad idea or not, no more complaining. He had made his decision, and he was going for it.

The instant he stepped in, the aroma snagged him. There was a rich smell in the air of roast meat and garlic, hitting him with more ferocity than the pelting storm—the aromas were so wonderful they made Nick weak at the knees.

The building had been gutted, leaving nothing but clouded windows, a concrete floor, and black girders holding up the floor above. Hanging from the ceiling was the source of the wonderful smell. Roast chickens, turkeys, and smoked fish hung from meat hooks. Entire salamis hung from strings.

"It's true then," said Allie in a charged whisper. "The Haunter can rip whatever he wants right out of the living world!"

"I'll never doubt you again," said Nick.

"Wow!" was all Lief could say.

They were so awed by the hanging feast, it took them a few moments to notice the small Afterlight sitting cross-legged in the center of the concrete floor. He looked frozen there, as if he hadn't moved for many years. His glow had a yellow tinge to it, and shimmered faintly against the gray walls.

"I've been waiting for you," said the Haunter.

Nick found his feet not wanting to move forward, until Allie whispered in his ear, "He probably says that to anyone who shows up."

"He's just a little kid!" said Lief, but Allie "shushed" him.

The three kids approached the seated figure. The light was dim, but as they got closer, they could see that even though he had died young, the Haunter was a very, very old spirit. Physically, he couldn't be any older than six, and yet there was such a sense of age in him, he might as well have been a withered old wizard. The clothes he wore barely looked like clothes at all. They were furs, stitched together—perhaps to protect him from an ice age that had passed twenty-thousand years ago.

"Tell me why you have come," the Haunter said in his high-pitched voice. He had only one visible tooth. Perhaps it was because most of his front baby teeth had come out shortly before he died.

"We . . . we heard you can teach people to haunt the living world," Allie said.

"I teach nothing," he said. "Either you have the skill, or you don't."

Then he reached into his lap, and produced a smooth stone the size of an egg. The Haunter looked at the stone for a moment, as if it held the wisdom of the world, then in one smooth motion, he hurled it at Nick. "Catch it!" he said.

Nick held up his hands, but the stone passed right through his chest, and hit the floor behind him! This wasn't an Everlost stone, it was an artifact of the living world!

The Haunter laughed in his very-old-little-kid voice. "Pick it up. Bring it to me," he said.

"How am I supposed to pick that up?"

"The same way I did," said the Haunter.

Nick went to the stone, leaned down, and reached for it. His fingers closed on it, but passed right through it, just as he knew they would. He tried again, concentrating this time. Nothing. The stone didn't even wobble. *Fine,* thought Nick. *He'll point out how completely useless we are, then he'll start teaching us.*

Nick stood up and turned to the Haunter, anxious to just get on with it. "I can't," said Nick. "I can't pick up the stone."

"In that case," said the Haunter, "your lesson is over." Then he snapped his fingers, and there came a thundering that had nothing to do with the weather. The steel door behind them slammed itself shut. Then, down a flight of old wooden stairs came a dozen figures wrapped from head to toe in black robes, and they headed straight for Nick. Before he knew what was happening, dark gloved hands lifted him off the ground.

"Stop! What are you doing!"

"The price of failure," the Haunter said calmly, "is an eternity to think about it."

And then they turned Nick upside down, and plunged him headfirst into a pickle barrel that had crossed over into Everlost along with the building. It was still full of slimy saltwater brine. Then they slammed the cover back on, and Nick found himself submerged in salty, liquid darkness. For a horrible instant, he thought he might drown there, but realized he couldn't. The brine was in him and around him. It sloshed through the place where his insides should be, it filled his mouth and nose, yet still he did not drown, and never would.

Allie stared at the barrel paralyzed with disbelief, listening to Nick's angry, muffled screams from within as the dark-robed figures nailed the lid on tight. So this was why no one ever returned from the Haunter. How could she have been so stupid to take this risk? To make her friends take the risk? *I did this to Nick,* was all Allie could think. *I made him come here.*

Allie looked at all the other barrels. Were those barrels full of others who failed the test, unable to die, yet unable to escape, left to pickle in their own thoughts for all time?

"The other boy next," the Haunter said.

Lief shook his head. "No. No, I don't want to! I just want to go."

"Bring me the stone and you can go."

He looked at the faces of the kids around him, but they didn't seem to have faces beneath the dark wrappings.

"I don't like this game," Lief cried. "I don't want to play."

"Let him go!" Allie demanded. "What kind of monster are you?"

The Haunter only gave her a single-toothed smile, then turned to Lief again. "The stone."

With no choice, Lief went to the stone, and tried to lift it. He grunted in frustration with each grasp, and Allie suddenly found herself thinking of that stupid arcade game, where a claw tried to scoop up a stuffed animal. The claw almost always came up empty-handed. And so did Lief.

"Nooooo!"

The Haunter's goons were on him, and although Lief and Allie tried to fight them, there were just too many of them. Lief was plunged into another barrel, kicking and screaming and sloshing brine across the floor, until they nailed on the lid. Allie could hear his sobs from within the awful brine.

Then the dark figures pulled open the lid of a third barrel, and waited.

"Bring me the stone," the Haunter said to Allie.

Allie always prided herself on being cool in a crisis, and coming through when it really mattered. She had to figure the angle here. She had to think them all out of this.

"I'll bring you the stone, if you release my friends."

The Haunter did not move. Did not bat an eyelash. Allie knew she was in no bargaining position, yet still the Haunter said "Agreed. Your friends for the stone."

So this was it, then. She had brought them here, and only she could get them out.

A stone on the ground. It seemed such a simple thing, but she reached for it with the same terror with which she would have reached for a burning coal.

Grabbing the stone was like trying to grab a shadow. Her fingers passed through it again and again, and she found herself angry at the stone: a stubborn piece of the living world, refusing to admit that she existed. "I *Am*!" She wanted to shout at it. "I exist, and I *WILL* move you!"

Still her fingers passed through it again, and again.

"Enough!" said the Haunter, and his goons advanced on her.

Move you stupid stone, move!

Allie forced every ounce of her will to the tips of her fingers and closed them again over the smooth rock, and again, her fingertips failed her.

But this time the stone wobbled.

Suddenly the goons stopped moving, and the Haunter stood up. The entire world seemed perched on the tips of Allie's fingers.

"Go on," the Haunter said.

Allie reached for the stone one more time. She had made it wobble. She had moved it. The knowledge that she had done it gave her an inkling of faith that she might do it again. This time she reached for it with not just her fingertips but with both hands, and she tried to scoop it up in her palms.

I will not leave my friends in those barrels, she told the stone. *I will not be a victim of this monsterchild. YOU WILL RISE OFF THE FLOOR!*

And it did! Although the stone sank deep into her ghostly hands, it came off the ground! Allie did not let her excitement break her concentration. She held her will in the palms of her hands along with that stone. It was heavy. It was perhaps the heaviest thing she had ever lifted, but she did not feel its weight in her muscles. This was a weight she could feel on her soul, and the strain was so great she felt her spirit would tear apart. Slowly she moved toward the Haunter, and his goons backed away.

"Here's your stone," she said. He held out his hand and she brought her hands over his. The stone lingered in her hands only an instant longer, then it fell right through, and into the Haunter's open palm. He closed his palm around it.

"Very good. A skill is best revealed when one has no choice but to show it."

"Free my friends."

"Five years of study," the Haunter said.

"What?"

"You have shown your skill. Now you must develop it, and discover what other skills you have—because where there is one skill, there are more. Study with me for five years, and then I shall free your friends from their barrels."

Allie took a step back. "That wasn't our agreement."

The Haunter showed no expression. "I said I would free them. I never said *when*."

This time, instead of coming up with a clever, well-thought-out approach to the situation, she found herself lunging for the Haunter, which of course did no good, because his goons were there to hold her back. Their strength seemed unnatural, even for Everlost spirits—and in a moment she found out why. In her struggle, she grabbed at the scarf covering one of their faces, and what she saw terrified her. She should have known something was wrong from the beginning. If Afterlights all wore the clothes they died in, what were the chances of finding a team of goons, all shrouded in black? These weren't Afterlights at all. They were shells—and when Allie peeled back the scarf from the face, she saw nothing behind it—just cloth curving around the back of a head that didn't exist.

Allie screamed, reached for the other faces, and one after another, she revealed them as empty, soulless soldiers. This trick was part of the Haunter's skill; wrapping clothes around empty air, creating soldiers out of nothing. The more Allie screamed, the louder the Haunter laughed.

Handless gloves gripped her tightly, and carried her to the door. "Come back when you are ready to learn," the Haunter said.

Then they pulled open the heavy iron door, and hurled her out into the street, slamming the door behind her.

She tried to push herself up on her elbows but found she couldn't, and realized she was sinking into the middle of the living-world street. She struggled to free herself, but only became more deeply embedded in the asphalt, which seemed more like tar trying to take her down. A garbage truck rolled over her, its wheels rolling straight through her head like it wasn't there, and it only made her angrier.

Angry enough that one of the rear tires blew as it crossed through her.

The truck slammed on its brakes, and pulled over to the side of the street up ahead.

Did I blow out that tire?

But if she did, she didn't care. Not now. With a heavy force of will, she pulled herself upright. Now standing waist-deep in the asphalt, she worked her legs, and pressed with her hands until she had pulled herself out of the street.

She ran to the door of the Haunter's lair. For a quick moment she forgot that it was not a living-world door, and slammed into it with full force, as if she could pass through it. She bounced off the solid steel, almost landing back in the street.

She pounded on the door over and over, ramming her shoulder against it. She tried to climb in through windows, but they were eternally blocked with security bars that had crossed into Everlost along with the rest of the building. For hours she tried to find a way in, and by dawn she was no closer to freeing her friends than she had been when she started.

As the jet-dark sky became the motley gray of a stormy morning, the rain turned to sleet, and the pinpricks of rain passing through her became sharp darts of ice. Discomfort, but not pain. Never pain, which just fed her rage. This dead/not-dead state robbed her of her right to feel with her body, and that made the anguish of her soul all the more severe.

Come back when you are ready to learn, the Haunter had said, but Allie already knew she would never be his student.

She was no monster, and neither would she study under a monster. She would be back, though. She would come with a force of three hundred kids. Mary's kids. They would tear the place down brick by brick if they had to, until there was not even a ghost of a ghost of a building.

Allie ran all the way back to the great marble plaza that marked the boundaries of Mary's towering domain, and hurtled straight through a revolving door, ignoring the surprised looks of the kids on lookout. She raced into the elevator with such speed that she hit the back wall. The entire elevator shook, the doors closed, and in an instant she was surging upward.

She and Mary might have had their little differences, but Allie had enough faith in Mary to know she would sacrifice herself for the safety of the kids in her care. Together they would take on the Haunter, and who knows, perhaps it would forge some sort of bond between Allie and Mary.

She began at the top floor, but Mary wasn't there. There were kids in the foodless food court, playing their morning games. "Mary! Where's Mary? I have to find her!"

Allie went to the arcade floor, the publishing room, the TV room, and everywhere she went kids followed, her commotion actually drawing kids right out of their routines, like a speeding train pulling a swarm of leaves behind it, caught in its draft.

Mary was nowhere.

Vari, however, seemed to be everywhere. Everywhere she went, Vari seemed to find a way to get there first.

"Mary knows where you went last night," Vari announced. "Everyone knows."

Allie looked around at the other kids, and Allie knew from the way they looked at her, and from the distance they kept, that she had suddenly become an outsider. Someone to be feared. Someone who could not be trusted.

"Mary doesn't want to talk to you," Vari said. "Ever."

"Listen, you little weasel, you tell me where Mary is, or I swear I'll take you straight out into the living world, and stomp you down so hard, you'll sink clear to China!"

When Vari didn't talk, Allie took things into her own hands. Allie had heard that Mary liked to wander the unused floors when something was troubling her. A quick trip to the elevator control room found all the elevators on the usual floors, except for one. There was a single elevator waiting on the fifty-eighth floor.

It was the emptiness that hit Allie first. She knew the unused floors of the great towers were empty, but some were more empty than others. When you stood in the concrete expanse of floor fifty-eight, you felt like the only person in the universe.

Mary was there all right, in a far corner looking out of the windows at the world below. When she turned to see Allie her expression hardened. Other elevators began to arrive, and kids piled out of stairwells to watch the situation unfold.

Mary strode toward her with such sternness about her, Allie felt sure Mary would slap her . . . but she didn't. Instead Mary stopped a distance away. *Dueling distance,*

Allie thought. The distance from which Aaron Burr must have shot Alexander Hamilton.

"I want to know where Nick is," Mary asked. Allie could see she had been crying, although Mary tried not to show it.

"I need your help," Allie said.

"First tell me where Nick is!"

Allie hesitated. This wasn't going to be easy. "Lief and Nick have been captured by the Haunter." At the word "Haunter," many of the little kids gasped, and clung to older children.

"See, didn't I tell you?" Vari said. "They brought this on themselves!"

"Shut up, Vari!" It was the first time Allie had heard Mary yell at him. It was the first time she heard her yell at anyone. Now she turned her anger toward Allie. "You deliberately went against my wishes, and my warnings!"

Allie was not about to deny it. "I know. I'm sorry, and you can punish me any way you like, but right now we have to rescue Lief and Nick."

"*Your* actions put them in harm's way."

"Yes," admitted Allie. "Yes, they did. I was wrong, but right now—"

Then Mary turned to all those gathered. "Let this be a lesson to everyone that nothing good can ever come from leaving this place."

Now Allie was getting frustrated. "Yes, fine. I am the poster child for bad choices. Now can we just get on with what has to be done!"

Mary looked at her with the same sadness her eyes held

when she looked out from her high window. A single tear came, and she wiped it away.

"There is nothing to be done."

Allie heard what Mary said, but was convinced she hadn't heard her right.

"What?"

"Nick and Lief are lost," Mary said. "*You've* lost them." And Mary turned to walk away.

Allie shook her head, and felt like lunging at Mary just as she had lunged at the Haunter, but she held herself back. "No! No—you can't just leave them."

Then Mary turned on her with a powerful vengeance. "Don't you think I want to save them? Do you think I want Nick spending an eternity imprisoned by that evil spirit?"

"Then do something about it."

"That would risk every child here, and I won't put them in danger. I protect them! I don't send them out to fight a war! The Haunter leaves us alone. We leave him alone. That's the way it is with all the monsters. Even the McGill." Again, nervous whispers at the mention of the McGill.

"The world out there is not a kind one, if you haven't figured that out," Mary said. "Sometimes we sink, and never come back. Sometimes we are captured and are never seen again. Losing Nick and Lief is tragic, and I will not make it more tragic by sending other defenseless children for the Haunter to enslave."

As breathless as someone who did not breathe could be, Allie said, "You're a monster. You're no better than the Haunter! You're telling me that you're going to do NOTHING? That Nick and Lief are 'acceptable losses.'"

"No loss is acceptable," Mary said. "But sometimes we have to accept it anyway."

"I won't!"

"If I can accept it, then so can you," she said. "If you want to stay here with us, you'll learn to live with it."

And all at once Allie knew what was going on here.

Mary was getting rid of her. She was hurling Allie out of the fold, but doing it in such a way that she could remain blameless. If Allie wanted to stay, then she had to accept the loss of her friends, and not even try to rescue Nick and Lief. Allie would never stay under those conditions, and Mary knew it. Maybe that's why Mary became calm, and in control again.

"I'm truly sorry this happened," Mary said. "I know what you must be going through right now."

What made it worse was that Mary's voice had genuine compassion in it. She honestly did care. Mary's caring, however, came with too high a price.

Allie swung her hand with all the strength she could muster, and slapped Mary across the face with such force that Mary stumbled backward. Vari caught her and in an instant a dozen other kids were all over Allie holding her back, pulling her down, tearing at her as if they could tear her apart.

"Leave her alone!" yelled Mary, and almost instantly the kids let her go.

"I wish you could feel pain," Allie said. "I wish you could feel the sting of that slap."

Then she turned, marched into an elevator, and took it down alone. She didn't know where she was going, only that she had publicly renounced Mary Queen of Snots, and was not coming back.

Mary stared at Allie's elevator door long after it had closed. Allie may not have known it, but Mary had felt the sting of the slap. Not on her face, but in her soul, where it hurt all the more. Even so, Mary had done the right thing. She had turned the other cheek.

"Go back to what you were doing," Mary told all the kids around her. "Everything's fine."

The crowd began to split up, and soon it was only her and Vari on the desolate floor.

"Why did you let her go?" Vari said. "She should be punished."

"Being alone in the living world is punishment enough," Mary said, and although Vari didn't seem satisfied with her response, he would accept it. They all would. Mary wondered if Allie had any idea how hard it was to allow Nick and Lief to be sacrificed for the sake of the other children. But the Haunter had powers that Mary did not. Just as it was foolish for them to go there in the first place, it would be doubly foolish to attempt a rescue. Foolish, and pointless. And now Nick was gone. Before she could really get to know him he was gone, and there was nothing she could do about it. For a moment grief threatened to overwhelm her. A gasp of remorse escaped her throat, but she fought it down, just as she fought down her tears. For the sake of all her children.

"You did the right thing," Vari told her.

She leaned over to kiss him on the head, but stopped,

knelt down, and kissed him on the cheek instead. "Thank you, Vari. Thank you for being so loyal."

Vari beamed.

As Allie's elevator went down, theirs went up. Mary's grief was heavy, but she would find a way to get past it. The turmoil that Allie had brought them would soon be gone. Soon there would be happy children playing ball and jumping rope, which was as it should be, and as it would be day after day, forever and ever.

In her book *Everything Mary Says Is Wrong,* Allie the Outcast writes: "There are mysteries in Everlost. Some of them are wonderful, and others are scary. They should all be explored, though—perhaps that's why we're here; to experience the good and the bad that Everlost has to offer. I really don't know why we didn't get where we were going, but I do know this much: being trapped doing the same thing over and over again for all time is no way to spend eternity—and anyone who tells you so is wrong."

CHAPTER 12

Learning to Surf

The sense of isolation Allie felt after leaving Mary's domain was as overwhelming and complete as if she had been sealed into a barrel herself. Being out in the living world left her infinitely lonely. Mary could act like the living world didn't matter anymore, but for Allie it was an ever-present reminder that she could witness, but not participate, in life. For days she tried to work out a plan for rescuing her friends from the clutches of the Haunter, and as she schemed, she walked, because she had to. She was like a shark, always having to stay in motion—and although she had found many dead-spots in the city where she could rest, she never lingered long. Then one day, she had a moment of clarity, and she realized that she had been drawn into her own endless loop. She had been walking the exact same streets in the exact same pattern, and she had been doing it not for days, but for weeks. She had thought she was immune to getting trapped in a ghostly pattern, but she was wrong. The sense of helplessness of it—the sense of inevitability—almost made her spirit cave in, and give in to the pattern. She almost continued in her repetitive weave of the streets, because it was easier than fighting it. It had grown comfortable. Familiar. It was the thought of Lief and Nick, still trapped in those barrels, that broke her out of it, because if she stayed in this rut, she would never find a way to free them.

The first step was the hardest. She turned left instead of right on Twenty-first Street, and an immediate sense of panic set in. She wanted to take back her step, and return to her old pattern—but she resisted, and took one more step, and another, and another. Soon the panic settled to mere terror, and the terror settled to normal fear. It only took one city block for her fear to fade into mild foreboding—the type of thing anyone felt when faced with the unknown.

Careful not to begin retracing her steps again, she forced herself to go places she had avoided. New York was a crowded city, but there were areas that were less traveled. These were the places Allie had stuck to, for she couldn't handle the crowds that would pass through her as if she wasn't there.

Now she forced herself to go to the crowded places. It was as she passed through midtown Manhattan during lunchtime that she discovered something Mary had probably never written about in her various volumes.

The streets were crowded. More than just crowded, they were packed. The midtown towers flushed out thousands of people during the lunch-hour rush, and of course, they all barreled through Allie as if she wasn't even there. It was terribly unpleasant to feel them pass through her—much worse than when something inanimate, like a car or a bus passed through, because a living person had a strange organic commotion about it. The instant a person passed through her she could feel the rush of blood, the beating of a heart, the rumble of intestines still digesting whatever they had eaten for breakfast. It was, to say the least, profoundly icky.

Much stranger, though, was the sudden disorientation that fell over her when a tightly packed gaggle of businessmen crashed through her. Her thoughts became strange and random—the way thoughts become just before sleep sets in.

—stock about to split/need that raise/no one suspects/ah, yes, Hawaii—

And when the businessmen had passed, all that remained were the high-decibel sounds of the city. She assumed she was just hearing little bits of their conversations, and left it at that. Then it happened again when a crowd of tourists tromped through her, on their way to the theater district.

—too expensive/aching feet/what is that smell/pickpockets—

This time she knew she wasn't hearing their conversations, because most of them were silent, and the ones who were talking were speaking French. Now she understood exactly what was going on. It was like channel-surfing—but she was channel surfing people's minds.

She flashed to that moment mired in the street outside of the Haunter's warehouse. A truck had passed through her—or at least its tires had. She had been angry—furious—and in that instant the tire blew out, as if her anger had caused it to burst. What was it the Haunter had said?

. . . You have to discover what other skills you have—because where there is one skill, there are more. . . .

Could this all be part of some innate talent in haunting? Was she special in this ability to intrude into the real world, rupturing a tire, and reading the minds of the living for brief moments?

And then she thought—could those moments be made to last . . .

The next time she mind-surfed, she did it intentionally, with hopes of catching the wave.

Allie found a girl who seemed to be about her age. She was a society-type girl, wearing a uniform from some ritzy prep school. Allie followed behind her for a few blocks, matching her pace. Then Allie took a sudden leap forward, and stepped right inside of her skin.

> *—i could but if i do it might not work and they might not like me but then they might and if i don't they certainly won't even notice me and this skirt is definitely too tight am i gaining weight oh there's that pizza place no i'm bursting out of this stupid ugly skirt but it smells so good—*

Whoa! The girl made a sharp turn right, and went into the pizza place, leaving Allie there on the street reeling from the experience. She had surfed the girl's mind for ten seconds at least. By the time Allie recovered, she was knee-deep in the street, and had to pull herself out.

I shouldn't have done that, Allie told herself, but even so, she wanted to do it again. That scared her, and so she left Sixth Avenue, ducking down a smaller side street, making sure she had absolutely no contact with another living person for the rest of the day. *I'll have to tell Nick and Lief about this*, she thought, and that reminded her that unless she rescued them, she would never get to tell them anything. They would spend the rest of their unnatural lives pickling.

The only way to rescue them was to find others who could help her, and she had to do it before a new routine set in. Mary and her little club were of no use, so Allie would have to gather her own allies. The question was, where would she find them?

She began looking for "ghosts" of buildings that had crossed over when they were demolished. Only a few buildings did. Maybe one out of every thousand that met the wrecking ball was deemed worthy by God, or the universe, or whatever, to cross into Everlost.

The old Waldorf=Astoria hotel was the most promising—after all, it was a hotel, so what better place for dead/not-dead kids to stay?

She pushed through the revolving door to reveal a lobby done up in plush art-deco spendor. Some singer, long dead, crooned through a big old-fashioned radio, singing "Embraceable You." There was a huge bar just off the lobby, but no bottles graced its cherrywood shelves. Instead a big sign read BAR PERMANENTLY CLOSED DUE TO PROHIBITION.

"Hello? Is anybody here?"

She called twice, and rang the bell at the reception desk. Nothing. The combination of 1920s music and the absolute emptiness of the place gave her the horror-movie creeps. The hotel wasn't merely deserted, it was soulless, like the Haunter's hollow soldiers. She left as quickly as she could.

She had to face the fact that most every Afterlight in the city ended up moving in with Mary. Safety in numbers. Mary's little kingdom was simply the place to be in this part of the world. But then, thought Allie, Everlost did have other territories. . . .

CHAPTER 13

Time in a Bottle

Lief was accustomed to being alone, but there was quite a difference between being alone in a lush green forest, and being jammed into a pickle barrel.

At first he felt sure Allie would rescue him right away. When it didn't happen in the first few minutes, or the next, or the next, he began to get scared. Then the fear turned to anger, and then the anger itself pickled into resignation. He could hear very little in the brine, and could feel even less.

Then, as the days went by, his mind began to play the most amazing trick on him. He was able to forget where he was. The darkness became a starless infinity that stretched into empty space. His spirit filled the emptiness from one end of infinity to the other. This, he knew, is what God must have felt like before creation. A single spirit in a formless liquid eternity. It was a feeling of such power, time itself seemed to stop in its tracks. Lief felt as if he was the entire universe, and nothing, at the same time. So glorious was this sensation of timelessness, that he was able to lock himself inside of it just as tightly as he was locked in the barrel.

Nick, on the other hand, was miserable.

CHAPTER 14

The Alter Boys

WELCOME TO ROCKLAND COUNTY! It was a road sign Allie was sure she'd never see again. The last time she had seen it, she was pushed into the Earth, and if it hadn't been for Lief and Nick, she wouldn't have made it out. *I must be crazy coming back here.* Well, crazy or not, here she was.

"Johnnie-O!" she called out at the top of her lungs. "I want to talk to you, Johnnie-O!"

Allie knew it wasn't just bad luck that had brought Johnnie-O and his little team of morons to them that night. The way Allie figured it, any new arrivals in Everlost in this area would follow the main highway, and would pass this way. If Johnnie-O wasn't here himself, chances are he had a lookout keeping an eye on this very spot, waiting for some poor unsuspecting Greensoul to rest beneath the WELCOME TO ROCKLAND COUNTY sign.

She figured right. It took a few hours of calling, and making noise, but finally word had been relayed back to Johnnie-O, and he showed up at around noon. This time he came with a dozen kids to back him up, instead of just four. Nothing was going to scare them away this time. The cigarette was still hanging out of the corner of his mouth, smoldering away, and Allie realized that cigarette was going to be stuck there until the end of time.

"Hey—it's that girl who tricked you!" said the kid with the purple lips, and the lump in his throat.

Johnnie-O hit him. "She didn't trick me," he said, and nobody contradicted him. He assumed a kind of gunslinger posture, like this was a showdown. He looked more comical than anything else, with his huge hands.

"I thought I sent you down," he said.

"You thought wrong."

"So what? Did ya come back so's I could send you down right this time?"

"I'm back with a proposition."

Johnnie-O looked at her, his expression stony. At first Allie thought he was doing it for effect. Then she realized he didn't know what "proposition" meant.

"I want your help," Allie explained.

Raggedy Andy tossed his weird red hair out of his eyes and laughed. "Why would *we* wanna help *you*?"

Johnnie-O smacked him, then crossed his heavy arms and said, "Why would *we* wanna help *you*?"

"Because I can get you what you want."

By now even more kids had arrived. Some were real little, others her age, maybe a bit older. They all had menacing scowls—even the little ones.

"We don't want nothin' from you!" Johnnie-O said, and his chorus of bullies grumbled their agreement. This was all posturing, Allie knew. He had to be curious—if he wasn't, he'd already have pushed her down.

"You attack Greensouls for the crumbs in their pockets, and prechewed gum."

Johnnie-O shrugged. "Yeah, so?"

"What if I told you I knew where you could get *real* food. Not just pocket crumbs, but whole loaves of bread."

Johnnie-O kept his arms crossed. "And what if I sewed your lying mouth shut?"

"It's no lie. I know a place where salamis and chickens hang from the ceiling, a place where you can eat all you want, and wash it down with root beer!"

"Root beer," echoed one of the little kids.

Johnnie-O threw him a warning glance, and the kid looked at his toes.

"There ain't no such place. Whadaya think I am, stupid?"

Well yes, Allie wanted to say, *but that's beside the point.* Instead she said, "Have you ever heard of 'The Haunter'?"

If the rest of the kids were any indication, they all knew about the Haunter. There were whispers, a few kids backed away from her, and the lump in Purple-puss's throat bobbed up and down like a fishing float. For a second Allie even thought she could see fear in Johnnie-O's eyes, but he covered it with a wide grin that tilted the tip of his nasty little Marlboro to the sky.

"First you tell me the McGill is your friend, and now the Haunter?" His smile turned into a frown, and the cigarette tipped downward. "I've had enough a you—you're going down!"

"Send her down!" the other kids started yelling. "Down! Down!"

They advanced on her. She knew she only had a split

second before mob mentality took over, and then nothing she could say would save her.

"I lied!" she shouted. "I lied about the McGill to stop you from sending me down—but this time I'm telling the truth." Johnnie-O put up his hand, and the kids hesitated, waiting for his signal.

"The Haunter captured my friends, and I can't rescue them alone! I need somebody strong," Allie said, looking right into Johnnie-O's eyes. "I need somebody smart."

Allie watched the tip of his cigarette. Would it tip up, or would it tilt down? It wavered for the longest time, and finally it tilted upward. "You came to the right guy."

They took Allie to the nearest town, the place Johnnie-O and his band of juvenile hoods called home. Johnnie-O made a point of crossing the main street several times, for no sensible reason.

"It's because of the Chinese restaurants," Raggedy Andy explained. "They're supposed to be bad luck or something—at least that's what Johnnie-O heard." And so they wove a serpentine path down the street, crossing to avoid all four Chinese restaurants in town, proving that superstition was not limited to the living.

They brought Allie to their hideout. Stupid that they called it a hideout, because they didn't have to hide from the living, who couldn't see them anyway. Like Mary, Johnnie-O had found a building that had crossed over, and had made it home. His was a white clapboard church—which struck Allie as funny. This kid probably never went to a church in his life, and now he was stuck living in one. At least there was some justice in the universe. There were about thirty kids total, all disciples of Johnnie-O, like he was running a tough-guy school. They called themselves "The Altar Boys," because they lived in a church, but the way Allie saw it, they were also "alter" boys—that is, every single one of them had something about him slightly altered from his living self; like Johnnie O's hands, or Raggedy Andy's hair.

"How come there are no girls?" Allie asked.

"Girls come by once in a while, wantin' to join," Johnnie-O said. "We send 'em packing." And then he added, "I don't like girls much."

Allie couldn't help but grin. "I think you died about a year too young."

"Yeah," Johnnie-O admitted. "And it really ticks me off."

Now that she was accepted by their leader, the other kids kept stealing glimpses at her, like she was some sort of exotic creature. *Great,* she thought, *I'm playing Wendy to a delinquent Peter Pan and the lost boys of Juvie Hall.*

She told them all about the pickle factory, and the Haunter's air-soldiers.

"His magic ain't no match for us," Johnnie-O said proudly. Allie wasn't entirely convinced, but beggars can't be choosers.

"The hard part will be getting in. There's a big steel door—not living-world steel, but steel that crossed over with the building. I pounded on it for hours and couldn't make a dent."

Johnnie-O wasn't bothered. "That ain't a problem. We'll use explosives."

"You've got explosives!?"

He called to a kid on the other side of the church. "Hey, Stubs, get your fat butt over here!"

The kid came running.

"A few years back," Johnnie explained, "Stubs here was sellin' illegal fireworks out of his garage. They caught on fire, and Stubs won himself a one-way trip to Everlost. Anyways, it turns out part of his fireworks stash came over with him." And then Johnnie added, "Which is more than I can say for most of his fingers."

"Yeah," said Raggedy Andy, laughing. "That's how come Stubs can only count to three."

Allie and the "Alter" Boys left at dawn, the members of the gang all carrying baseball bats, chains, and various other makeshift weapons that had somehow crossed over. They would have been terrifying in the living world, but with the threat of pain and death not applicable in Everlost, it was all pretty much for show; fashion accessories for bad boys who didn't get where they were going.

All the while as they marched south toward the city, Purple-puss kept giving Allie dirty looks. Not too long into their journey, he broke his silence. "I don't like this, Johnnie-O," he said, the bulge in his neck ping-ponging up and down. "She's not one of us, we shouldn't oughta be trusting her."

Johnnie-O smirked. "Heimlich here don't trust nobody."

"For all we know," Heimlich said, "she could be leading us straight to the Sky Witch."

"Shut up," said Johnny-O, "there ain't no such thing."

"Sky Witch?" asked Allie.

Johnnie-O waved it off. "Just a stupid story they tell to scare little kids about some witch who lives in the skies over Manhattan."

"She devours kids' souls," said another kid.

"Yeah," said Raggedy Andy, baring his teeth and hooking his hands like claws. "She grabs you and takes a deep breath sucking your soul right up her nose. That's why they also call her the 'Queen of Snot.'"

Johnnie-O gave them a Three Stooges–like slap that got all three of them. "What, were you born stupid or did you just die that way?" He turned to Allie. "Some kids will believe anything."

Allie, wisely, said nothing.

"We should make her skim," said Raggedy Andy. "That way we'll know whether she's worthy."

Johnnie-O explained that all prospective members of the Altar Boys had to take a coin and skim it on the Hudson River. If it skimmed at least twice like a stone, then you were worthy of joining the Altar Boys. You had to use a coin you crossed with, and you only got one chance because once your coin sank, it was gone for good.

Allie was confused. "But . . . how can you skim an Everlost coin on living-world water? It wouldn't work—it would just fall straight through."

"Well," said Johnnie-O with a wink, "I'm the one who decides whether or not I saw it skim."

The next morning, they came to the George Washington Bridge, which crossed the Hudson into the northern tip of Manhattan. There they halted. Allie looked back to see them all milling around near the on-ramp.

"We don't do bridges," Johnnie-O said and Allie smirked.

"Oh, are you scared?"

Johnnie-O narrowed his eyes into a glare. "If you ever tried to cross a bridge you'd know how easy it is to sink right through it, and fall into the river. But I guess you ain't bright enough to figure that out."

Allie was about to fire right back at him, about how she had already crossed this bridge, and maybe his name should be Johnnie-Zero, instead of Johnnie-O, because he had zero guts—but then Raggedy Andy said, "We lost more than twenty kids once trying to cross the Tappan Zee bridge. It was awful."

Everyone looked down sadly, realized their shoes were sinking into the road, and began to shuffle around again.

"Old news," said Johnnie-O, clenching his fists, "but we don't cross bridges no more."

Allie swallowed everything she was about to say. She wondered if she, Nick, and Lief would have sunk through this bridge, if they hadn't been wearing their road-shoes.

"Maybe she is working for the Sky Witch," said one of the little kids. "Maybe she wants us to sink."

The others looked at her now with frightened eyes, but the look quickly mildewed into threatening.

"Johnnie-O's right," Allie said, "we shouldn't risk it."

"We'll take the tunnel," Johnnie-O announced, and led the way.

Flurries were falling by the time they reached the Lincoln Tunnel four hours later. Although there was a narrow service catwalk along the side, Johnnie-O led his crew right down the middle of the road, intentionally letting oncoming traffic barrel right through them.

The Everlost version of macho, thought Allie. Although she would have much preferred the catwalk, she didn't want to show any signs of weakness, so she walked side by side with Johnnie-O, ignoring the annoying sensation of through-traffic.

By the time they reached the Manhattan side of the tunnel, the flurries had grown into a full-fledged snowstorm, the first of the winter. A violent wind tore at the coats of the living.

Snow felt different than rain or sleet as it passed through Allie. It tickled. As for the wind, she felt it, and it was indeed cold. But like all other weather conditions, feeling it and being affected by it were two different things. The cold did not, could not, make her shiver. And yet as unpleasant as it seemed for the living people fighting the snowstorm, Allie wished she could be one of them. But Johnnie-O, like Mary, had no interest in the living. Allie wondered how long until she became like that.

The going was slow, because it seemed every single city block had a Chinese restaurant, and Johnnie-O was making them cross the street, or turning down side streets again and again to avoid them.

"This is ridiculous," Allie said. "Chow mein does *not* carry the plague." The next time, she refused to cross the street, and walked right in front of Wan Foo's Mandarin Emporium.

"Wow, she's brave," said one of the little kids, and so Johnnie-O was forced to do the same, just to prove he was just as brave as Allie.

When they finally reached the Haunter's place, Allie could tell something was wrong. The steel door that had been so securely sealed now hung wide open and was slightly bent.

Johnnie-O looked to Allie as if she could explain, but she only shrugged.

Maybe, she thought, *Nick and Lief fought their way out.*

Johnnie-O, for all his swagger and big-fisted boisterousness, wasn't about to be the first one in, so Allie took the lead and cautiously stepped inside.

The scene inside was not at all what Allie expected. There was no longer food hanging from the ceiling. Instead, half-gnawed carcasses of roast chickens and pieces of meat lay strewn about the floor.

"My God," said Allie.

"You said it," said Johnnie-O. "I haven't seen so much food in fifty years!"

Unable to control himself, he raced forward and the Altar Boys followed, grabbing the carcasses and meat off the floor and shoving them into their mouths. There was no need to fight because there was enough for everybody.

"No!" yelled Allie. "The Haunter! He could be anywhere!"

But they weren't listening.

Allie braced for the moment the Haunter's hollow minions would descend on them, slapping them into barrels, but as she looked around she realized the barrels were all gone. All, that is, but one single barrel that sat in the center of the mess.

Allie noticed shredded bits of black cloth mixed in among the scraps of food—and then something else caught her eye. It was a turkey—a big one—a twenty-five pounder, maybe. It was a bird the Haunter had probably ecto-ripped into Everlost right off someone's Thanksgiving dinner table. One thing though . . . the turkey had a bite out of it. A huge jagged bite. It was as if a dinosaur had sunk its teeth into it and ripped it apart—you could still see the teeth marks.

What, thought Allie, *could leave an awful bite mark like that*?

Suddenly her attention was drawn to the single barrel in the center of the room. Someone was inside it, pounding and screaming. She couldn't make out the words but she recognized the voice. Just hearing it chilled her far more than the blizzard ever could.

"Johnnie-O! Over here!" she called.

With a chicken in each of his fists and grease dripping down his chin, Johnnie-O looked a bit more comical and less menacing than usual. Reluctantly he handed his chickens to Heimlich with a look that said, *You eat them, you're dead.*

He came over to the barrel, and both he and Allie knelt down, putting their ears close to the wood.

"Who's out there?" the voice inside said. "Let me out, let me out and I shall give you whatever you want!"

It was the Haunter.

Johnnie-O looked to Allie for direction. She had, after all, led them to the biggest feast of their afterlives, so she was now held in some sort of reverence.

"Let me out!" yelled the Haunter. "I demand you let me out!"

Allie spoke loudly enough to be heard through the wood and brine. "What happened here? Who did this to you?"

"Let me out!" screeched the Haunter. "Let me out and I shall rip food from the finest restaurants in the living world and lay it at your feet."

But Allie ignored him. "Where are the other barrels?"

"They were taken."

"By whom?" Allie demanded.

"By the McGill."

Johnnie-O gasped, and his mouth dropped open in astonishment. His cigarette would have fallen out if it could. "The McGill?!"

"His ship's in the bay, out past the Statue of Liberty," the Haunter said. "Let me out and I will help you fight him."

Allie considered it, but then she looked around. The strips of black cloth were squirming on the ground like snakes. Frantically they danced about, and Allie realized what the Haunter was doing. Even from within the barrel, the Haunter was trying to bring his air-warriors together to capture them. They tried to reassemble themselves, but it was useless. The McGill had shredded them far too well for even the Haunter to put them back together again.

Allie looked at the barrel and tried to find some compassion for this creature inside, who had so mercilessly imprisoned her friends. In the end she found her compassion did not reach that far.

"Leave him in there!" she said loudly enough for him to hear. "Let him stew in his own juices."

"NO!" the Haunter screamed within the barrel, and around the room bones and bird carcasses began to fly like meteors, randomly tossed about by the Haunter's rage.

Allie didn't care. She turned to Johnnie-O. "Can you

and the Altar Boys come with me?" she said. "I won't be able to fight the McGill alone."

But Johnnie-O backed away. "We got what we came for," he said. "Ain't nothing anyone can say, living, dead, or otherwise that would get me to fight the McGill. You're on your own."

And then, almost as an apology, he reached down and grabbed a leg from the turkey that had been bitten by the McGill. He ripped the leg free and held it out to her, almost like a peace offering.

"Here, take it," Johnnie-O said. "You deserve to eat too."

And so she did. She dug her teeth into the turkey and relished its flavor—the first flavor she had tasted in all her months here. It was like being in heaven.

Yet as good as it was, it couldn't outweigh the hell she knew she would soon have to face once she tracked down the McGill.

She turned to leave, but before she could, Johnnie-O called to her. "You never told us your name," he said, then tilted his Marlboro up with a grin. "I gots to know it if we're gonna tell stories about how you went off to fight the McGill and all."

Allie found herself oddly flattered. Johnnie-O had decided she was worth being turned into a legend.

"My name is . . ." and for a moment she couldn't remember. But the moment passed. "Allie," she said.

Johnnie-O nodded. "Allie the Outcast," he said.

Allie had to admit she liked it. "That's right."

"Good luck," Johnnie-O said. "Hope you don't get eaten or anything."

Allie left and headed toward Battery Park—the tip of Manhattan, where she was sure to see the McGill's ship, if it was still there. She was terrified, and yet at the same time, she felt ennobled. Fighting to free her friends had felt like a desperate mission for a lone girl, but now she was Allie the Outcast, on her way to battle the McGill. Kids would tell her story, whatever that story might be. This was no longer just a mission; it was a quest. And she was ready.

PART THREE

The McGill

CHAPTER 15

The Brimstone Ship

On February 7, 1963, a ship called the *Marine Sulphur Queen* left the world of the living. A few days after setting sail from Beaumont, Texas, the ship vanished off the coast of Florida without as much as a single radio message. All they found was an oil slick, a few life jackets, and the persistent smell of brimstone—the awful odor associated with rotten eggs, and, coincidentally, the smell also associated with hell.

There was, of course, a perfectly logical and nondemonic explanation for the smell. The *Sulphur Queen* was an old World War II tanker that was now being used to transport liquid sulphur—also known as brimstone. However the eerie smell, combined with the fact that the ship mysteriously vanished in the Bermuda Triangle, naturally led people to consider a dark, supernatural end to the unlucky brimstone barge.

In truth, the death of the *Sulphur Queen* was extremely bizarre, but not exactly supernatural. Stated simply, the *Sulphur Queen* was overcome by a very large ocean fart.

On that fateful February day, a massive ball of natural gas, two hundred feet wide, burst up from beneath the ocean floor, and when the bubble surfaced, the entire ship dropped into it in less than a second. The bubble burst, water rushed in, covering the ship, and it was gone. The *Sulphur Queen* was very literally swallowed by the sea.

There were the expected few moments of utter panic and mortal terror as the crew of the tragically submerged vessel made their final journey down that path of light, to wherever they were going. Then, less than a minute later, the ship itself got to where it was going—namely the bottom of the sea.

But that wasn't the end of it.

Because what no one knew was that the old vessel was the last of its kind. It was the final ship built by a failing shipyard, which closed down the day the *Sulphur Queen* first launched out of dry dock. The workers, knowing an era was coming to an end, built the ship with as much care as a team of shipbuilders could muster. Their love of this ship was welded into every rivet. Such an ignoble death to this well-loved vessel could not be suffered lightly by the fabric of eternity. And so, when the waters surging about in the methane-heavy air finally settled, a ghost of the *Queen* remained, permanently afloat in the half-world of Everlost.

Since no soul had crossed over with it, the ghost of the *Sulphur Queen* drifted for years; no crew, no passengers. It drifted, that is, until the McGill found it, and turned it into the greatest pirate ship ever to sail the waters of eternity—and, except for one nasty run-in with the *Flying Dutchman*, its supremacy on the seas had never been challenged.

Since the evil smell of brimstone still surrounded the vessel, the McGill found it useful for inspiring fear, because the McGill knew that when it came to being a monster, image was everything. One only needed to sniff the brimstone to be convinced that the *Sulphur Queen* was a ship from hell, rather than a ship from Texas.

The McGill had remodeled the tanker into as proper a pirate ship as possible. It wasn't too hard to make it menacing, for the ship was already rusted and rancid when it crossed into Everlost. That, the smell, and the McGill's fearsome reputation were all it took to make the *Sulphur Queen* the floating terror of Everlost.

On the open deck, the McGill had fashioned himself a throne made from pieces of this and that: pipes torn from the ship, fancy portrait frames, curtains from old buildings that had crossed over. The throne was studded with jewels that were glued on with old bubble gum. It was, in short, a monstrosity—just like the McGill himself—and it suited him just fine.

The McGill's most recent adventure had been a raid in New York. He had long heard rumors of the Haunter, and his mystical little dojo where he taught kids to haunt, with weird discipline, like it was some sort of martial art. The McGill had no patience for legends that didn't involve him. As far as he was concerned, such legends were competition, and needed to be silenced.

The Haunter was silenced well. Oh, he had put up a fight, levitating, and summoning up wraiths in black robes that walked like human beings—as if any of this could impress the McGill. He had learned early on that one's physical strength in Everlost had nothing to do with muscle mass. It had all to do with the strength of one's will—and the McGill was surely the most willful creature that ever lived. After he had shredded the wraith-warriors with his claws, the McGill took on the Haunter himself. The little Neanderthal had put up a fight—but in the end he was no match for the McGill.

"If you ever get out of there," he had shouted at the barrel where the Haunter had been sealed, "you had better NEVER cross my path again. Or I'll find something worse for you."

He wasn't sure if the Haunter had even heard him, because he never stopped cursing from within the barrel.

The McGill had dined royally on the spread of food that this Haunter had somehow pulled from the living world. He feasted for hours, and threw his scraps to his associates, who were happy to have them. That's what he called his crew: "associates."

Now, still full from the feast, they had returned to the ship with a dozen barrels, leaving behind only the one that contained the Haunter.

"So what do we do with them?" asked Pinhead, as the McGill sat in his throne, looking at the barrels now arranged haphazardly on the deck. Pinhead was the McGill's chief associate. Somewhere along the line, Pinhead had forgotten the correct proportion of a human head to its body, and so the size of his head had receded like an apple left on a windowsill. The difference was not so profound that he looked like a complete freak. It was subtle. When you looked at Pinhead, you knew something was wrong, but you weren't quite sure what it was.

"Sir? The barrels—what should we do with them?"

"I heard you," the McGill snapped.

He rose from his throne, and loped in his awful crooked stride toward the barrels.

"According to the Haunter, there's someone inside every single one of them," Pinhead told him, with a certain excitement in his voice. In life, Pinhead must have been the kind of kid who would rip through a cereal box to get to the prize at the bottom.

"We'll see," the McGill snapped.

"And I'll bet these kids have been pickling for so long," Pinhead said, "that they'll worship whoever sets them free."

This gave the McGill pause for thought. He stroked his chin, a bulbous thing as rough and unshapely as a potato. It was an interesting idea. Others feared him, but never was he the subject of worship and complete adoration. "You think so?"

"Only one way to find out." And then Pinhead added, "If they're ingrates, we'll put 'em back in the barrels and dump them into the sea."

"All right, then," said the McGill, and he gestured to his associates lurking in the shadows. "Open them up."

Although not even the Haunter knew this, Afterlights were very much like wine when sealed in a barrel. The longer a wine is left to age, the better it gets. . . . unless of course something goes wrong, and it turns to vinegar.

Neither Nick nor Lief had turned to vinegar, however. Both had adapted in his own unique way to their situation.

While Lief became like a baby in a womb, and lost any sense of time and space, Nick did the opposite. He was aware of every passing moment, never forgot exactly where he was—and didn't even forget WHO he was, so those stupid little pieces of paper he had written his name on weren't an entire waste of time.

Nick found he could pass the time by taking an inventory of everything he remembered from his life, and his afterlife. Even though some key memories had already been lost, he was still close enough to his earthly existence to remember quite a lot. He tried to list alphabetically every single song he knew, and sang each one. He cataloged every movie he remembered ever seeing, and tried to watch them in his head. With nothing to reflect on but himself, he came to realize that he had spent far too much time complaining and worrying. If he ever managed to get out of that barrel, he knew he'd be a different person, because nothing—not even sinking into the Earth—could be worse than this. And so, both Nick and Lief had been profoundly changed by their pickling experience: Lief had found a bizarre state of spiritual bliss, and Nick became strong and fearless.

Nick felt the commotion of his barrel being removed from the Haunter's lair. He had no idea where he was being hauled off to, but the very fact that there was activity around him was a hopeful sign. Counting out the seconds in his mind, he waited for something momentous to happen.

Nick had counted 61,259 seconds from the time his barrel had first begun to move until the top was pried off. The tops were pried off of three barrels simultaneously. Nick stood up right away, ready to thank his rescuer. Having had nothing but darkness and pickle brine in his eyes for many weeks, he couldn't really see much of anything at first. There were other kids around him. To his left was an open barrel with someone still submerged beneath the surface. To his right standing up in another barrel was a kid Nick did not recognize, who began screaming and never stopped. Nick stood there in amazement, wondering how his lungs could hold out—he sounded like a human air-raid siren. Then he realized that since the kid didn't actually have lungs anymore, being a spirit and all, he never had to stop for breath. He could just scream until the universe ended, which might have actually been his plan. This kid had clearly turned to vinegar in his barrel.

"Get the screamer out of here!" said a slobbery voice. "Take him and chime him!" Several kids nearby took the screamer out of his barrel, and carried him away. All the while he never stopped screaming. *Poor kid,* thought Nick. *That could have been me.*

But it wasn't. And it was a great consolation to know that he had survived his time in pickle purgatory. Nick blinked, and blinked again, forcing his eyes into focus, ready to face whatever situation he would now find himself in. He was on the deck of a ship that was sprinkled with crumbs of some sort. There were crewmen around him, all of them kids, and standing in front of an ugly throne was what could only be described as a monster.

Lief did not know the top of his barrel had been pried off. He didn't know much of anything. He heard a kid screaming, but it sounded far away. Not in his universe.

Not his concern. Lief now existed without time or space. He was everything and nothing. It was wonderful. Then when someone grabbed his hair and hauled him upright, he found that the place of infinite peace he had discovered within himself did not leave him. Whether he had lost his mind, or had become "one with the universe" was a matter of opinion.

"Who are you?" a wet, distorted voice asked. "What can you do? What use will you be to me?"

Lief was still on the first question.

"His name is Lief," said a familiar voice. He remembered the voice belonged to someone named Nick. All at once Lief's memories came back to him. He remembered his journey from the forest, his time in front of the video game, the fact that he had been in a barrel.

Someone approached him. No, not someone, some "thing." It had one eye the size of a grapefruit, filled with squiggly veins. The other eye was normal-size, but dangled from its socket.

"I don't like the look of him!" the monster said. "He looks like someone made him out of clay, and forgot to finish him."

"I think he's forgotten what he looks like," said a boy with an unusually small head.

The monster raised a three-fingered claw and pointed it at Lief. "I order you to remember what you look like!"

"Leave him alone!" shouted Nick.

"I order you to remember!"

Lief suspected he knew what this creature was, and he knew he should have been terrified of it, but he was not.

The creature moved closer to Lief. When it opened its mouth, a tongue lashed out that forked into three octopus tentacles. "I order you to remember what you look like, or you're going overboard."

Lief smiled happily. "Okay." Then he closed his eyes, and rummaged around through his mind until he found a memory of his face. The moment he did, he could actually feel his features changing. When he opened his eyes, he knew he was himself again—or at least something close.

The creature studied him with his huge eye, and grunted. "Good enough," he said.

Nick, still waist-deep in his barrel, watched the creature closely, ready to fight it if necessary. Then something occurred to Nick that almost crushed his newfound courage. "Are you . . . Are you . . . the McGill?"

The creature laughed, and limped across the deck over to Nick, crumbs crunching beneath his fungus-ridden feet as he walked.

"Yes, I am," the creature said. "You've heard about me! Tell me what you heard."

Nick grimaced from the creature's awful stench. "I heard that you were the devil's pet dog, and you chewed through your leash."

That was the wrong thing to say. The McGill roared, and kicked Nick's barrel so hard it shattered, spilling brine all over the deck. "Pet dog? Who said I was a dog? I'll put *them* on a leash!"

"Just some kid," Nick said, trying not to look at Lief. "If you're not a dog, then what are you?"

The McGill poked a sharp claw against Nick's chest.

"I'm your king and commander. I own you now."

Nick didn't like the sound of that. "So . . . we're slaves?"

"Associates," said the boy with the unusually small head.

The McGill ordered their pockets checked for anything of value, and when nothing was found, the McGill raised his claw, and pointed to the hatch. "Take them below!" he said to a group of associates. "Find out what they can do, and make them do it."

The McGill watched them go with one eye, and kept the other eye trained on Pinhead. Once the two new kids were gone, the McGill waved a clawed hand. "Open the next one."

Pinhead did as he was told. The next barrel, however, was empty, as was the next, and the next. Just brine with no one inside.

"I can't understand it," Pinhead said. "The Haunter said there was someone in each barrel."

"He lied," the McGill grunted, and retired to the captain's quarters, which were just behind his great open-air throne.

Fourteen barrels, and only three occupants. It did not sit well with the McGill. This wasn't the first time such a thing had happened. If he had a nickel for every time he expected to find an Afterlight and didn't, he'd be a rich monster.

It was the thought of nickels that made the McGill turn to his safe. It was a bulky iron thing built right into the wall. Only the McGill knew the combination. It had taken him more than a year of trying until he found the right one, and now the safe was his prize possession. He turned the wheel, feeling the familiar rattle of the tumblers, then he closed his claw around the lever, and pulled it open.

Inside was a bucket filled with coins so worn it was impossible to tell their denominations, or what country they had come from. The coins had been taken from enemies or associates—and anyone who was not an associate was an enemy. It was common knowledge that money in Everlost was of no real use, but the McGill kept the coins, all the same.

"If they're so worthless, why do you keep them in your safe?" Pinhead had once asked.

The McGill had chosen not to answer him, and Pinhead was wise enough not to ask again. The easy answer was that the McGill kept everything. . . . but the real answer was that the coins were the most plentiful objects in Everlost, and as such were of special interest to him.

The only other item he kept in the safe was hidden beneath the bucket of coins. It was a small slip of paper half an inch wide, and two inches long. On the tiny paper were printed the following words:

A brave man's life is worth a thousand cowardly souls.

He would read and reread that slip of paper to remind him why he patrolled the shores and went on raids of Everlost encampments. Then he would return it to its hiding place beneath the bucket of coins. Although few knew it, there was more to the McGill than mindless looting and pillaging. That little slip of paper was a constant reminder to him that he had a larger goal.

* * *

Nick, still disoriented from his rebirth into the world of the almost-living, stumbled from the light of the deck into the dim, narrow corridors of the ship. The McGill's "associates" prodded him and Lief forward, while around them the rest of the McGill's crew jeered at them as they passed. Lief waved and smiled like some returning hero, and it just made Nick mad.

"Will you stop that?" Nick demanded. "What are you so happy about?"

The jeering kids, Nick noticed, all had crooked teeth and mismatched features; ears slightly off, noses twisted, tweaked, or flattened, like their faces were putty that the McGill had played with. Some were girls, some were boys, but in truth, it was impossible to tell the difference anymore. Nick dubbed them "Ugloids," and wondered if they were as ugly inside as out. They all seemed somewhat dimwitted—perhaps service to the McGill had made them that way—and since none of them seemed too highly motivated, Nick took a calculated risk. He pulled out of the grip of the two Ugloids holding him, grabbed Lief's hand, and began to run. As he suspected, the Ugloids were slow on the uptake, and by the time they took to chasing them, Nick and Lief had a nice lead down the hall.

"Where are we going?" asked Lief.

"We'll know when we get there." The truth was, Nick had no idea. Courage and spontaneity were new to him. It hadn't occurred to him until after he had run from the Ugloids that perhaps he had confused courage with stupidity. He should have had a plan for escape—after all this was a ship, and there were a limited number of places they could go. But now he was committed, so he kept on running, turning down corridors and climbing through hatches hoping he wouldn't take a wrong turn, which, of course, he eventually did.

With the Ugloids gaining on them, Nick pushed open a hatch, and found that it opened onto one of the ship's holds—a cavernous space thirty-feet deep, forty-feet long, and smelling horribly of rotten eggs. There was a steep iron stairway winding down into it, but he had come through the hatch with such speed that he and Lief missed the stairway completely, flipped over the railing, and dropped into the depths of the hold.

The fall would have killed them, had they been alive, but things being what they were, it was merely a nuisance. They crashed loudly into furniture and picture frames and statues, and when they managed to get their bearings, they found themselves in the middle of the McGill's grand treasure trove. It looked more like a dragon's hoard than anything else. Shiny things like chandeliers, thrown together with chests of drawers, and automobile axles—like several moving trucks had just dumped the contents of a city-wide garage sale here, and left. *Mary would know what to do with all of this*, Nick thought. She would organize it, distribute it, put it to good use. Clearly the McGill had no purpose beyond hoarding it—as evidenced by the fact that everything was painted with the words PROPERTY OF THE MCGILL. His purpose was greed, nothing more. Nick could imagine the McGill capturing Finders and taking everything they had. Maybe he even forced the Finders to work for him, collecting items that had crossed over, just so the McGill could store them here.

By the time Nick and Lief had made their way through the treasure trove to the nearest hatch, Pinhead was there, with plenty of associates to back him up.

"Hi," said Lief, all sunshine and joy, "did you miss us?"

Pinhead took Lief's weirdness as sarcasm, and tossed Lief aside. Then he grabbed Nick and pushed him against the wall. "The McGill wants to know how you can be useful to him."

"We're nobody's slaves," Nick said.

Pinhead nodded. "I knew you'd be too defiant to be of any use."

"Does that mean I can go back into my barrel now?" asked Lief. Pinhead ignored him.

"Chime them!" Pinhead ordered. "Chime them along with all the other useless ones." Then the crew came forward, grabbing them, forcing them through the hatch and down a narrow dim hallway toward another hatch labeled CHIMING CHAMBUR with sloppy childlike paint strokes. Nick struggled against them, but it was no use—and although his first instinct was to try to talk his way out of this, he wasn't going to give Pinhead the satisfaction of seeing him plead.

Pinhead pulled open the hatch. "Have fun," Pinhead said with a nasty snicker. Nick suspected there was no fun to be had at all.

"There is only one rule for swimming in Everlost," writes Mary Hightower. "Don't. Large bodies of water are very dangerous for us Afterlights—for if the land is like quicksand, then water is like air. If you happen to fall into a lake, river, or ocean, you'll find the water about as buoyant as clouds to someone falling through the sky. You'll hit the bottom with such speed, you'll find yourself embedded twenty feet into the sea floor before slowing down to regular sinking velocity, and that will be that.

"Ghost ships are the only exception to this rule. Like the Everlost buildings that remain on land long after leaving the 'living world,' ghost ships still do what they were built to do; that is, float—and nothing, not tidal wave, nor hurricane, nor torpedo could ever sink them. Just don't get thrown off of one."

CHAPTER 16

A Dangerous Crossing

Allie knew the risks of traveling on water before she climbed aboard the Staten Island Ferry, but seeing the McGill's ghost ship right there in the bay made her realize she had to take a chance. If she didn't, there was no telling where that ship would go next, and no telling if she'd ever find it again.

She had raced from the old pickle factory to Battery Park, and from there she could see, just as the Haunter had said, the McGill's ship. She knew it was a ghost ship because it left no wake behind it as it powered forward. She knew it was the McGill's, because painted in sloppy black letters beneath the words "*Sulphur Queen*," were the words PROPERTY OF THE MCGILL. The only way to reach it, though, was on another vessel. The Staten Island Ferry seemed the best candidate for the job.

Allie made her way to the ferry landing, and pushed through the bustle of people piling on and off the boat, ignoring the thoughts that shot like bullets through her mind each time someone passed through her. All their thoughts were about the wind and the snow, which made no difference to her. She didn't let herself slow down, because she could already tell the ferry deck was as treacherous for her as the surface of a bridge. It was like walking on tissue paper; every footfall left her ankle-deep in the floor, and she had to step quickly to keep from sinking too far into the deck.

The toot of a horn, and the ferry pulled away from the dock, bound for Staten Island. The way Allie figured it, the bay was large, but not all that large. Living-world boats would often have to adjust their courses to avoid collision. Right now, the McGill's ship was in between them and Staten Island, invisible to the ferry's pilot. With any luck, the ferry would pass right though it, delivering Allie to her destination.

All around her, living folk spoke of meals and sales, inconsiderate husbands and unsatisfied wives. Small talk now seemed so small from her perspective, she wondered how people could engage in it altogether. Such pettiness filled the lives of the living. She could begin to see why Mary would have nothing to do with it.

Mary. Almost reflexively, she turned to look back at the city. Through the falling snow, the buildings of the city were just a faded shadow, but the Twin Towers of Mary's domain were bright and bold, as if painted on the skyline, standing in proud defiance of everything Allie once thought she knew about the nature of the world. *Someday,* thought Allie, *I will write a book too*. It wouldn't be a book of rules and etiquette, but one of experience, because each day in Everlost brought a fresh experience. How Mary could think she knew so much, without ever leaving the comfort of her tower, was one of the greatest mysteries of Everlost.

But now there were other things to deal with, like the ghost ship looming closer before her. In her excitement Allie tried to lean against the ferry's rail, only to lean right through it. She spun her arms, trying to catch her balance, and nearly fell off the ferry into the bay. She saved herself by letting her knees buckle, and falling backward, but that didn't turn out to be a good thing either. Her rear hit the deck, and passed through it. She reached out her hands, but they went straight through the wood and the steel beneath that. She could feel the warmer air of the lower deck on her fingertips and felt herself sinking even farther.

As she tried to right herself, her body kept falling, and she dropped right through a row of benches on the lower deck, not as much as ruffling the pages of a man's newspaper as she fell through him. She didn't stop there. The force of her fall left her embedded in the floor of that deck. Frantically she tried to pull herself up, but again, only succeeded in sinking farther.

She fell through the lower passenger deck, right into the auto deck, where cars sat, their engines off as they crossed the bay. Even the steel of cars didn't stop her, and now she began to panic.

"Help!" she screamed, "Somebody help me!"

But of course there was no one to hear her cries, and she cursed herself for not thinking to make herself a pair of road-shoes before attempting this crossing.

She fell through the floor of the auto deck into the engine room. Gears grinded, pistons pounded, echoing all around her, and as she tried to stand up, her feet passed through the hull of the boat.

She could feel the icy bay water around her ankles,

and then her shins, and she knew that if she didn't think of something fast, she would sink straight through the bottom of this boat and, as Mary wrote, "that would be that."

"Help me!" she screamed again, if not to anyone in the living world, then to some force in the heavens as invisible to her as she was invisible to the living.

There was a man in the engine room with her. Unkempt gray hair, two-day beard stubble; his blue uniform told her he was part of the ferry crew—one of the ferry's pilots on break. He quietly sipped coffee, raising and lowering his eyebrows as if in some silent conversation with himself.

Allie was up to her waist now, her legs dangling through the bottom of the boat, into the water. That's when something occurred to her.

The preppie girl at the pizza place!

When Allie had "surfed" that girl, she had felt like a kite lifted off the ground by the girl's thoughts. What if Allie could do that again—this time with the old man?

It was a long shot, but she had to try. Slogging her way through the steel of the ship's hull took everything she was worth. The hull was thick enough to slow her descent, but also so thick that pulling herself through it took a huge effort of will. In the end, she had to resort to kicking her feet in the water below and moving her hands through the air, as if she were swimming. She was down to her belly button by the time she got near the man, who sat in his chair, oblivious to her. She could feel the cold water of the bay passing through her middle, filling the spot where her stomach had once been.

Just a few more moments and I'll be gone, she thought.

And so with a last bit of strength she leaned forward,

toward the man in the chair, and touched him. She felt a rush of blood, the pumping of a heart, and she became a kite lifted into the air. Allie could no longer feel the cold of the water, and—

—i'll never win i have to win i have no chance i have every chance numbers numbers which numbers lucky numbers four twenty-five birthday seven twelve fourteen ages of the grandkids thirty-nine years we've been married eighteen million and if i win that lottery i'll never go to staten island again—

Allie couldn't feel her feet, she couldn't feel her hands, she couldn't feel anything, and all she could hear were his thoughts. It was as if her body had suddenly ceased to exist and she was just pure spirit, cocooned within another person's being. She opened her eyes, not realizing she had even closed them, and now what she saw seemed very different from what she'd seen before. There had been a green coffee mug on the table, but now looking at it, she couldn't tell whether it was green or red. Her eyes jerked toward a red light above the engine involuntarily, only the light wasn't red anymore, just pale white. Now she finally realized what was going on.

I am seeing through his eyes, and he's color-blind. She watched the coffee cup come up to her lips and then back down again. She could almost taste the coffee.

—win gotta win numbers all in the numbers—

His lottery thoughts assaulted her mind and he didn't even know she was there. The next time he brought the coffee cup to his lips she could swear she actually tasted the brew, and then in a few more moments she began to feel something spectacular: she felt hot. Hot from the coffee, hot from the heat of the engine. She could feel fingertips touching the handle of the mug, the pressure against skin, the tag of the shirt at the back of the neck. There was a numbness about it, true—as if her entire body had been shot with novocaine—but there was no doubting that she was feeling with the nerves of living flesh once again. It was all so startling, she forgot for a moment why she was there.

—numbers numbers lucky numbers, the man's thoughts droned on, *i have as good a chance as any ten times the chance if I buy ten tickets—*

And then it hit her that she had spent at least a minute here, while the ferry was still moving. She may have already missed her chance to intercept the McGill's ship! She could leap out of him now, but the fear of sinking through the bottom of the hull was so great in her that she didn't dare. If only the pilot would go to the upper decks instead of just sitting here, he would carry her with him.

—numbers, lucky numbers what if I add them all together and divide by 7?—

Her frustration kept on building. *"Stop thinking about the stupid lottery and get up!"*

And suddenly the man put down his coffee cup and stood.

Was it coincidence? Allie didn't know for sure.

The man remained standing for a moment, then slowly settled back down in his chair, slightly bewildered.

If her thoughts had made him get up, maybe she could

do it again. Allie filled herself with the same frustration and determination. *"Stand up!"* she insisted. Again the man stood.

—numbers lottery numbers why did i just stand up?—

Okay, thought Allie. This was something new. It was clear that the man still had no idea she was there, and he couldn't tell the difference between her thoughts and his own. Allie tried to take advantage of that.

"Go to the upper deck," Allie said. *"You always take your break down below, and you never enjoy the view."*

*—it's too hot down here anyway, i should go on deck—*the man thought.

Allie felt the strange, numb sensation of fabric against skin as he rose and climbed the stairs. The cold of the auto level hit Allie suddenly. She couldn't actually feel the chill, but she could feel *him* feeling cold, and she realized she had pushed him up here with such a strength of will, he had forgotten to take his coat.

"Next deck," Allie whispered. He obeyed.

The first passenger deck was warm, although not as warm as the engine room. He continued climbing up to the top level, which was open to the snowy day. Now, through this man, Allie could lean against the railing without falling through it.

But when Allie scanned the waters she was shocked to see the McGill's ship was no longer there! She could see nothing but the shore of Staten Island in the distance. She panicked for a moment, until understanding set in.

I'm seeing through his eyes, she reminded herself, *and he can't see the ghost ship.*

She stepped out of him. It was easy, like slipping out of

an overcoat, and the second she did, the nature of the world changed again. The McGill's ship reappeared now that she was viewing the world through her own ghostly eyes. The McGill's ship was off to the right, but the ferry was moving too fast. At this rate the ferry would pass in front of it, not coming any closer than a hundred yards!

Filled with a sense of fury and despair, she turned to the old ferry pilot, but he was no longer there. She found him heading toward the ferry's bridge. She hurried after him, and stepped right back into the old man, stealthily. Immediately the world she saw became his color-blind living world, as he opened the door to the bridge, and went in.

The ferry's bridge was small and smelled of old varnish. Another, younger pilot was at the controls.

"Winds are killer today," said the younger ferryman. "They oughta make these things more aerodynamic."

"Yah," said the old man, absently.

The younger man glanced over at him for a second. "Something wrong?"

"Nah, nah," he said, "it just . . . nothing, I don't know. Something weird."

Allie knew he was sensing her. Even though she was hiding beneath the threshold of his understanding, he was feeling the hint of her presence. A plan was forming in her mind, but if he was becoming aware of her, she would have to make her move quickly, or it would be too late.

"Tell him to take his break early," Allie demanded. *"Take over the controls."*

Suddenly Allie felt the body of the old man turn, looking around as if searching for someone behind him. "What the—?"

"Something bite yah?" asked the younger pilot. "I'll tell yah, the bugs here don't know it's winter. They breed down in the engine room, and crawl up here between the bulkheads."

"Do it!" Allie insisted. *"Take control of the ferry now!"*

But the old man said—

—no!—

There was a panic in his thoughts and Allie knew she had been exposed.

—who are you? what do you want?—

In her panic, she considered leaping out of him, and right into the other pilot—but she had never done a person-to-person leap before. No, it was best to stay where she was and work with the old man. She calmed herself down, and spoke to him through her thoughts.

"That doesn't matter," she told him, *"all that matters is that you take the wheel and change course."*

"No!" He said it aloud, this time.

The other man looked at him. "No, what?"

"No . . . uh . . . it wasn't a bug," he said. "At least not the kind you're talking about."

The other guy didn't know what to make of it, so he just turned his attention forward.

"Never mind who I am," Allie thought. *"You have to take the wheel! You have to change course!"*

But he wouldn't. That's when Allie made a calculated move. This was a battle of wills, and although she was a stranger in his skin, her sense of touch didn't seem as numb as it had before. Maybe . . . just maybe . . .

Allie thrust a hand forward and found that the hand

moved. It wasn't her hand but the old pilot's. His fingers quivered as two spirits struggled to control it, but in the end Allie won. She wasn't just mind-surfing now, she was *body-surfing*, and could use this man's body as if it were her own. She grasped the shoulder of the younger pilot and spoke, but when her voice came out it was the dry, raspy voice of a man who had smoked two packs of cigarettes a day his whole life.

"You can go below," Allie heard herself say in the old man's voice. "I'll finish off this run." The younger ferryman offered no argument. He nodded and left, happy for some break time.

Inside her thoughts, the old pilot clawed for control of his limbs again.

"Patience!" Allie told him. *"Patience, it will be over soon."*

But that only made him more terrified.

Gripping on to the wheel Allie pulled to the right. Now she could not see where the McGill's ship was, but she remembered the spot where it had been. The boat began a turn that took it off its well-run course.

All at once it occurred to Allie, *I am alive again! I am flesh, blood and bone.* Is that what the kid had meant when he said there were other ways to be alive again? She knew she had discovered something major here, but she couldn't deal with that right now.

She held the new course for a full minute. By the time that minute had passed, the body she wore was shaking with the force of the man's spirit trying to reclaim himself, and finally she let him, because she had done what she had set out to do.

The moment she stepped out of his body, the man

yelped, then quickly gained control of himself. He blotted his sweating forehead, and rather than letting the shock of what had happened fill him, he instead turned his attention to the wheel, quickly pulling it back on course toward Staten Island. She did, however, hear him praying beneath his breath, whispering a series of Hail Marys. She wanted to tell him that it was okay—that this was a one-shot deal that would never happen to him again, but with the McGill's ship so close, she didn't have time.

Her change of course had brought them right into the path of the oncoming ghost ship. The bow of the McGill's huge vessel rammed right into the ferry's starboard side, but rather than slicing it in half, it simply passed through, as if the ferry wasn't there. Around her the details of the ferry seemed to fade into nothing, as the Everlost reality of the ghost ship cancelled it out, plowing forward—and Allie remembered what Mary had said about how hard it was to see two things occupying the same space.

The bow of the McGill's ship hit her, catching her solidly, and she realized she could not pass through this steel! If she didn't find something to hold on to, the McGill's ship would push her out of the ferry, and right into the sea. She reached for anything that she could grab on to and finally the anchor hanging from a hole in the bow swept past. She grabbed it, held on to it, and was lifted out of the ferry's air space. In a moment the ferry was gone, chugging steadily toward Staten Island, and Allie was clinging for all she was worth to an anchor suspended above the churning water of New York bay. Silently thanking her parents for forcing her to stay in gymnastics for four years, she climbed the anchor chain, and deftly flipped onto the deck of the ghost ship.

She surprised a team of unlikely pirates, who grabbed her the second she was on board. They were even more unpleasantly distorted than the Altar Boys. They practically carried her to the highest deck, where something slouched on a gaudy throne.

The thing on the throne was far from human. Allie found it horrifying to look, yet harder to look away. It had sharp, three-fingered talons for hands, and skin as red as a lobster and pocked like the moon. Its mismatched eyes wandered of their own accord, and its nasty tuft of spidery hair looked like it might crawl off the creature's head at any moment. This *thing* was beyond grotesque—so far beyond that Allie found her fear balanced by fascination. How could something so horrible exist?

"What are you?" she said. She thought she said it to herself but realized she had spoken aloud.

"I am the McGill," it said. "Hear my name and tremble."

And Allie laughed. She didn't mean to, but that line was so goofy, she couldn't help herself.

The McGill frowned, or at least she thought it frowned. It waved a dirty claw, and all the assembled "pirates" scrambled away like rats, except for the small-headed one standing beside her.

"I will make you suffer in ways you cannot imagine," the McGill said, and although Allie believed it, she wasn't going to let this beast see her fear the way she had let the Haunter see it. If there was one thing she had learned, it was that monsters only had the power that you gave them. But she also knew that monsters didn't deal well with blatant disrespect. She had already disrespected the McGill once; she would probably not get away with it again.

"I've heard that you are the greatest creature in all of Everlost." She nodded respectfully. "Now I see that it's true."

The McGill smiled, or at least Allie thought it smiled. It turned its dangling eye toward the misproportioned boy beside her. "What do you think, Pinhead, should I throw her overboard, or something worse?"

"Worse," answered Pinhead. Somehow Allie knew he'd say that.

The McGill shifted in its throne, trying to make that unsightly body more comfortable, which seemed an impossibility. "But first I want to know how you snuck on board my ship."

Allie grinned. "No one's ever done that before, have they?"

"Actually, no," said Pinhead, and the McGill threw him a burning gaze before turning back to Allie.

"How did you do it?" demanded the McGill.

"I'll tell you, but only if—"

The McGill didn't let her finish. It waved a clawed hand. "'Only if' nothing, I don't make deals. Throw her overboard, I've lost interest in her."

Pinhead moved to grab her, but she slipped out of his grasp.

"No," said Allie. "Wait—I'll tell you how I got on your ship."

Pinhead hesitated. She thought she might get what she wanted if she played this right, but realized that she could not play at all. The McGill did not play games, and truly intended to toss her over. The best she could do was to stall with hopes of finding some way to bargain for the lives of Nick and Lief . . . assuming they hadn't already been hurled overboard themselves.

"I took the Staten Island Ferry," she said quickly, "and I slipped on board as it passed through your ship."

Suddenly both of the McGill's wandering eyes zeroed in on her. It gripped the edge of the throne with its claws and pushed itself up.

"That ferry changed course," the McGill said, "almost as if it was intentional. Did you do that?"

Allie wondered which response would keep her from being thrown overboard, yes or no. In the end she realized her answer was really the best of both worlds. "Yes and no," she said.

The McGill took a step closer. "Explain."

"I couldn't make the ship turn myself, so I sort of leaped into the pilot's body and took over for a few seconds."

The McGill maintained its hideous stare in silence. "You expect me to believe this," it finally said.

"Believe what you want, but I'm telling you the truth."

The creature eyed her for a few moments more. "So then, you're telling me that you know how to usurp, possess, and control the living? You can actually *skinjack*?"

Allie didn't like the sound of that. Is that what she had done? Had she *possessed* the pilot? Had she *skinjacked* him? It sounded so . . . criminal. "I prefer to think of it as 'body-surfing.'"

The McGill laughed at that. "Body-surfing. Very good." It scratched thoughtfully for a moment at the stalk of its smaller, dangling eye. "What's your name?"

"Allie," she answered. "Allie the Outcast."

The McGill, not at all impressed by her title, dug a single claw into its oversized nose, pulling out a booger the size of a roach, and flicked it to the wall where it stuck. Allie grimaced.

"Take her below," the McGill told Pinhead.

"Shall I chime her with the others?"

"No," the McGill said. "Put her in the guest quarters."

Pinhead nodded obediently and took Allie's arm with slightly more respect than he might have a moment ago. Allie, however, sensing her bargaining position had now changed, shrugged Pinhead off.

"You took two of my friends from the Haunter."

The McGill became very attentive. "Friends," the monster said slowly.

"Are they here?"

"Maybe they are, and maybe they aren't. For now you will go to your quarters. When I want you, I'll call for you."

She sighed, knowing she couldn't push it any further. "Thank you for being so . . . merciful," Allie said. "But I would appreciate it if Pea-brain here would keep his hands off me."

"That's Pinhead," corrected the boy. "Pea-brain works in the engine room."

The McGill waved a hand in dismissal, Pinhead bowed to Allie in a mock gesture of courtesy, and she was led to the guest quarters with more dignity than any Afterlight had experienced on the *Sulphur Queen* since its crossing into Everlost.

* * *

Once the girl was gone, the McGill lumbered back to his throne and sat down. From the little perch where the throne sat, he had a view of the ocean before him. They had crossed beneath the Verrazano Bridge, and the *Sulphur Queen* would soon be out in the Atlantic, on its endless journey up and down the Eastern Seaboard.

The McGill rarely allowed himself flights of fancy—he kept his existence pessimistic, always expecting the negative, and reveling when the worst didn't come to pass—but this girl had struck a chord in him.

Skinjacking! This was a power more useful than any of the powers he already possessed. To be able to leap from one body to another at will; intruding into the living world, then finding new flesh to inhabit whenever it suited him—how powerful that would make him! Could this girl teach him how to do that? If so, it would be worth putting all of his other plans on hold. Yes, this new associate offered some exciting possibilities.

The closest Mary Hightower comes to mentioning the McGill is in her book *Caution, This Means You!* Between paragraphs on the dangers of gravitational vortexes and reality television, Mary writes, "If you find a dead-spot containing something of great value, like jewelry, food that has crossed over, or any other object that seems too good to be true, chances are that it is too good to be true. Stay away from these places, or you may find yourself in a very unpleasant circumstance."

It is commonly believed that she is referring to the McGill's Greensoul traps, which are rumored to be strategically placed up and down the East Coast. Of course, their existence has never been proven. . . .

CHAPTER 17

The Chiming Chamber

Unlike Mary Hightower, the McGill did not write any books. The way he saw it, information was best hoarded, much like the objects in his treasure hold. The less information others knew, the more power he had over them. Still, the McGill secretly read every book that Mary Hightower had written. At first he found it all very amusing, because Mary's information was wrong as often as it was right. The more he read, however, the more he realized that Mary was not getting her facts wrong at all. She was deliberately distorting what she knew when it suited her. In this way, she was very much like the McGill, holding all the best information in.

The fact that Mary did not mention the McGill in any of her writings was a constant thorn in his side. He was a legend. He was, after all, the One True Monster of Everlost, and he deserved at the very least a chapter. Was that so much to ask? Someday, he would take on this Mary, defeat her, enslave her, and then force her to write an entire encyclopedia about him. But for now his interest was in a different girl.

* * *

Allie knew her welcome on board the *Sulphur Queen* would last only until the McGill got tired of her or got what it wanted. What *he* wanted, because Allie was reasonably certain this beast was male. Either way, her time was limited. Besides, she didn't have the patience to wait; she simply had to find out if Nick and Lief were here. Once in the "guest cabin," Allie waited until the sound of Pinhead's footsteps faded, then she quietly opened the door and snuck out.

The ship was large and the McGill's crew was small, so she was able to slip through the hatchways and corridors unseen. On the occasions that she did encounter the McGill's ugly young minions, they made so much noise that Allie had plenty of time to hide.

A ship has many places to stow prisoners, so she methodically explored every dark corner, ignoring the hideous rotten-egg smell, which grew as she went deeper into the bowels of the ship. Finally she found the ship's massive holds. By the stench and the yellow residue on the ground, Allie suspected the holds once carried sulphur, but now they held the spoils of the McGill's pillaging raids. She marveled at what she saw in each of the chambers, wondering how these things had crossed over. Had someone died in this leather recliner? Was this stained-glass window so lovingly made that it crossed over when the church burned down? And what about this armoire, complete with wedding dress and tuxedo hanging inside? Did the bride and groom "get where they were going" on an ill-fated wedding night? Was their love, like Romeo and Juliet's, not meant for the living world?

Each object held a story that no one would ever know,

and the fact that the McGill treated these things with such thoughtless disrespect made Allie hate the creature even more.

She opened the door to the fourth and final hold, expecting to find more piles of the McGill's treasure. This room was different, however.

As she peered in, her mind did not entirely comprehend what she saw. Her first impression was that of a giant hanging mobile, like something she once saw in the Museum of Modern Art. Large, lumpy objects hung from chains, all at different heights, all glowing dimly like low-wattage lightbulbs.

Then one of the objects spoke.

"What time is it?" the glowing lump said.

Allie let out a yelp, stepped back, and hit the steel bulkhead behind her. The wall rang out with a dull, hollow thud.

"What time is it?" the lump said again. It was a boy, maybe a year or two younger than her, wearing gray flannel pajamas, hanging upside down from his ankles around five feet from the ground. His pj's had a dorsal fin on the back, and a cartoon of a shark on the front.

"I . . . I don't know . . . ," Allie answered.

"Oh. Okay." The boy didn't seem disappointed. He just seemed resigned.

"Careful," said a girl hanging next to him. "He's a biter."

The pajama-boy smiled, showing a set of razor sharp, sharklike teeth, like the picture on his pajamas. "It's in a sea predator's nature," he said.

Only now did the truth begin to dawn on her as she took in the larger scene around her. The hanging lumps were Afterlights. Every single one of them. There had to be hundreds of kids, all hanging upside down.

The act of chiming was invented by the McGill and he was proud to claim responsibility for the idea. Since it was impossible to hurt someone in Everlost, and since the McGill so wanted to inflict distress, he came up with a whole new form of torture, functional in several different ways: first, because it provided an efficient way of storing those Afterlights he had no immediate use for, and second, because he created a hopeless sense of abject boredom in his victims.

Simply stated, the act of chiming was to hang someone upside down from their ankles by a long chain, or rope. It didn't actually hurt the spirit being chimed, but it was a pretty dull way to spend one's days, and if boredom was the closest thing to suffering that the McGill could inflict, he would have to live with that. In any case it was entertaining for him, because he would often go down to the hold and begin swinging people. They would collide into one another, grunting and oofing as they bumped, like human wind chimes, and hence it became known as "being chimed."

When Nick was first chimed, he wasn't sure whether it was better or worse than being in the pickle barrel. The rotten-egg smell was certainly worse than the garlic and dill of the pickle brine, but then, at least here, he did not feel so alone. Lief, who had reached a state of nirvana in his barrel, took it in stride, smiling all the while, and Nick eventually decided being alone would be better than hanging upside down next to a happy camper—but then, it was better than being next to the screamer, or that kid who was trying to turn himself into a shark.

As soon as the Ugloids had finished stringing them up, they painted numbers on their chests in black. For reasons Nick could not figure out, he was number 966, and Lief was number 266, although the kid had drawn the two backward.

"Your hair looks funny," Lief said, as soon as the Ugloids had left. "It stands straight up."

"No," said Nick, intensely irritated, "it's hanging straight down."

Lief just gave him an upside-down shrug. "Up is down in China and you're part-Chinese."

"Japanese, dweeb!" Nick reached out and slugged him on the shoulder, but that just started them both swinging into the others who were around them.

"Hey watch it," some kid said. "It's bad enough when the McGill comes down here to swing us. We don't need a couple of idiots making us chime, too."

His dangling comrades also complained each time Nick tried to climb his own rope, to get to the grate high up above. Through that grate he could see the sky, and he knew if he could get out on the open deck, he'd figure out a way to escape. Unfortunately, the ropes had all been greased, and he never got more than ten feet up his rope before falling down again and swinging into the kids around him, setting off a chain reaction of whining, which in turn reminded the screamer to start screaming, and everyone blamed Nick.

So aside from the occasional fight, and group sing-along, there was nothing to do but wait until the McGill found a use for them. Nick had this fantasy that Mary would come with a hundred of her kids to rescue him. He never dreamed that his rescuer would be Allie.

* * *

"Oh my God!"

Allie stood there on the sulphur-dusted floor of the chiming chamber, still unable to believe what she saw. She tried to count how many of them there were, but there were simply too many to count. There were numbers scrawled on their chests, and some of those numbers were up in the high hundreds.

"Are you here to free us?" girl 342 asked.

Since Allie didn't know if a rescue of this many Afterlights would ever be possible, Allie didn't answer her. Instead she asked, "I'm looking for two boys. They wouldn't have been here long. One is named Nick, the other Lief."

Then a voice from high above called down to her.

"They're on the other side." It was an older boy in a Boy Scout uniform, with rust-colored hair sticking straight down like an upside-down flame. His was the shortest rope; he hung about fifteen feet above the floor, making him the highest one, and the one with the best view of the chamber. "All they do is talk talk talk," he said. "Tell them to shut up, it's annoying."

Allie pushed her way forward into the mass of "chimed" kids. They swung like pendulums as she pushed through them, all of them grumbling and griping at having been disturbed. She tried to be gentle, but the forest of dangling spirits clearly did not appreciate her intrusion.

"Shut up, you idiots," the high-chimed Boy Scout said. Allie wondered if being strung the highest made the kid the automatic leader of the group, or did it merely make him high-strung?

"I said shut up!" he yelled more loudly. "Keep making noise, and you'll set off the screamer."

And next to Allie, the screamer, once more reminded of his job, began to wail in Allie's ear. Reflexively Allie clapped her hand over his mouth. "That," she said, "is totally uncalled for. Don't do that again. Ever." The screamer looked at her with worried eyes. "Are we clear on this subject?" said Allie. The screamer nodded, and she removed her hand.

"Can I scream a little?" he asked.

"No," said Allie. "Your screaming days are over."

"Darn." And he was quiet thereafter.

"Hey," someone called out. "She shut down the screamer!" The chamber rang out with upside-down applause.

"Allie, is that you?" It was Nick. She pushed her way past a few more danglers, and found both of them. Nick hung about five feet from the ground, his head at about eye level. Lief hung about a foot higher.

"How did you get here?" Nick asked. "I thought for sure the Haunter put you in a barrel, too!"

"I got away before he could," Allie explained.

"And you just left us there?!"

Allie sighed. They had no idea what she had gone through to get here, and now was not the time to tell them. She looked at Lief, who smiled and gave her an upside-down wave with his dangling arms. "Hi."

Lief's calm acceptance of his plight just made Allie feel all the more miserable. "This is horrible! How could the McGill do this!?"

"He's a monster," Nick reminded her. "It's what monsters do."

"Are you going to hang here with us?" Lief asked, happily. "There's room next to me!"

"Ignore him," Nick told Allie. "He's completely lost it." Nick squirmed, and bent his knees until his hands could get a grip on his ankles. "Can you cut us down?"

Then the kid up top called down to them. "If you free them, the McGill will throw all three of you overboard. He may get so mad, he'll throw us *all* overboard."

Allie knew he was right. The McGill was both mean-spirited and unpredictable—and besides, if she cut them down, where would they go? Even if they got out of the hold, they were still trapped on the ship.

"I can't free you now," she told them, "but I will soon. Hang tight." She grimaced at her poor choice of words.

"So you're just going to leave us here?" Nick said.

"Don't be a stranger!" Lief said, merrily.

"I'll be back soon. I promise."

"You promise? You also promised the visit to the Haunter wouldn't be dangerous," Nick reminded her. "And look how that turned out."

Allie made no excuses because he was right. This was all her fault. Allie rarely apologized for anything, but when she said "I'm sorry," this time, it carried the weight of all the apologies she had never given when she was alive. Then she hugged them awkwardly, setting them both slightly swinging, and left before her emotions could get the better of her.

CHAPTER 18

Skinjacking for Dummies

The *Sulphur Queen* hugged the shore of the East Coast, stopping now and again to send out a landing party in a lifeboat to see if any of the McGill's Greensoul traps had snagged any new Afterlights. They were simple devices really; camouflaged nets tied to Everlost trees. A Greensoul would see a candy bar, or a bucket of popcorn, or whatever else the McGill was able to use as bait, but the second the kid grabbed it, the trap sprung, and there the kid was caught until the McGill's crew came to cut him down. Easy as catching a rabbit.

The McGill was pleased with the current state of his world. Things were coming together nicely. He had to believe that finding this girl Allie was no coincidence. Forces in the universe were conspiring in his favor. Whether they were forces of light or forces of darkness . . . well, that was yet to be determined.

The morning after Allie's unexpected arrival, the McGill went down to her quarters, and found her there, reading one of those blasted books by Mary Queen of Snots.

When he entered, Allie casually glanced at him from her

bed, then returned her attention to the book. "Mary's books are *sooo* annoying," she told the McGill. "You can't tell the truth from the lies. Someday I'll set her straight."

It was hard for him not to smile. She disliked Mary, just as he did. This was a good sign.

The McGill tossed his head in a calculated gesture of disdain. His greasy hair whipped around, and flung some slime against the wall. "You will teach me how to skinjack now."

She turned a page in her book, ignoring him. "I don't follow orders."

The McGill paused, not sure whether to spit worms at her, or treat her with uncharacteristic patience. He chose patience. "You will teach me how to skinjack now . . . *please*."

Allie put down the book and sat up. "Well, as long as you used the magic word, sure, why not."

She did not appear disgusted in the least when she looked at him. This was troublesome. Everybody, even his own crew, found him utterly repulsive. His power to repel was a matter of pride. He made a mental note that he would have to come up with new and inventive ways to disgust her.

What the McGill didn't realize was that Allie *was* disgusted, but she was extremely good at keeping her emotions to herself when she wanted to. Allie had decided that the McGill already had enough power over her; she wasn't willing to give him the satisfaction of nausea.

"The art of skinjacking," Allie began; "lesson number one."

"I'm listening."

Allie hesitated. She had truly painted herself into a corner here, because if there was ever a spirit that should not know how to skinjack, it was the McGill. She barely knew how to do it herself, having only tried it once with the ferry pilot—but the McGill didn't know that. As far as he knew, she was an expert. As long as she acted like an expert, she could get away with just about anything.

"Possessing the living is a very complicated thing," she said with authority. "First we must find . . . uh . . . a Vortex of Spirit."

"A Vortex of Spirit," repeated the McGill. "I don't know what that is."

Neither did Allie, but that really didn't matter.

"Do you mean a place that's already haunted?" the McGill asked.

"Yes, that's it."

"A place that's haunted without explanation?"

"Exactly!"

The McGill stroked his swollen chin as he thought. "I know a place like that. A house in Long Island. We went there in search of Afterlights to capture. We didn't find a single one, but the walls of the house kept telling us to get out."

"Okay," said Allie. "Then that's where our lessons will begin."

The McGill nodded. "I will call for you when we arrive."

Once he was gone, Allie let her revulsion out, shivering and squirming, and then she returned to her bed, disgusting herself further with Mary Hightower's volume of misinformation. She hoped that couched between Mary's useless tips there might be a clue to defeating the McGill—the trick was finding it.

The McGill, being an arrogant creature, believed he could see through anyone who was lying. It was that arrogance that kept him from seeing how completely Allie was tricking him. He strolled along the deck, pleased with this new wrinkle in his existence. Around him, his crew did their busywork on deck. There was little point to all the cleaning, the swabbing, and the polishing the crew did. What was rusty now would always be rusty. What was covered in sulphur dust would stay that way, no matter how much the crew tried to wipe it away. The best they could do was to clear away the cookie crumbs the McGill often left behind. Still, the McGill insisted that his ship be like a real ship, his crew like a real crew, and cleaning is what crews did. It was always the same crew members cleaning the same things, and at the same time of day. Routine. It's what made a ghost ship a ghost ship. Allie, however, was a break from the routine.

He proudly strolled past his crewmen, flicking little black bugs at them, or spitting on their shoes—just to remind them who was boss. Then he returned to the bridge and ordered the ship turned around, heading back toward Long Island and the haunted house he had told Allie about. Then he sat in his throne, reaching toward a tarnished brass spittoon that sat next to it. The bowl was originally used for spitting tobacco, phlegm, and other vile things, but it served a different function here. The McGill dug his claw in, and pulled out a fortune cookie—one of many that filled the copper pot.

Mary Hightower was not a fan of fortune cookies, and

told her readers so. Just thinking about it made the McGill laugh. What Mary didn't tell her readers is that fortune cookies were plentiful in Everlost—not quite as plentiful as those faceless coins, but far more useful. For once, Mary had done him a service. If others stayed away from the cookies, it meant there were more for him!

The McGill crushed the fortune cookie in his fingers, hurling the crumbs out on the deck for his crew to fight over like seagulls, then he settled into his throne and read the small slip of paper that had been hidden in the cookie.

Out of the water will come your salvation.

Allie had come to him out of the water, hadn't she? He leaned back, well satisfied with himself.

The house on Long Island did, indeed, tell them to get out.

It told them loudly, it told them often. It was an annoying house. It was, however, all bark and no bite. There was a young couple living in the house—and although it yelled at them, too, they apparently could not hear it as they were both deaf. Since the house had no appendages by which to communicate in American sign language, it was profoundly frustrated. It must have been very satisfying for the house to finally have spirits within its walls who *could* hear it—even if they weren't inclined to listen. Regardless, Allie had to admit it was the perfect location for her first bogus lesson in skinjacking.

"Okay," Allie told the McGill, "first find a dead-spot in the room," which was not very difficult since the whole house was spotted with them like Swiss cheese. Apparently many people had died here. Allie didn't want to think about it.

The McGill took a spot near a window facing the sea. "Now what?"

"Close your eyes."

"My eyes don't close," the McGill reminded her.

"Right. Okay then, keep your eyes open. Face the ocean . . . and wait for the sun to rise."

"It's noon," the McGill pointed out.

"Yes, I know. You have to stand here, and wait until tomorrow when the sun rises, then stare into the rising sun."

"Get . . . Owwwwwwwwt," said the house.

"If we have to be here at dawn, why didn't you tell me that before we came?"

"You know what your problem is?" Allie said. "You have no patience. You're immortal, it's not like you're going anywhere. Skinjacking takes patience. Stand here, and wait until dawn."

The McGill gave her an evil eye, spat out a wad of something brown on her shoe, and said, "Fine. But you wait with me. If I have to listen to this stupid house, then so do you."

So they waited, ignoring the pointless activities of the people who lived there, and turning a deaf ear to the house.

The next morning however was overcast, and instead of a rising sun, the horizon was filled with a ribbon of gray.

"You'll have to wait until tomorrow," Allie told the McGill.

"Why? What does this have to do with possessing the living?"

Allie rolled her eyes as if the answer was obvious. "Staring at the sun at dawn gives you soul-sight. Not every living person can be possessed. Soul-sight allows you to see which ones you'll be able to skinjack, and which ones you won't."

The McGill looked at her doubtfully. "And this is how you learned?"

"Well," said Allie, "it's the first step."

"How many steps are there?"

"Twelve."

The McGill regarded her with his wandering, mismatched eyes, then asked, "Is anyone in this house possessible?"

Allie thought back to when she caught glimpses of the occupants speaking to one another by means of complex hand gestures. In truth, anyone was possessible, but she wouldn't let the McGill know that. The whole point of this was to make sure she didn't teach the McGill anything at all. The whole point was to stall long enough to learn the McGill's weaknesses. If she could drag him through twelve ridiculous steps, convincing him that at the end he'd learn how to skinjack, she might find the key to defeating him—or at least, a way to free her friends. Either way, she knew she'd have to make a quick escape when it was all over, because when the McGill finally figured out that he was being duped, his fury would reverberate through all of Everlost.

"The woman is possessible," Allie told the McGill.

"Show me," the creature said. "Skinjack her now."

Allie clenched her teeth. Her experience taking control of the ferry pilot had been exciting, but frightening. It had been an intense experience, but also fundamentally gross—like wearing someone else's sweaty clothes. Still, if she were going to keep stringing the McGill along, she would have to deliver.

"Okay, I'll do it. But only if you tell me why you've got all those kids strung up in your ship. And why you put numbers on them."

He considered the question, then said, "I'll tell you AFTER you skinjack the woman."

"Fine." Allie rolled her shoulders like a runner getting ready for a race, then approached the woman in the kitchen. Stepping in was easier this time than it had been with the ferry pilot, perhaps because she and Allie were the same gender, or perhaps because practice made perfect. The woman never quite knew what hit her. What struck Allie first was the absolute silence. She almost panicked, thinking something was wrong, until she remembered the woman was deaf. The world around Allie now was brighter—the way it appeared to the living—and she could feel the seductive density of flesh. She flexed her fingers, and found that it had only taken a few moments to push the woman's consciousness down, and take control. Allie looked around. Through the woman's eyes she could no longer see the McGill, but she knew he was there. If he wanted proof that she could possess people, he would have proof. She rummaged around in the kitchen drawers until she found a permanent marker, then went to the wall and wrote in big block letters:

BEWARE THE MCGILL

Then she hopped out of the woman, not wanting to spend a second more there than she had to. The living world faded into the muted colors of Everlost, her hearing returned, and there was the McGill smiling through sharp, rotten teeth. "Very good!" he said. "Very, very good."

"Now tell me about the Afterlights in your ship."

"No."

"You promised."

"I lied."

"Then I won't teach you what I know."

"Then I'll throw your friends over the side."

"Get . . . Owwwwwwt!!!!"

Allie clenched her fists and let off an angry growl that only made the McGill laugh. She might have held some of the cards, but the McGill would not let her forget that he held all the aces.

"We will come back each morning," the McGill said, "until we have a bright sunrise. Then we will go on to step two."

Allie had no choice but to agree. She rode the lifeboat in furious silence back to the *Sulphur Queen*, even more determined than ever to outsmart the McGill.

As for the woman Allie had possessed, once she regained control of her body, she took one look at the words scrawled on the wall, and concluded that all the stories about this house were true. She immediately contacted her Realtor, and put the house up for sale, determined that she and her husband would move as far away from Amityville as possible.

"Beware of fortune cookies that cross into Everlost," Mary Hightower writes in her book *Caution, This Means You!* "They are instruments of evil, and the proper way to deal with them is to stay far away. AVOID TEMPTATION! Don't even go near Chinese restaurants! Those wicked cookies will rot off the hand of anyone who touches them."

CHAPTER 19

Evil Chinese Pastry of Death

The McGill followed Allie's lead, letting her direct him through the first three steps of human possession. He supposedly now had "soul-sight," allowing him to see which humans were possessible and which were not, however when he looked at the living, he saw no difference between them. He wouldn't tell Allie this, though. Soul-sight would come, he convinced himself. Once he worked his way through the remaining steps it would come. It had better.

The second step was to follow the actions of a living person for twenty-four hours. "The point," Allie explained, "is to become in tune with the things living people do." It was a deceptively difficult chore, because the living could travel through the world in ways that the McGill could not. Every single time the McGill chose someone to follow, they would eventually get into a car, or a train, or, in one strange instance, a helicopter, and be carried away too quickly for the McGill to follow on foot.

It took several days until he finally settled on someone who wasn't going anywhere; an inmate at a local jail. He spent twenty-four hours observing the prisoner's various limited activities, and the McGill returned to the *Sulphur Queen* triumphant.

The third step, however, was much more difficult. According to Allie, he was required to commit an act of selflessness. The McGill didn't think it was possible.

"You could release one or two kids from the chiming chamber," Allie suggested.

But the McGill flatly refused. "It wouldn't be selfless," he told her, "because I'd be doing it to gain something."

No—if selflessness was what was required then it would be a difficult task indeed. This required consulting with the cookies. After Allie had gone to her quarters, the McGill once more pushed his hand into the spittoon and withdrew a fortune cookie, crushed it, and pulled out the slip of paper. This time it read:

The answer comes when the question is forgotten.

Annoyed, the McGill threw the cookie crumbs over the side, rather than giving them to his crew.

The McGill wasn't the only one annoyed by this turn of events. Allie silently cursed herself for not being more clever. Did she actually think the McGill would be tricked into releasing her friends? True, the challenge of this "third step" bought her time, but if the McGill was truly incapable of selflessness, it would only serve to make him angrier and angrier.

She now had freedom on the ship—more than any of the McGill's actual crew—but something was happening to her. Each time she looked in a mirror, her reflection looked a little off. Did one ear look larger than the other? Was this bottom tooth always crooked? She wondered how long it would be until she became no better than the rest of his crew. Allie pondered all this as she stood on deck one afternoon, looking toward shore—only she couldn't find it. The sky was clear, but all she could see was ocean. It seemed to her that the *Sulphur Queen* always hugged the coastline, but now they were out in the open sea. It was unsettling, for although she knew she could no longer be a part of the living world, seeing it gave her some connection to the life she once had. By her calculation, they should have been off the coast of New Jersey—the southern part of the state, where her family lived—but the shore was nowhere in sight.

As she stared out at the horizon, the McGill approached her, lumbering in that awful way of his.

"Why are we all the way out here," Allie asked him, "if you're supposed to be checking your traps?"

"I have no traps in New Jersey," was his only answer.

"But what's the point of coming all the way out to sea?"

"I didn't come here to answer stupid questions," he said.

"Then why *did* you come?"

"I was on the bridge," the McGill said, "and I saw you staring over the side. I came down to see if you were all right."

Allie found this show of concern even more disturbing than the slime that so freely oozed from the McGill's various bodily openings. The McGill brought his flaking three-fingered claw to her face and lifted her chin. Allie took one look at that swollen, turgid finger, purple and pale like a dead fish three days in the sun, and she pulled away from him, revolted.

"I disgust you," the McGill said.

"Isn't that what you want?" Allie answered. From the start she knew he took great pride in his high gross-out factor. He never passed up an opportunity to be repulsive, and was skilled at thinking up new disgusting things to do. At that moment, however, he didn't seem pleased with himself at all.

"Perhaps my hand could use a softer, gentler touch," he said. "I'll work on it."

Allie resisted the urge to look at him. *Please don't tell me the monster is falling in love with me,* she thought. She was simply not the compassionate kind of girl who could handle it. "Don't try to charm me," she told him. "The 'Beauty and the Beast' thing doesn't work with me, okay?"

"I'm not trying to charm you. I just came down here to make sure you weren't planning to jump."

"Why would I jump?"

"Sometimes people do," the McGill told her. "Crew members who think sinking would be better than serving me."

"Maybe they have the right idea," Allie told him. "You won't release my friends, you won't answer my questions—maybe I'd be better off down there."

The McGill shook his head. "You're just saying that because you don't know—but I know what happens when you sink." And then the McGill became quiet. His dangling eyes, which never seemed to be looking in the same direction, now seemed to be looking off somewhere else entirely. Somewhere no one else could see.

"It may begin with water," he said, "but it always ends with dirt. Dirt, then stone. When you first pass into the Earth, it's stifling dark, and cold. You feel the stone in your body."

Allie thought back to the time Johnnie-O had almost pushed her down. She remembered that feeling of the earth in her body. It was not something she ever wanted to experience again.

"You feel the pressure growing greater all around you as gravity pulls you down," the McGill said. "And then it begins to get hot. It gets hotter than a living body could stand. The stone glows red. It turns liquid. You feel the heat. It should burn you into nothing but it doesn't. It doesn't even hurt, because you can't feel hurt, but you *do* feel the intensity of the heat . . . it's maddening. All you see is the bright molten red, then molten white the hotter it gets. And that's all there is for you. The light, and the heat, and the steady drop down and down."

Allie wanted to make him stop, but found she couldn't, for as much as she didn't want to know, she felt she *had* to know.

"You sink for years, and from time to time, you come across others," the McGill said. "You feel their presence around you. Their voices are muffled by the molten rock. They tell you their names, if they remember them. And then in twenty years time, you reach a place where the world is so thick around you with sunken spirits, you stop. Once you're there, once you've stopped falling and realize you're not going anywhere anymore, that's when you begin waiting."

"Waiting for what?"

"Isn't it obvious?"

Allie didn't dare guess what he was talking about.

"Waiting for the end of the world," the McGill said.

"The world . . . is going to end?"

"Of course it's going to end," the McGill told her. "Probably not for a hundred billion years, but eventually the sun will die, the Earth will blow up, and every kid who's ever sunk to the core will be free to zoom around the universe, or do whatever it is Afterlights do when there's no gravity to deal with anymore."

Allie tried to imagine waiting for a billion years, but couldn't. "It's horrible."

"No, it's *not* horrible," the McGill said, "and that's what makes it *worse* than horrible."

"I don't understand."

"You see, when you're at the center of the Earth, you forget you have arms and legs, because you don't need them. You can't use them. You become nothing but spirit. Pretty soon you can't tell where you end, and where the Earth begins . . . and you suddenly find that you don't care. You suddenly find that you have endless patience. Enough patience to wait until the end of the world."

"'Rest in peace,'" Allie said. "Maybe that's what they mean." It was perhaps a great mercy of the universe, that lost souls who could do nothing but wait were blessed with everlasting peace. It was kind of like the weird bliss Lief had found in his barrel.

"I could never imagine being that patient," Allie said.

"Neither could I," said the McGill. "So I clawed my way back to the surface."

Allie snapped her eyes back to the McGill, whose eyes were no longer far away—they were both looking right at her.

"You mean . . ."

The McGill nodded. "It took me more than fifty years, but I wanted to be back on the surface again, and when you want something badly enough, you can do anything. No one has ever wanted it as much as me; I'm the only one who's ever come back from the center of the Earth." Then the McGill looked at his gnarled claws. "It helped to imagine myself as a monster clawing my way up from the depths, and so when I finally reached the surface that's exactly what I was. A monster. And it's exactly what I want to be."

Although nothing about the McGill's horrible face had changed since he began his tale, Allie could swear he somehow looked different. "Why did you tell me this?" Allie asked.

The McGill shrugged. "I thought you should know. I thought you deserved a little bit of truth in return for all your help."

And although the picture the McGill painted was not a pretty one, it somehow made Allie feel a bit better. A bit less in the dark. "Thank you," she said. "That was very thoughtful."

The McGill lifted his head. "Thoughtful . . . Do you think maybe it was selfless?"

Allie nodded. "Yes, I think it was."

The McGill smiled wide enough to show his rotten gums. "The answer was found when the question was forgotten, just as the fortune cookie said."

"Fortune cookie?" asked Allie. "What do you mean?"

But the McGill ignored her. "I've achieved the selfless act," the McGill said. "I'm ready for step four."

* * *

Allie dug through what writings of Mary's she could find, until she discovered the entry on fortune cookies—how they were evil, flesh-rotting little pastries, and should be avoided like nuclear waste. If Mary was frightened enough of fortune cookies to ban them, Allie knew there must be something important about them.

Allie sought out Pinhead. He was down in the mess hall with the rest of the crew, who were all entertaining themselves with the same games they played over and over again. They flipped and traded old baseball cards from long-dead players. They argued over who was cheating in checkers. As in Mary's world, these crew members, if not rousted from their games by the McGill, would sit in their eternal ruts, and get into the same fights over and over again. *Remember that,* Allie told herself. *Don't let your guard down. Don't let yourself fall into routine again.*

When the crew saw her enter the mess hall, either they ignored her, or they scowled at her. She was not well loved among the crew. Mostly they resented the fact that she had found the McGill's favor, where they had not. Still, they had to grudgingly admit that since she had been on board, their situation had improved. The McGill was distracted and was far less demanding on them now.

Pinhead, more than any of the others, understood the value of having Allie aboard. At first she had thought he'd be resentful the way Vari had been resentful of Nick, but since Pinhead was often the scapegoat for the McGill's anger when things didn't go his way, Allie was a bit of a savior to Pinhead. She could hardly call him a friend, but neither was he an enemy. One thing Allie was certain of:

he had more brains than his small head would suggest, and was pretty much the glue that held things together around the *Sulphur Queen*.

Pinhead stood in a corner acting as referee for two other young crewmembers who were playing the flinching game—the one where you slap each other's hands, and get a free slap if your opponent flinches.

"Tell me about fortune cookies," she said. He immediately left the two flinchers to their game, and took Allie aside, sitting down with her at a table where they could talk without being overheard.

"What do you want to know?" Pinhead asked.

"Mary Hightower says they're evil. Is that true?"

Pinhead laughed. "Mary must have had a bad fortune."

"So tell me the truth."

Pinhead looked around as if it was some big secret, then said quietly, "Fortune cookies all cross over."

Allie took a moment to process that. "What do you mean *all*?"

"I mean all. Every single fortune cookie that was ever made anywhere in the world crosses into Everlost. Living people might break them open, but the *ghosts* of all those cookies cross over, unbroken, just waiting for some Afterlight to find them."

"Interesting," Allie said, "but why is that such a big deal?"

Pinhead grinned. "It's a very big deal," he said, and then he leaned in close. "Because in Everlost, all fortunes are true."

* * *

Allie wasn't sure whether to believe Pinhead. Just as Mary's information had been wrong, it was possible Pinhead's was wrong as well. It was just rumor. It was just myth. There was, however, one way to find out: She had to open one up.

Since the McGill had talked about the cookies, she reasoned that he must have a stash somewhere, so while the McGill was off inspecting a trap on the coast of Maine, Allie went up to his throne deck, and began the search.

They weren't too hard to find. In fact, she would have found them sooner, if she didn't have a certain disgust at getting anywhere near the McGill's spittoon. It was only after a pause for thought that she realized the McGill had no reason to actually have a spittoon. Since he prided himself on his repulsiveness, he never actually used it. Instead, he spat everywhere else. That being the case, the spittoon was probably the most mucous-free object on the entire ship.

It turned out that she was right. She reached into the spittoon and found the McGill's collection of fortune cookies.

She held one in her hand, grit her teeth, and watched what happened, hoping that Mary was wrong about her hand rotting off. Her hand didn't rot. It didn't wither. Allie was not at all surprised.

Now there was a sense of anticipation in her as she held the little pastry. She had never believed in fortune-tellers, but then, she had never believed in ghosts either. She closed her eyes, made a fist around the cookie and squeezed. It crumbled with a satisfying crunch, then she pulled the little slip of paper out from the remains.

Selfish ambition leaves friends in a pickle.

Allie wasn't sure whether she was more amazed or annoyed. It was like the universe wagging an accusing finger at her for having brought Nick and Lief to the Haunter. She tried another one, because the first only spoke of what had been, not what will be. Perhaps this second one would be more helpful. She broke another cookie, and read the fortune.

You shall be the last. You shall be the first.

Since it made no sense to her, she went for a third.

Linger or light; the choice will be yours.

It was like eating pistachios, and she found herself getting into a rhythm of cracking open one after another . . . until she reached for the fourth one, broke it open, and the fortune said:

Look behind you.

CHAPTER 20

The Day the McGill Got Chimed

The McGill held his temper as he stood behind Allie in the throne room, watching her steal his fortunes. Never before had anyone pilfered his fortune cookies, and his fury at her was deep, but for once he resisted the urge to lash out. He had successfully completed the first four steps. Only eight remained. If his temper caused him to be rash and hurl the girl over the side, he would never know the secret of possessing the living. But since anger was the only way the McGill knew how to react, he just stood there, not reacting at all.

The girl, her back still to him, suddenly stiffened as she read her fourth fortune, and slowly turned around to see him there. The moment she saw him, he recognized the look of fear in her eyes. It was the first time he had seen her show fear since arriving on the ship. At first it had troubled the McGill that she seemed unafraid of him, but now, he found himself troubled by the fact that she was. He didn't want her to be afraid of him. This new sensitivity in himself was deeply disturbing.

"Explain yourself!" The McGill's voice came out in deep guttural tones, like the growl of a tiger at the moment it pounces.

Allie stood straight and opened her mouth to speak, but hesitated. The McGill knew what that hesitation meant. *She's going to lie,* he thought—and he knew if she did lie, there would be no containing his temper. He would hurl her with such force, she would reach the mainland like a cannonball.

Then, after a moment, she relaxed her shoulders, and said, "I just learned about fortune cookies, and wanted to see for myself if it was true. I guess I got carried away."

It smelled of honesty—enough honesty for the McGill to keep his temper in check. He lumbered toward her, keeping one eye trained on her face, and the other on the spittoon. "Give me your hand," he demanded, and when Allie didn't do it, he grabbed her hand, holding it out.

"What are you going to do?" she asked.

He didn't answer. Instead he reached into the spittoon with his free claw, grabbed a fortune cookie and placed it in her palm, then closed his hand around hers. "Let's find out what our fortune is," he said. The McGill squeezed Allie's hand so hard, not only did the cookie shatter, but her knuckles cracked as well. Then the McGill released her hand, and pulled out the fortune slip with his sharp nails.

Forgiveness keeps destiny on track.

The McGill found his anger slipping away. The cookies never lied. "Very well," he said. "I forgive you." He sat down on his throne, satisfied. "Now get out of my sight."

Allie turned to leave, but stopped at the threshold. "Forgiveness is the fifth step," she said, and then she left.

* * *

Allie's brain—or her memory of a brain—or whatever you called the thought processes of an Afterlight—was working overtime. Granting the McGill the fifth step had been an impulsive thing to do, but at the moment it had felt like the *right* thing to do. But what was she thinking? There was no right thing, because there *was* no fifth step! All this stalling was buying her nothing, and in all her time here, she was no closer to freeing her friends. If they were to have any hope, she would have to find the McGill's weakness—and Allie suspected if he had one, it would lie in the questions he refused to answer.

"Why does the McGill stay away from New Jersey?" Allie asked Pinhead, the next time she caught him alone.

"It's something he doesn't like to talk about," Pinhead told her.

"That's why I'm asking you, not him."

Pinhead held his silence as a few crew members passed by. When they were gone, Pinhead began to whisper.

"It's not all of New Jersey he stays away from," Pinhead said. "It's just Atlantic City."

Allie knew all about Atlantic City. It was the Las Vegas of the East Coast: dozens of hotels and casinos, a boardwalk full of fudge and saltwater taffy shops. "Why would the McGill be afraid of a place like that?"

"He was defeated there," Pinhead told her. "It happened at the Steel Pier. See, there are two amusement piers in Atlantic City that burned down years ago, and crossed over into Everlost. The Steel Pier, and the Steeplechase Pier. They became a hangout for 'The Twin Pier Marauders,' a gang of really rough Afterlights—probably the nastiest gang there is. Anyway, the McGill raided them twenty years ago, and they fought back. It was a terrible battle, and in the end, they had hurled the McGill's entire crew into the sea, and captured the McGill."

"Captured him?"

Pinhead nodded. "They took him to the Steeplechase Pier, and chained him upside down from his feet to the parachute-drop ride, and up and down he went every thirty seconds for four years . . . until one of the Marauders turned traitor, and set him free."

"I'm surprised he told you something like that."

"He didn't," Pinhead said. "I was the one who set him free." Then Pinhead looked at her, studying her face. "I've answered your questions," Pinhead said. "Now I have a question for you. I want to know if you really are teaching the McGill to skinjack."

Allie carefully sidestepped the question. "Well, it's what he wants."

"The McGill shouldn't always get what he wants."

She wasn't expecting that response from Pinhead. "But . . . don't you want your master to have that skill?"

"He's my captain, not my master," Pinhead said, some indignance in his voice. He thought for a moment, looking down, then returned his gaze to Allie. It was now a powerful gaze, full of urgency, and maybe a little accusation. "I don't remember a lot from my living days, but I do remember that my father—or was it my mother—worked in a madhouse."

"A mental institution," Allie corrected.

"When I was alive, they didn't have such nice words for them. Sometimes, I would get to go in. The people there were very sick—but some were more than sick. Some were possessed."

"Things have changed," Allie pointed out. "They don't think that kind of thing anymore."

"It doesn't matter what they think; I know what I know."

Pinhead's thoughts drifted away for a moment. Allie couldn't imagine what it would be like to walk through an old-world asylum. She didn't want to know.

"Even when I was alive, I knew the difference between the sick ones and the possessed ones. You can see it in their eyes. My mother—or was it my father—said there was no such thing as possession, but you know it happens, because you've done it yourself."

"I didn't drive anyone crazy."

"Well," said Pinhead, "all I know is that if I were a living, breathing person, I wouldn't want something like the McGill living inside of me."

"Why should you care? If he skinjacks someone and leaves Everlost, you get to be captain."

"I'm not the captain type," he said, and he offered her a slanted mudslide of a grin. "Don't have the head for it."

Allie went back to her cabin and lay down, running what Pinhead had said about the Steel and Steeplechase Piers over and over again in her mind, until an idea came to her: a way to defeat the McGill, or at least a way to distract him enough for her and her friends to escape. The plan was simple, and it was dangerous, but it was the best hope she had.

All she needed was a small slip of paper . . . and a typewriter.

* * *

Although the McGill liked no one, he was beginning to suspect that if he ever *did* like someone, it might be Allie. This troubled him, because he knew she would abandon him and escape with her friends if she could. The McGill, however, believed in the power of blackmail. As long as he had her friends dangling like carrots before her, she would do what he wanted. He knew he would never trust her, because, for the McGill, trust had been left behind with the human condition. The McGill trusted no one but himself, and even then, he was often suspicious of his own motives. He wondered, for instance, if he believed Allie's twelve-steps-to-possession only because he wanted it so badly. Or worse, did he believe her only because he had begun to like her?

Since he couldn't trust himself, he decided he needed verification of Allie's honesty, and so, once Allie was below deck, he called up an oversize kid known as Piledriver. Piledriver's claim to fame was that he had died in a living-room wrestling mishap, while costumed as his favorite professional wrestler. The McGill often brought him along on shore raids to inspire fear in Greensouls who had not yet realized that pain and joint dislocation were no longer an issue. Today, however, the McGill had a different mission for Piledriver.

"Take two crewmen and a lifeboat," the McGill told him, after he explained the nature of the mission. "Leave in the middle of the night, when the rest of the crew is below. Don't tell anyone, and once you find what you're looking for, meet us at Rockaway Point. I'll hold the *Sulphur Queen* there until you return."

Piledriver dutifully left, pleased to be given such an important task.

The McGill reclined in his throne, picking at the jewels on the armrests. If Piledriver did the job right, they would soon know if Allie was telling the truth.

In her book *Everything Mary Says Is Wrong, Volume 2,* Allie the Outcast has this to say about the nature of eternity: "Mary may have invented the term 'Afterlights,' but that doesn't mean she really understands what it means to be one. Maybe there's a reason why we're here, and maybe there's not. Maybe it's an accident, and maybe it's part of some big-ass plan that we're too dumb to figure out. All I know is that our light doesn't fade. That's got to mean something. Finding answers to questions like that is what we ought to be doing, instead of getting lost in endless ruts."

CHAPTER 21

Web of the Psychotic Spider

Down in the chiming chamber, Nick had grown more and more determined to throw off his shackles. So much of his life had been a game of follow the leader. During his living days he had followed friends and trends, never sticking his neck out to do anything on his own. Then, when he first arrived in Everlost, he had followed Allie, because she was the one with momentum. She had always been the one with a goal, and a plan to reach it, however misguided it might be. His time in a pickle barrel had certainly changed his perspective on things. During all that time, he could do nothing but wait for rescue to come from the outside. Nothing was worse than that limp, lonely feeling that he had no power over his own fate—and yet here he was again, strung up like a side of beef, just waiting for someone else to help him.

So many of the kids chimed beside him had grown to accept this. Lief, with his weird post-traumatic bliss, was a constant reminder to Nick that he, too, might someday just leave his will behind, and grow as passive as a plant, waiting for time to do whatever time does to Afterlights. The thought frightened him—

it made him anxious, and that anxiety spurred him on to action.

"I'm finding a way out of here," he announced to any of the other chimed kids who cared to listen.

"Ah, shut up," said the high-strung kid. "Nobody wants to hear it."

A few others echoed their halfhearted agreement.

"You new chimers just complain, complain, complain," said some kid from deep in the middle of the chiming chamber—perhaps a kid who had been there for many years, and had lost anything resembling hope.

"I'm not complaining," Nick announced, and he realized that, for once, he wasn't. "I'm *doing* something about it." Then he began to bend at the waist and swing his arms, making himself move like a pendulum.

Lief smiled at him. "Looks like fun," he said, and he joined Nick, until they were both swinging together, bounding off of all the other kids around them—kids who were not at all pleased to be jostled out of their semivegetative state. Grumbles of "Stop it!" and "Leave us alone," began to echo around the chamber, but Nick would not be deterred.

He couldn't quite swing to the door, and even if he could, it was locked from the outside, so that was out of the question, and there were so many kids, he couldn't build up the momentum to swing free, like a true pendulum. In the end, he wound up accidentally locking elbows with Lief as he swung past him, and they spun around each other, like an upside-down square dance. Their ropes tangled, and they ended up pressed to one another like dance partners.

The high-strung kid laughed. "Serves you right!" he said. "Now you'll be stuck like that!"

Their ropes were hopelessly tangled, and now they were even farther from the ground than when they started.

Farther from the ground . . .

A stray thought sparked through Nick's mind so sharply and suddenly, it burst out of his chocolate-covered mouth before he understood what he meant.

"Macramé," he said.

"Huh?" said Lief.

One day long ago, when Nick was home from school, too sick to do much of anything else, his grandmother gave him some twine, and showed him how to weave it together into fancy patterns. It was called macramé. He had made a hanging-plant holder that was probably still holding a big old spider plant in his living room.

"Lief!" he said. "Twist around me some more." And without waiting for Lief to respond, Nick grabbed him and made Lief twist around him again and again until the torque of their tangled ropes made them spin backward, like a rubber band that was wound too tight. But before they could spin too far, Nick said, "Just follow me—do what I do."

Nick reached out and grabbed another kid.

"Hey!" complained the kid.

Nick ignored him and twisted the kid's position so that high above their upside-down feet, their ropes tangled. Lief did the same to a kid next to him. By now there were mumbles of kids around them taking notice. This wasn't just your run-of-the-mill swinging—this had purpose and design. This was something new.

"What are you doing down there?" demanded the high-strung kid.

"Everybody!" Nick shouted. "Grab the people around you and start crossing your ropes. Get as tangled as you can!"

"Why?" the high-strung kid said.

Nick tried to think of something the high-strung kid would understand. As he was wearing a Boy Scout uniform, Nick figured he knew just the thing. "Ever make a lanyard at Boy Scout camp?" Nick asked. "You know—those plastic strings you weave together to make whistle chains, and stuff?

"Yeah . . ."

"You start with tons and tons of string, right? But when it's done it's really short, once all the strings are woven together."

"Yeah . . . ," said the kid, beginning to get it.

"And if we keep tangling and tying up our ropes like a lanyard, we'll get higher and higher off the ground—and maybe if we're high enough, we could reach that grate up there and—"

"—get out!" said the kid, finishing Nick's thought.

"I don't wanna get tangled," whined some kid far off.

"Shut up!" said the high-strung Boy Scout. "I think it might work. Everybody do what he says. Start tangling yourselves!"

All it took was an order from their leader for every single kid to start tangling. It was a strange dance of kids weaving in and out of one another, grabbing hands, pulling, swinging, stitching their ropes together, and with each stitch made, the collection of hanging kids rose farther off the ground.

It took more than an hour, and when it was done, and there was not an inch of give left in their ropes, they had risen at least twenty feet. The result was hardly a lanyard, or even a macramé plant holder. Their ropes were a tangled mess, and the kids themselves were all tied up inside it like flies caught in the web of a large, psychotic spider. From where Nick hung, he could see the opening above them, so much closer now, only about ten feet away. If he were free from that blasted rope, he could climb up the tangle, and get out. If only there were rats to chew through these ropes.

He looked around him. None of the kids who had been near him before were near him now—he was faced with an entire new set of neighbors. In fact everyone was chatting; those who remembered their names were introducing themselves. This was more life than any of these kids had shown for years. Even the screamer, who had pouted ever since Allie forbid him to scream, was happily talking away. Still, while the tangle brought some much needed variety to their dangling existence, it hadn't freed anyone. Nick had to think—there had to be more he could do. And then, among all the chatty voices he heard one kid ask:

"What time is it?"

Through the interwoven ropes, he saw the kid in pajamas who everyone called Hammerhead. An idea came to him, and it amazed Nick that no one in the chiming chamber had thought of this before, being so deep and docile in their upside-down ruts. But then, Nick himself hadn't really been thinking outside the box until today, had he? There wasn't much slack left in Nick's rope, but he pulled his way through the clog of kids, and got them to shift positions, enabling him to inch forward until finally he was just a few feet away from Hammerhead, who smiled at him, showing his pointy teeth. "This is more fun than a feeding frenzy!"

"Uh . . . right. Hey, how'd you like to help me out?"

"Sure. What do you want me to do?"

It took Hammerhead less than five minutes to gnaw through Nick's rope.

"There's a problem in the chiming chamber," a nervous crewman told the McGill.

The McGill sat forward in his throne. "What kind of problem?"

"Well . . . sir . . . they all seem to have gotten . . . tangled."

"So untangle them."

"Well . . . it's not as easy as it sounds."

Frustrated, the McGill came out on deck, and went over to the grate above the chiming chamber. He pulled it open, and looked down into the depths to see the situation for himself. His captives weren't just tangled, they were talking. They sounded . . . happy. This was entirely unacceptable.

"Do we have something vile to pour on them?"

"I'll go check," said the crewman, and he ran off.

The McGill looked down at the tangled mob of kids again. "They look very uncomfortable," he said. Certainly they were talking now, but in time, they'd grow tired of this new situation, and realize how much more unpleasant this tangle was than simply hanging upside down.

"Pour something on them, then let them be," the McGill told the crewman when he returned. "They'll be miserable again soon enough."

As he walked off, for an instant the McGill thought he caught a whiff of chocolate somewhere on the open deck, but decided it must have just been his imagination.

CHAPTER 22

Member of the Cabinet

Nick had made it out, but there was nowhere on the *Sulphur Queen* for him to go. Everywhere, at every staircase, every gangway, every hatchway was some Ugloid cleaning. True, the ship was full of dark corners in which to hide, but dark corners were useless to him, because he couldn't douse his Afterlight glow. A corner was no longer dark once he was in it. He didn't have a plan yet for getting off the ship, but maybe if he could find Allie they could work together. By now she must know the ship better than he did. The problem was, he had no idea where she was, and he wasn't in any position to go traipsing around the ship looking for her. In the end, he retreated back into the bowels of the ship. Not the chiming chamber, but one of the treasure holds. It was the best place to hide, for no one dared to come down and disturb the McGill's possessions. He would hide here until the night hours, when the crew was down below, engaged in games, or brawls, or whatever. Those were the hours when he could more easily sneak around the ship. Then he would search for Allie. But for now, he found himself a large oak cabinet. He slipped inside, pulled the doors tightly closed and waited.

The dragon's hoard in the central treasure hold was a treacherous mountain of mismatched booty. Allie, who had been here several times hunting for books worth reading and other things to pass the time, knew she had seen an old-fashioned typewriter, she just wasn't sure where. The stuff in the chamber was a mixture of pure junk and treasure. The McGill did not discriminate; if an object crossed over, and he could get his hot little hands on it, it came onboard, and got dumped here. Jewels sat side by side with empty beer bottles.

The McGill was currently in his "war room," planning a landing party to a Greensoul trap in Rockaway Point. As he was occupied, this gave Allie time to search. Climbing between the old filing cabinets and car tires, coat racks, and bed frames was no easy chore, and with no light but her own glow to guide her through the debris, it was rough going. She nearly got pinned beneath an airplane propeller, and flattened by an iron lung, but finally she found the typewriter beneath an old table. It was made of black dull metal. The keys were faded from many years of use before it had crossed over. A little emblem on its face said "Smith-Corona."

Her grandmother had an old-fashioned typewriter like this one—she still used it. "Words aren't words unless you pound them out," she used to say. Allie found a slip of paper among the mess, and figured out how to load it into the machine.

Typing, Allie discovered, was a lot like keyboarding, with none of the speed and five times the effort. She shuddered to think of people spending day after day plunging their fingers against the little circular keys, which sank down a whole inch before flinging up an iron arm to smack the ribbon and leave a single letter imprinted on the page. She was thankful she had only a short phrase to type, but even so, she made enough mistakes to slow her down. The little typing arms kept getting stuck together like too many people trying to fit through a door. It took her four attempts before she had typed her message perfectly, then she put the typewriter back where she found it, and went looking for scissors. In the end she had to settle for the tiny scissors on a Swiss army knife she had found on the floor. When she was done, she slipped the little piece of paper into her pocket. She was about to put down the Swiss army knife when she heard the voice behind her.

"Admiring my treasure?"

She spun so fast, the Swiss army knife flew from her hand and embedded itself in the McGill's dangling eye. He pulled it out and dropped it to the floor. The wound healed instantaneously, as did all wounds in Everlost.

"Careful," he said. "You'll put out an eye with that thing."

Allie gave him a weak little chuckle.

"If you're trying to steal something, I wouldn't if I were you," he said. "Anything you steal I will make you eat. It might not hurt but you'll feel it sitting heavy in your stomach forever."

"I'm not stealing," Allie told him. "I'm just exploring."

The McGill turned to look toward the door leading to the chiming chamber. "I'm surprised you're not visiting your friends."

"I don't need to visit them," she said. "You'll free them soon enough."

"Are you so sure of that? How do you know I'll keep my word?"

"I don't. But what choice do I have but to trust you?"

The McGill pulled his lips back in a smile, and reached a hand toward her. She grimaced, not wanting to feel his dry bloated touch, but instead her cheek was met by something soft. She looked down to see that his right hand was no longer covered in peeling scales, but instead in soft, minklike fur. The fingertips still had sharpened yellow nails, but the hand itself was soft.

"As I said, I've been working on giving myself a soft touch."

Allie still pulled away. "Don't change yourself for me."

"I'll change myself anyway I like."

"It's still monstrous."

"Good. That's how I like it."

The McGill looked around proudly at his treasure trove. "There are girls' clothes in here. You could find something nicer to wear."

"I can't take off what I'm wearing. It's what I died in."

"You can wear something over it."

Then the McGill spotted a big oak cabinet. "I think there might be something in here," and with both hands he grabbed the handles and pulled it open wide.

Nick had heard the whole conversation between Allie and the McGill, and through it all he counted the seconds until the McGill would leave. When he heard the McGill mention the cabinet, his heart sank. It was just his luck wasn't it? If the McGill opened the cabinet and saw him, he'd probably hurl the entire thing over the side with Nick still in it. Nick pulled his knees to his chest, tried desperately to hide behind a wedding dress that was hanging there, and closed his eyes.

The cabinet creaked open, and Allie, who was standing a few feet back, saw Nick immediately. She gasped. She couldn't help it. The McGill, however, standing right in front of the cabinet, had a view of the wedding dress, and not the boy behind it. The McGill turned to Allie, obviously thinking her gasp was about the gown.

Allie forced her eyes away from Nick, so the McGill couldn't follow her gaze. The tip of Nick's shoe was sticking out from under the dress, so Allie approached it, and fluffed the petticoat out a bit, pretending to admire the lacy fabric. It hid the tip of the shoe from view. Thankfully the dress was thick enough to hide Nick's glow, and the cabinet had a strong camphor stench of mothballs, which overpowered any hint of chocolate in the air.

"I won't be a monster's bride," Allie said, then she grabbed the doors of the cabinet and forced them closed, nearly catching the McGill's hand in the process. The McGill glared at her. "Who said I'd ask you?" Then he stormed away.

Allie waited until she was sure he was gone, then waited twice that long again before she returned to the cabinet and pulled it open.

"What are you doing in here! Do you know how dangerous it is? If they find out you escaped—"

"They won't find out. There are hundreds of kids in there—it's not like they count us all the time."

"If you're caught, you're history."

"So I won't get caught."

Allie looked around. "Did Lief come with you? Is he hiding somewhere else?"

Nick shook his head. "He's still in there with the others." Then he smiled. "It's a mess in there, I got them all tangled up."

"How is hiding in here any better than hanging in there?"

"I'm not staying in this cabinet. As soon as I can, I'm getting off this ship, and I'm bringing back help."

"And exactly how are you going to do that?"

"That's the part I haven't figured out yet."

"*I'm* the one with the plan," said Allie. "Escaping now will just screw things up!"

"We've been waiting on your 'plan' for weeks."

Weeks, thought Allie. *Has it been weeks?* "The best plans take time," she told him.

Nick took a moment to look her over, then said, "I think you like it with the McGill. You've got some kind of power over him, don't you? I don't know what it is, but you do, and you like it."

Allie wanted to just grab him and shake him. It was an insulting suggestion. It was preposterous. It was true.

"I have a scheme to get us all out of here, if you just wait."

"I'm not waiting anymore. And anyway, two schemes are better than one."

Allie clenched her fists and growled, sounding more like

the McGill than she cared to admit. "Even if you get off the ship, who do you think is going to help you?"

"Mary," Nick said.

Allie laughed at that, and realized how loud her voice had gotten. She looked around to make sure they were still alone, then brought her voice down to an intense whisper. "She didn't help us before, and she won't help us now."

"I can convince her to. I know I can."

"You're an idiot!"

"We'll see who's the idiot!"

As frustrating as this was, Allie did not want to stand around and argue. Every moment they spoke was another moment they were in danger of being caught.

"I can steal a lifeboat," Nick said.

"Once they realize it's gone, it won't take long to figure out who took it. The McGill will punish Lief, and probably me, too."

"We can cut Lief down—all three of us can go!"

Allie thought about it, but shook her head. "The McGill thinks I'm teaching him how to possess people. The second he realizes I'm gone, he'll come after me." No, thought Allie. The best way to get Nick off the ship would be to do it secretly, and in such a way that there were no telltale signs that he had gone.

"How about this?" Allie said. "Tomorrow morning the McGill is sending out a landing party to check one of his Greensoul traps. If you can somehow get aboard that boat when it heads for shore . . ."

"Okay. That might work."

"I'll stay on deck, and try to keep anyone there distracted.

But it's up to you to find a way to hide on that boat." Allie thought about it. "I'll put some blankets in the boat—maybe you can hide beneath them." Allie looked around again, and leaned closer to Nick. "If you get through to Mary, tell her that if she wants to face the McGill, then she has to go to Atlantic City. There's a gang there that can help her fight the McGill, if she can convince them to join forces." Allie shut the doors to the cabinet, closing Nick in once more. "Remember—tomorrow at dawn."

"How will I know when it's dawn?" said Nick from inside. She left Nick to work that one out for himself. She climbed up to the quarterdecks, then out into the open air. It was twilight, and the McGill was at the bow, watching the sun set over the land. He did this each day. The McGill was such an odd beast; reveling in his own putrescence, and yet taking joy from the beauty of a world he was no longer a part of.

Nick said they had been there for weeks, and Allie couldn't deny it. For the life of her she had no feel for the time that had passed. Well, she had stalled long enough. Nick was right; it was time for action.

She quietly went to the McGill's throne, dipped her hand into the spittoon and pulled out a fortune cookie. Gently she found a corner of the paper inside, and carefully pulled it out, crumbled it, and inserted the fake fortune that she had typed. Then she dropped the cookie back in the container, where it sat like a little time bomb, waiting for the McGill's grubby, greedy claw.

At dawn the following day, the McGill and a crew of five left the *Sulphur Queen* on a lifeboat for a brief trip to

Rockaway Point. Someone had left several blankets in the corner of the boat, and the McGill removed them, ordering they be thrown into the hold with the rest of his belongings. There was no need of them here. The boat was lowered to the water, the McGill ordered the motor started, and they were off.

No one paid much attention to the mooring rope tied to the lifeboat's bow, which dragged in the water. Had they pulled that rope in, they would have found Nick, submerged beneath the waves, holding on with the rope wrapped around his arm twice as the boat powered its way to shore.

CHAPTER 23

Outrageous Fortune

There was one flaw in Allie's plan. She had no idea when the McGill would get to the particular fortune cookie she had planted. She thought she would have to add a few more to the mix to better her odds, but before she could, her whole situation changed.

Just before she planned to leave for the treasure hold to write more fortunes, Pinhead and four Ugloids broke into her room without knocking.

"He wants you on deck," Pinhead said. "He wants you on deck now."

This wasn't unusual. The McGill called for people on a whim, as if all the clocks in Everlost were set by his personal schedule. This was the first time, however, that Pinhead had barged in without as much as knocking.

"What does he want?"

"You," was all Pinhead said, and although he had been helpful to her in the past, he offered no hint of an explanation, not a wink, not a grin. "You'd better not keep him waiting."

When Allie came to the throne deck, the McGill sat

there, his claws clenched together, the look in his terrible eyes more terrible than usual. Next to the McGill stood a large Afterlight Allie hadn't seen for a while. The one dressed in that ridiculous wrestler's outfit.

"Good evening," the McGill said.

"You wanted to see me?" said Allie.

"Yes. I would like to know steps eight through twelve."

"Finish step seven," Allie said, "and then I'll let you know step eight." Allie had really come up with a good one for step seven. As the McGill was so fond of bullying people around, Allie decided that the seventh step would be a seventy-two-hour vow of silence. So far the McGill couldn't even make twenty-four. "You just spoke," she said. "I guess you'll have to start all over again."

The McGill motioned to the wrestler kid. "Piledriver, you can bring it out now."

Piledriver dutifully went into a side room, and came back rolling a barrel that he set in the center of the room.

"Are you putting me in there?" Allie asked. "Is that it? If you do you'll never know the last four steps."

The McGill nodded to Piledriver again, and he pried open the barrel. It was full of liquid—but there was also something else in the barrel—something that glowed—and once the lid was off, it rose out, dripping in slimy pickle juice. The moment Allie saw who it was, she knew she was in serious, serious trouble. It was the Haunter.

"You!" said the Haunter, the moment he saw Allie.

The McGill stood up. "I am the one who brought you here," the McGill told the Haunter. "You will answer my questions."

"And if I don't want to?"

"Then I'll seal you back in that barrel."

The Haunter held up his hand, and various loose objects began to fly around the room, striking the McGill.

"Stop that, or your next stop is the center of the Earth!" the McGill roared. "Your skill at moving objects does not impress me, nor does it bother me. I bested you before, and if you fight me, I'll do it again—and this time I'll show no mercy." Slowly the flying objects fell to the ground. "Good. Now you will answer my questions."

The Haunter looked at him with hatred so strong it could have warped time. "What do you want to know?"

"Don't believe a word he says!" Allie blurted out.

The McGill ignored her. "Tell me about this girl and her friends. Tell me what she knows."

The Haunter laughed. "Her? She knows nothing! I offered to teach her, but she refused."

"I didn't need him!" Allie countered. "I was taught by someone else."

"There is no one else who teaches the things I teach," the Haunter said, arrogantly. "You knew nothing when you came to me, you know nothing now."

"I know how to get inside people!" Allie told him. "I know how to skinjack." She tried to sound strong and sure of herself, but her voice came out crackly and weak.

"It's true," said the McGill. "I saw her do it."

The Haunter climbed out of the barrel and approached her, leaving a trail of salty brine where his moccasins fell. "It's possible," he said. "She does have an undeveloped skill to move objects, so it's possible that she may also have the skill to skinjack."

The McGill came closer to the two of them. "What I want to know is this: Can the skill be taught? Can she teach it to me?"

The Haunter didn't bat an eye. "No, she cannot."

The McGill pointed a crooked, sharp-nailed, furry finger at the Haunter. "Then *you* teach me how to skinjack."

The Haunter shook his head. "It can't be taught. Either you have the skill, or you don't. You've been in Everlost long enough to know what your skills are. If you have not possessed the living by now, then you never will."

Allie could feel the McGill's anger like the heat of a furnace. "I see." Like the heat at the center of the Earth.

"He's lying!" Allie shouted. "He just wants to win you over, and get you to trust him, so he can betray you the moment you're not looking! I'm the one who's been helping you all this time. Who are you going to believe, him or me?"

The McGill looked at both of them, the Haunter on his left, Allie on his right.

"Who are you going to believe?" Allie asked again.

The McGill regarded Allie for a moment more, then turned to Piledriver, and the other crewmen present. "Seal him back in the barrel, then throw him overboard."

"What?" the Haunter shouted.

"There is only room for ONE monster in Everlost," the McGill growled.

The Haunter raised his hands, and objects began to fly once more—but although he had powerful magic, he was small and outnumbered. No shower of objects could save him from being shoved back in the barrel. "You will suffer," the Haunter shouted. "I will find a way to make you suffer!" But soon all that came out were angry gurgles from within the barrel. Piledriver put the lid back on and hammered the nails back into place. Then he and Pinhead grabbed the barrel, and heaved it over the side. It disappeared beneath the waves without as much as a splash, sinking to the sea floor, and beyond. Thus, the Haunter met his destiny.

Once he was gone, Allie felt relief wash through her like a cleansing rain. "There," she said. "Now that that's over with, you need to get on with step seven. No—don't speak. You can start now. Seventy-two hours. I know you can do it."

And the McGill didn't speak. Instead he reached out and a crewman handed the McGill a paintbrush dripping with black paint.

"What are you doing?" Allie asked.

"What I should have done the moment you came on board."

Then he painted the number 0001 on her blouse, and said: "Chime her."

The McGill had not felt his temper rage this powerfully for a very long time. He had forgotten how good it felt.

Anger!

Let it fill him. Let it rage like a dance of flames. Anger at her for her lies, anger at himself for allowing his feelings to cloud his judgment. Anger enough to cauterize any vulnerability, burning closed the wound she had left in his twisted heart by her deception. This girl had played him for a fool, but that was over.

With the addition of Allie to the chiming chamber, his collection was now complete. He went down below to watch.

The crew had untangled them, and now they all swung free again. He watched as they turned Allie upside down, so that the 0001 on her shirt read 1000.

A brave man's life is worth a thousand cowardly souls.

From the first time he read that fortune years ago, he knew what it meant. He could have his life back, in exchange for a thousand Afterlights. Souls were the currency with which he could buy back his life. Imagine it! Flesh and bone, blood and breath. For a short while, he had thought skinjacking would be better, but that option had never really existed, had it? No, there was only one way to return to the world of the living. This bargain: his life for a thousand souls. Whether the bargain was with deity or demon, it didn't matter to the McGill. All that mattered were the terms. Well, he had satisfied the terms. He had a thousand souls for payment. Now all he needed was a location to make the exchange.

So he returned to his throne room, and went straight to the spittoon. He reached in, pulled out a cookie, and smashed it against the arm of the throne, extracting the piece of paper. He held the fortune with anticipation for a moment, before gazing upon its words. The instant he saw the message, he knew what it meant, and for the first time in many years, the McGill was afraid . . . because the fortune said:

Your victory waits at the Piers of Defeat.

Ignoring all the warnings in his mind that told him it was a bad idea, the mighty McGill set the *Sulphur Queen* on a course toward Atlantic City.

PART FOUR

A Thousand Souls

CHAPTER 24

Nick's Journey

Over a treacherous bridge, and across the entire breadth of Brooklyn, Nick marched from Rockaway Point to Manhattan. He had no way of knowing that even as he crossed that first bridge, Allie was being chimed by the McGill.

His mission was clear, but by no means simple: get help. More specifically, get help from Mary. That was the hard part, because Allie had already told him how Mary had refused to put her children at risk before. As much as it hurt Nick that Mary chose to leave him in a barrel, he admired the selflessness it implied. Her motto wasn't "leave no child behind," it was "put no child in danger." It made getting help from her tricky.

Nick encountered no Afterlights on his trek toward Mary's domain. Certainly there were many dead-spots on the way, and perhaps there were Afterlights hiding here and there, but he wasn't looking for them. He was single-minded.

He marched down the center of Flatbush Avenue, cars and pedestrians passing through him. Unlike Allie he had no skill for connecting with the living world, and he found that the more he ignored that world, the more it slipped into shadow. The living world was as insubstantial to him as beams of light from a movie projector, and the living themselves were like the movie on the screen; only important if he chose to watch. He could see how Mary had come to see Everlost as the *real* world. The *true* world. It would be easy to trick himself into believing the same thing—but did he want to do that?

For a moment he chose to focus on the "movie" of the living; a child and mother crossing the street to catch a bus; an old woman taking her time, and a cabbie who honked at her, only to get a rap on the hood from her cane. It made Nick laugh. Even if he was not a part of it, that world was charged with a vibrant spark that Everlost didn't have. No, the living world could not be dismissed or ignored, and for the first time he began to wonder if perhaps Mary's disregard for the living world was nothing more than envy.

As he neared Manhattan, his memory of a heart began to pound in anticipation. What would Mary do when she saw him? Would she be reserved and dignified? Would she scold him for having left in the first place? He knew he still had feelings for her that could not be destroyed by barrel or beast, but did she have any real feelings toward him? He had thought to learn a skill from the Haunter—a skill Mary could use. Well, Nick had no new skills to offer her, but he *had* been changed. He was fearless—or if not truly fearless, then at least no longer fear*ful*. By the time he got to Manhattan, he was running and he didn't stop until he reached her towers.

* * *

Mary knew something must be horribly wrong. She knew because of the look of anguish on Vari's face. She'd never seen him look so bleak.

"Vari, what is it? What's happened?"

"He's back," was all Vari said. Then he shuffled away, hanging his head low in a dejected defeat she didn't quite understand. Before she could ask him anything else, she saw someone she thought she'd never see again, standing in her doorway.

"Nick?"

"Hi, Mary."

There was more chocolate on his face now than before. As with many Afterlights, changes weren't always the desired ones, but Mary didn't care, because he was here, and beneath the chocolate there was a smile just for her.

It was rare that Mary lost herself, but this was one occasion where the control and poise she prided herself on flew out the window. She ran to Nick and hugged him tightly, not wanting to let him go. It was only now in this moment that Mary realized the fondness she had felt for him was more than that. It was love—something she had not felt in all her years in Everlost. It had been easier to suppress it when she thought he was lost, but now the emotion came in a wellspring, and she kissed him, giving herself over to the heady smell and rich taste of milk chocolate.

Nick was not quite expecting this. Maybe in his wildest dreams, but his wildest dreams had a tendency not to come true. For a moment he found himself going limp like an opossum playing dead, before finally putting his arms around her waist and returning the embrace. It occurred to Nick that since they didn't actually have to breathe, they could stay like this forever. If it was inevitable for Afterlights to lock themselves in ruts, this was a rut he could handle.

But the moment ended, as such moments do, and Mary took a step back, regaining her composure.

"Wow," said Nick. "I guess you missed me."

"I thought I lost you," Mary said. "Can you ever forgive me for not coming after you? Do you understand why I couldn't?"

Nick found himself slow to answer. He understood, but that didn't mean he could completely forgive it. "I won't talk about it if you won't," Nick said, and left it at that.

"How did you escape?" Mary asked.

"It's a long story, but that's not important. I need your help."

Nick sat her down and told her about the McGill, his ghost ship, and his cargo of captured Afterlights. "I know you never really believed in the McGill. . . ."

"No," said Mary. "I've always known he existed—but like the Haunter he kept away."

"Allie's figured out a way to defeat him."

"Allie!" Nick could hear the disdain in her voice. "Allie's a very foolish girl. She's learned nothing from what happened with the Haunter, has she?"

"I believe her," Nick said. "No matter what you think of her, she's smart. When I left, she practically had the McGill eating out of her hand."

Mary sighed. "So then, what does she want me to do?"

This was the hard part. Nick knew he had to sell this,

and sell it right. "She wants you to bring your kids to Atlantic City. It'll take all of them to fight the McGill."

Mary shook her head. "No! I can't do that. I won't put my children in danger."

"Allie says there's a powerful gang there—a gang that defeated him before, so we won't be alone."

"She doesn't know what she's talking about!"

"Then all the more reason to help her, if you know things she doesn't." And when Mary didn't say anything more, Nick put his cards on the table. "If you don't help then I'll go there without you."

"That," said Vari, slumped in a chair in the corner, "is the best idea I've heard yet."

They both ignored him. "The McGill will destroy you," Mary said. "You can't fight him."

"You're probably right, but if you won't help, I'll have no choice but to go alone."

Mary turned away, and pounded a fist against a window. Nick couldn't tell if she was angry at him or herself. "I . . . I . . . can't . . ."

Nick was not bluffing, and soon Mary would realize that. He knew his feelings for her were strong, but he also knew that some things were stronger. "I love you, Mary," he said, "but there are things I have to do, even if you won't." And he turned to leave.

She called to him before he reached the door. Nick had truly thought she wouldn't, because, in his experience, when Mary made up her mind, the case was closed. But maybe she was changing, too.

"I won't put my children in danger," she said again,

fiddling nervously with the locket around her neck. "But I can't leave a thousand children in the McGill's hands either. So I'll go with you."

"What!" said Vari.

Nick wasn't expecting that either. "But . . . but that won't help. We need an army to fight the McGill."

But apparently Mary knew better, as Mary always did.

Mary had a secret cache of clout that ran deeper than anyone knew. In other words, she could get her hands on things that most Afterlights could only dream about, were they able to dream. Today, she had arranged luxury transportation: a ghost train out of old Penn Station.

She did not say good-bye to the children, because she didn't want to worry them. She left Meadow in charge, and Vari, who refused to be left behind, became the third member of their traveling party. "Do you think I'm going to let you take all the glory?" Vari told Nick as the three of them trudged uptown. "One way or another I'm going to end up on top. Just see if I don't!"

"Personally," said Nick, "I think you'd look best hanging upside down by your ankles."

Vari sneered at him. "You've got more chocolate on your mouth than ever. Pretty soon it'll cover your whole stupid face."

Nick shrugged. "Mary doesn't seem to mind."

Nick suspected that if Vari had had his violin he would have kabonged him over the head.

"Will you two stop," chided Mary. "We're supposed to fight the McGill, not each other."

Actually, Nick found himself enjoying his bickering with Vari—maybe because he finally had the upper hand.

It was dusk by the time they reached old Penn Station—a glorious stone-faced, glass-domed building that had been torn down half a century ago, in the questionable name of progress, and replaced with a miserable underground rat warren beneath Madison Square Garden. The new Penn Station was generally considered the ugliest train station in Western civilization, but luckily, the old Penn persisted in Everlost, if only out of its own indignation.

Nick was duly impressed—and also impressed that Mary was willing to ride a train, considering the nature of her death. As for the conductor, he was an old friend of Mary's: a nine-year-old Afterlight who called himself Choo-Choo Charlie. In life he was obsessed with model trains, and so to him, old Penn Station, with its many ghost trains, was as good as making it to heaven.

"I can't take you to Atlantic City," he told them. "On account a' there's no dead tracks down there. I can get you halfway, though, is that okay?"

"Can you get us as far as Lakehurst?" Mary asked. "I have a friend there who can take us the rest of the way."

Then, with Charlie in the engine, the ghost train lit out on the memory of tracks, heading for New Jersey.

They arrived in Lakehurst a few hours later, but it took the rest of the night to seek out Mary's friend there: a Finder named Speedo. After meeting him, Nick decided he preferred a chocolate eternity to an eternity in a wet bathing suit. Nick figured Speedo must have been a pretty good

Finder though, because he had himself a late-model Jaguar.

"It's a sweet ride," he told them, as he drove them around the dead-roads of an old naval air station, showing the car off, "but it can only go on roads that don't exist anymore—do you know how hard those are to find?" Then he threw an accusing look at Mary. "You never told me about that when you gave me the car!"

Mary smirked. "You never asked."

Speedo told them it would take weeks to navigate a dead-road course all the way to Atlantic City, but Mary didn't seem concerned.

"Actually," she said, "it's your other 'sweet ride' that I'm interested in."

"Yeah, I thought you'd say that," said Speedo, as they pulled onto a huge airfield tarmac. "But I drive."

When Nick saw the ride they were talking about, even in his amazement he had to smile. Miss Mary Hightower didn't travel often, but when she did, she sure knew how to travel in style!

CHAPTER 25

The Piers of Defeat

As the *Sulphur Queen* pulled into Atlantic City, a dense morning fog blanketed the shore, hiding the many beachfront hotels from view—but the two dead piers sliced through the fog, jutting out like two arms reaching to grasp the approaching ghost ship.

The Steeplechase Pier stood on the left, with its dozens of rides, all still whirring and spinning like a great gear work churning out time. The Steel Pier was on the right, a grand showplace of the rich and famous. Its signs still advertised in giant letters its golden days before fire burned it into the sea: "Tonight Frank Sinatra," "Dancing till Dawn in the Marine Ballroom," and, of course, "Come See Shiloh, the World Famous High-Diving Horse."

The living world could no longer see the piers, of course. All the living saw were the casinos that sucked their money away like a riptide, and the garish new Steel Pier, built near the ruins of the original—but like the old and new Penn Stations, there was no comparison. When Everlost eyes looked upon Atlantic City's sandy shore, the two dead piers stood apart, just as the two lost towers stood apart from the skyline of New York, like grand beacons of eternity.

The crew of the *Sulphur Queen* gathered on deck to watch as they neared the piers.

"We're going to crash into them!" Pinhead said.

"No we won't," said the McGill, with the confidence of a monster certain of his own destiny. The two piers were only twenty yards apart from one another, leaving a space between them that was just the right size for the *Sulphur Queen* to dock. It was the perfect berth, as if it was an intentional part of some greater design. It was another indication to the McGill that the universe and he were in perfect alignment—and just as the McGill predicted, the *Sulphur Queen* slid smoothly between the two piers with just a few feet to spare on either side. A perfect fit.

"Kill the engine," he told his bridge crew, and they waited until the *Sulphur Queen*'s forward momentum grounded it in the sandy bottom of this huge dead-spot, bringing them to a halt.

"What now?" asked Pinhead. His apprehension rolled off him like sweat from the living. After all, Pinhead had abandoned the cutthroat gang that called themselves the Twin Pier Marauders. They would not take kindly to a traitor if they got their hands on him.

The McGill knew that the battle today would be the greatest of his death, but he would be triumphant. The fortunes didn't lie.

"Prepare to lower the gangway to the Steel Pier," he told Pinhead. "The rest of you come with me." Then the McGill led his entire crew down to the chiming chamber.

* * *

All this time, Lief hung by his ankles, patiently waiting for something to happen. Very little ever happened in the chiming chamber—and even less since Nick left. It was nice that Allie had joined them, although she didn't seem too happy about it.

Lief did not share her frustration. Things made sense to Lief now. It was like his whole existence was a jigsaw puzzle that finally had every single piece in place. No matter what image the puzzle showed, be it the darkness of a pickle barrel, or the image of a thousand kids hanging upside down, it didn't matter because the puzzle was complete. *He* was complete, and *that* mattered more than his circumstance. No amount of unpleasantness could take away that sense of absolute completion. He couldn't explain this to Allie—any more than he was able to explain it to Nick. All he knew was that he felt no real desire to leave the chiming chamber, or to stay for that matter. He was content to simply . . . *be*.

He knew there were others here like him. Many of the chimed kids had also found their peace.

Through the forest of souls, Lief caught sight of Allie watching him with sadness in her eyes. Lief pulled up a dangling hand to wave to her. He felt sorry for Allie. She had not found her peace. Neither had Nick. They fought so hard against everything: so full of fear, loneliness, resentment, anger. Lief remembered feeling those same things, but the memory was fading, as so many other memories had. He didn't fear the McGill, because there was only one feeling left to him. Patience. Patience to wait for whatever came next.

"We should have stayed with you in your forest," Allie said.

Lief smiled gently. "It would have been a fun forever." Then he looked at the kids all around him. "But that's okay. I don't mind. I'm ready."

"Ready for what?" Allie asked.

Lief found himself perplexed by the question. "I don't know," he said. "Just . . . ready."

That's when the drone of the *Sulphur Queen*'s engines died. A few moments later the entire chimed mob swung forward, then back as the ship ran aground.

"We've stopped," said the high-chimed Boy Scout.

"We always stop," said another.

"No, this is different."

"Quiet," shouted Allie. "Listen!"

There came the sound of far off footsteps on metal that quickly grew louder. It wasn't just one person descending into the bowels of the ship, but dozens.

Allie was the last. Allie was the first. Just as the fortune had said: She was the last to be chimed, and the first cut down.

The McGill burst into the chiming chamber with the full complement of his crew behind him. He came straight to Allie.

Allie found the McGill even more hideous when looking at him upside down. She could see into his massive misshapen nostrils full of metaphysical nastiness. Fortunately she didn't have to look for long, because with a single slash of his razor-sharp claws, he cut Allie's rope, and she fell headfirst to the sulphur-dusted floor. She got up quickly, determined to stand eye to eye with the beast.

"Where are we?" she asked. "Why did we stop?"

The McGill never took his eyes off her, but he didn't answer her either. Instead he spoke to his crew. "Cut them all down," he said, "and use the ropes to tie their hands behind their backs."

"You're setting us free?" asked the high-strung Boy Scout, to which the McGill answered, "I'm sending you to your reward."

"Yay!" cried Lief.

"It's not that kind of reward," Allie told him.

Lief gave her an upside-down shrug. "Yay, anyway."

The McGill grabbed Allie's arm, and although she tried to shake him off, he held tight. "You will come with me, and you will do exactly as I say." Then he brought her up on deck.

Allie had lived in South Jersey before her fateful car crash—Cape May to be exact, the state's southernmost tip. Yet even though it was only an hour from Atlantic City, Allie had never been. Her parents despised the crowds and general vulgarity, and so they avoided Atlantic City as if they were making a political statement.

Still, Allie knew where she was the moment she came onto the deck of the *Sulphur Queen*. She had to hide her excitement or the McGill might be suspicious. Her plan had worked! Or at least it had worked so far. There was a long way to go—a dozen things that could go wrong—but there was one thing she knew she could count on: the McGill's arrogance, and his blind faith in her false fortune. Perhaps that would give the Twin Pier Marauders the edge they needed to defeat him again. *My enemy's enemy is my friend,* thought Allie. No matter how savage the Marauders were, if they brought down the McGill, they would be good friends to have.

The McGill led her to the gangway. The ramp sloped down sharply from the *Sulphur Queen*'s deck to the boardwalk surface of the Steel Pier. "You first," he said, and prodded her along. So she was the bait. "Go!" he demanded, and so Allie stepped down the gangway and onto the vast boardwalk of the pier.

"Keep walking," the McGill said. He waited with his crew just off the gangway—perhaps ready to make a quick escape if the situation called for it. Allie strode forward, past shops and signs: Schmidt's Beer, Planter's Peanuts, Saltwater Taffy, Chicken in a Basket. They were all empty. If any food had crossed over when the pier had burned down, that food was long gone.

At first the only sounds were seagulls and eerie calliope music coming from the Steeplechase Pier. The utter soullessness of the place reminded her of the feeling she got when she had walked the lobby of the Waldorf=Astoria hotel. Then she spun at the sudden clatter of hoof beats on wood, and saw the strangest thing. Toward the end of the pier, a horse leapt from a platform that had to be fifty feet high, into a tank of water with a great splash. Then the horse climbed a ramp out of the tank and wended its way up the ramp toward the high dive again. This diving horse was part of the pier's memory, and was the only animal Allie had seen that had crossed into Everlost. She felt an intense pity for the creature and its peculiar eternity.

"Ignore it!" said the McGill. "It does what it does. Keep walking."

Allie kept walking forward, but saw no one. The Marauders must have known they were there, but they were keeping quiet.

"Hello!" she called out, but no one answered. "Anyone here?"

Then to her right she heard the long slow creak of a rusty hinge. She turned to see the dark gaping entrance of some grand ballroom, but a sign taken from one of the steeplechase rides hung crookedly over the entrance. The sign read THE HELL HOLE. This, she realized, was the den of the Marauders. Out of the darkness stepped a boy, his face stretched into a pit bull snarl. He wore a black T-shirt that said "Megadeth," and held a baseball bat with metal spikes sticking out all over it.

"Get off my pier!" he growled.

Then the McGill stepped forward. "I am the McGill and I am calling you out!" he turned and shouted to the entire pier. "Come out from hiding, you cowards! Come out and fight . . . or flee."

Allie knew what would happen next. The kids who were hiding in the woodwork everywhere, dozens upon dozens of them, would come out. They had to have powers if they had defeated the McGill before—they'd have even more powers now. They would surround the McGill and his crew. The McGill wouldn't stand a chance.

But that's not how it happened.

The lone marauder with the pit bull snarl stood there posturing for a few more seconds. Then he dropped his spiked bat, turned tail, and ran like a frightened puppy as fast as his legs could carry him toward the shore, disappearing into Atlantic City. Fight or flee, the McGill had said. The boy had made his choice.

The McGill began to laugh loudly for the whole pier to hear, but still no delinquents came from secret hiding places. "The Mighty Marauders! Hah!"

The crew checked every inch of both piers, and even the barnacle encrusted pilings beneath. The dead piers were truly dead. The Marauders were gone, and Allie's hope plunged with the same horrible heaviness of Shiloh, the diving horse.

It is virtually impossible to read all of Mary Hightower's books, because she has simply written so many, and since they were all scribed by hand, copies are hard to come by the farther one gets from her publishing room. Neither the McGill nor Allie had read Mary's book entitled *Feral Children Past and Present*. If they had, they would have come across this choice nugget in chapter three:

"Well known for their savagery are the Twin Pier Marauders, who ruled Atlantic City for many years, until they vanished. Although reports are sketchy, more than one Finder has come to me with a story of how the Marauders were lured off their piers and into living world casinos by the seductive ca-ching of the slot machines. Once there, the Marauders were hypnotized by the spinning oranges, plums, and cherries, and sank into the quicksand carpet never to return—which proves beyond a doubt that gambling is very, very bad for you."

CHAPTER 26

Oh, the Humanity

The McGill's glorious moment had come, and he was ready for it. He had been preparing for this day for more than twenty years. With no one to challenge his dominion, he began to unload his cargo of Afterlights, and soon the pier had filled with all the kids the McGill had collected, blinking in the light of the hazy morning, with hands tied behind their backs. The fighting instinct had left so many of them, they simply waited for whatever doom the McGill had in store for them.

The McGill took in the sight of his thousand souls, pleased with himself beyond measure, and, clutching his two most valuable fortunes in his hand, he readied himself to complete the bargain.

He looked up into the gray fog shrouding the sky, and called out to the heavens for a sign of whoever it was that had set this bargain before him.

"I'm here!" cried out the McGill, but the sky did not answer. He waved his fortunes in the air. "*The life of one brave man is worth a thousand cowardly souls!* I have the thousand souls—and I've brought them here, just as the fortunes instructed."

No answer. Just hoof beats, a whinny, and a splash. It was as if the pier itself was mocking him. He yelled even louder. "I've lived up to my end of the bargain—now return my life to me! Free me from Everlost, and give me back my life."

The McGill waited. The crew waited, the thousand souls waited. Even the off-key calliope music from the Steeplechase Pier sounded muted and hushed by the gravity of the moment.

And then another sound began to pierce through the music. It was a faint hum, like a distant chorus of moaning angels, growing louder and louder until it could be felt as much as heard.

Then something materialized out of the fog. Something huge.

"Oh my God!" said Allie. "What *is* that!"

It was so massive, it didn't just assault the eye, but the mind as well, until it blocked everything else out.

"I'm here," cried the McGill in absolute joy. "I'm heeeeeeeere!" And he spread his arms wide, opening his entire soul to receive his reward as it descended in glory from the heavens.

Not everything that meets an untimely end crosses into Everlost. Like the atmospheric conditions that lead to a tornado, conditions must be right for crossing. The love of the living, and the occasional sunspot both play a part—but perhaps the most consistent factor is the persistence of memory. There are certain things and places that the living will never—*can* never forget. These are the things and places that are destined to cross over.

In Everlost, Pompeii is a pristine city, and the great library of Alexandria still houses the wisdom of the ancient world.

In Everlost the *Challenger* is still on a Florida launchpad, forever hopeful of a successful blastoff, and the *Columbia* is on the end of the runway, basking in the moment of a perfect landing.

The same is true of the world's largest airship.

Zeppelin LZ-129, better known as the *Hindenburg*, crossed into Everlost in May of 1937 in a fiery hydrogen blaze that sent thirty-five passengers where they were going, and brought one German boy with it, crossing him into Everlost. Thus, the great airship was reborn, flight ready, filled with a memory of hydrogen gas, and freed from the swastikas on its tail fins, which were denied admittance into Everlost when the rest of the ship crossed.

As for the boy, he eventually took on the name Zepp, and had the distinction of being Everlost's first airship pilot. His plan was to offer rides to any Afterlights he happened to come across, in exchange for whatever they could give him. However, like so many in Everlost, he fell victim to his own rut, and for reasons no one has ever been able to explain, he did nothing for sixty years but fly the thing back and forth between Lakehurst, New Jersey, and Roswell, New Mexico.

It caused quite a stir when sunspot activity briefly made it visible, but that's another story.

Eventually Zepp traded the *Hindenburg* to the Finder known as Speedo for a few cases of bratwurst, and Speedo became the proud owner of the largest airborne vessel ever constructed by man. A sweet ride, if ever there was one.

* * *

The nose of the great gray zeppelin seemed to materialize out of the fog as if arriving from another dimension.

"I'm here!" cried the McGill in absolute joy. "I'm heeeeeeeeere!"

Most of the airship's eight-hundred feet were shrouded in fog as it settled down gently on the Steel Pier, right in front of the McGill. It used its own tiny piloting gondola, which hung beneath, as a makeshift landing gear.

A gangway opened in the airship's superstructure in front of the pilot's gondola, revealing that the great gray balloon was not a balloon at all, for it was filled with structure. It was all silver flesh stretched over a steel skeleton, and massive lungs holding their hydrogen breath, giving more than a hundred tons of lift against gravity. It was a marvel of engineering, but the McGill did not see a zeppelin at all. He saw a chariot of the gods.

"I'm here!" said the McGill again, but such was his awe that this time it came out as barely a whisper.

The lowering gangway touched the deck of the pier, and the McGill waited to get a glimpse of the being with magic enough to give him back his life. It didn't matter that the living world had moved on without him, or that anyone he knew would be long dead—he barely remembered any of them anyway. Once his spirit was housed in a living body again, he would adapt to this twenty-first century, reclaiming the right to grow, and grow old—a right that death had denied him.

Three figures descended the gangway, but it was the first who seized the McGill's attention. A girl in a green velvet dress. As she stepped onto the pier, and strode toward him, the McGill's crooked jaw went slack, his arms went limp, and the two tiny fortunes he clutched in his claw fell to the ground. This could not be. It simply could not be!

"Megan?"

The girl smiled at the sound of the name. "Megan," she repeated. "Now I remember. That was my name." She stood there ten feet away from the McGill, and as she looked at him the smile faded from her face, but not entirely. Only now did he notice the other two who had come out with her. A small boy with curly blond hair, and another boy with a face smudged brown. Hadn't the McGill chimed that boy?

"Megan," she said again, clearly enjoying the memory of the name. "But that was a long time ago. Now my name is Mary Hightower."

The veins in the McGill's mismatched eyeballs began pulsing. "*You're* Mary Hightower? No! That's not possible!"

"I knew you'd be surprised. But I've always known who you were, Mikey. How could I help but know?"

Through the crew, and even among the captive kids, a whisper rolled like an ocean wave. . . . *Mikey Mikey she called him Mikey . . .*

"Don't call me that!" yelled the McGill. "That's not my name! I am the McGill: the One True Monster of Everlost!"

"You," said his older sister, "are Michael Edward McGill. And you're no monster. You're my little brother."

A second wave rolled through all those gathered, this time a bit louder. . . . *Brother brother he's Mary's brother . . .*

The McGill was filled with so many conflicting emotions, he felt he would blow into a thousand pieces, and didn't doubt that such a thing was possible for an Afterlight who was tormented enough. He was filled both with joy at seeing his sister again, and the fury that this was not the deliverance he had waited for. He was filled with humiliation at having been exposed for who he truly was, and the dread of being forced to face it.

"I have a gift for you, Mikey," she said. "It's a gift I should have given you a long time ago." She reached up and opened the silver locket she wore around her neck, then held it out toward him the way a priest might hold a cross up to a vampire—and although the McGill tried to look away, the gaze of his eyes, both the large and the small, was transfixed by what he saw.

In one half of the locket was an old-fashioned tin picture of his sister, looking exactly as she looked now. And in the other half was a picture of the boy named Michael Edward McGill.

"No!!!" screamed the McGill, but it was too late; he had seen the picture, and knew it for what it was—he knew it right down to the core of his being. "Nooooo . . . ," he cried, but the slithery slipperiness of his voice had already begun to change, because Mikey McGill suddenly remembered what he looked like.

To those around him—to Nick, to Allie, to the crowd and the crew, the transformation was nothing short of miraculous. The McGill went from beast to boy in seconds. His head shrunk, and his spidery tuft of hair coiffed into a short, neat cut. His dangling eye drew back into his face, and his swollen one deflated. He sprouted five manicured fingers where once claws had been. Even the fetid rags that covered his body stitched themselves back into the memory of the clothes he wore in the photo, and when it was done, the McGill was nothing more than a clean-cut fourteen-year-old boy who could have been his mother's pride and joy.

Mikey touched his face, realizing what had happened and screamed. *"You can't do this to me! I am the McGill! You can't do this!"* But it had already been done. The monstrous image he had taken years to cultivate was gone, replaced by his own humanity. Mary closed her locket. Mission accomplished.

Allie could only stare. This boy, this Mikey—could this be the same person who had captured and chimed a thousand kids? Allie had to remember that humanity had returned to his face, but it would take much more than a photograph to return it to his soul.

While everyone else just gawked, it was the high-strung Boy Scout who saw this moment for what it was. This was the moment of their liberation. And the moment of their revenge.

"Get him!" he screamed, and he raced forward. With his hands still tied behind his back, he hurled himself at Mikey McGill, knocking him to the ground. The others were quick to follow, and in a few seconds, a thousand kids were pushing forward. With their feet their only weapons, they began kicking him, and with so many of them, they could have kicked Mikey clear into the next world.

"No!" yelled Mary, "Stop!" But mob mentality had taken over, and no one was listening to her. The crowd became louder, wilder, as if the spirit of the Twin Pier Marauders had filled them.

In the middle of it all, Mikey suffered the stomping and kicking of this nightmare dance. It could not kill him. It could not even bruise him—but the pain of his absolute humiliation was far greater than any physical pain could have been.

"Stop them!" he yelled to his crew, but he had no power over them now. Instead of obeying his orders, his entire crew deserted, running from the pier in a panic, escaping into Atlantic City just as the lone Marauder had. Mikey was now truly alone.

Then someone began cutting the ropes that bound his captives' hands, and they weren't just kicking him anymore, they were swinging and pulling and trying their best to tear him apart.

This was not what the fortune predicted. The fortune was wrong! How could the fortune be wrong? It was only now, whipped and beaten down by the fury of the Afterlights he had enslaved, that he came to see the truth. He was not the brave man the fortune spoke of. He was the cowardly soul.

With what strength Mikey McGill had left in him, he fought through the angry mob, toward the far end of the pier—because jumping into the sea and sinking back to the center of the Earth would be a better fate than this.

There were very few who did not participate in the punishment of Mikey McGill. Allie, Nick, and Lief did not. Neither did Mary, Vari, or even Pinhead, who was the only crewman with the courage to stay. They didn't join the mob, but they didn't stop it either. Mary did keep calling to the crowd, begging them to calm down and leave her brother be, but her voice was not even heard. In the end, she could only turn away.

"He's getting what he deserves," said Nick.

"But we should do something," said Allie. "This is awful!"

"No," said Pinhead, sadly. "He came here to find his destiny, and he did. We have to let destiny take its course."

They watched the mob push closer to the end of the pier with Mikey somewhere in the middle, and Allie found, like Mary, she couldn't look. Instead she turned to Pinhead, who picked up the two fortunes Mikey had dropped.

"*'Your victory waits at the piers of defeat,'*" he read. "You wrote this, didn't you?"

"Yes," Allie admitted, "but that one about the thousand souls—that was real."

"Not exactly," said Pinhead. "You see, I found that old typewriter long before you did."

Allie was both impressed and horrified. Pinhead shrugged. "I had to think of something to keep the McGill busy for the last twenty years."

The mob was almost down to the far end of the pier now. Allie almost hoped that Mikey would find a way to escape back onto the *Sulphur Queen*, but that wouldn't really be escape at all, because the mob would simply chime him, and spend the rest of time using him as an unbreakable piñata.

Allie could do nothing to help Mikey McGill, and so rather than pondering his fate, she tried to fill her mind with the job that was now at hand. *Her* plan. *Her* goal. Allie knew what she had to do now, because she had imagined it and worked out every angle even before arriving in Atlantic

City. Although Mikey McGill didn't know it, by coming to Atlantic City, he was bringing her within sixty miles of home—the closest she'd been since arriving in Everlost.

Allie had freed her friends, and now she was free from the McGill. All that remained was for her to complete her journey home.

"Gotta go," she said, catching the others by surprise. She quickly hugged Lief, and then Nick, thanking him for everything, and for being her accidental companion on the journey.

"Allie, I—" but Allie put up her hand to shut him up. She despised long emotional good-byes, and refused to let this turn into one.

Then she turned to Mary. In spite of everything that had gone on between them, she gave Mary a respectful nod, and glanced at the *Hindenburg*. "You win the award for Best Grand Entrance."

"We've got a lot to do here," Mary told her. "Why don't you stay and help us?"

"I would, but I've got other plans."

Mary accepted it without asking what those plans were. Allie figured she knew. "We could have been friends," said Mary, with some regret.

"I don't think so," Allie said, as politely as she could, "but I'm glad we're not enemies."

Then Allie turned, and, forcing herself not to look back, she strode past the giant airship, and left the pier.

The mob levied its fury on Mikey McGill as he fought his way toward the end of the pier to escape. He was fully prepared to take the plunge once more.

Fate, however, had other plans for him.

As he neared the end of the pier a sound came to his ears, faint behind the raging mob, but he heard it all the same. Hoof beats. A whinny. A splash. He turned to see, through the flailing arms and legs of the mob, Shiloh, the Famous Diving Horse, climbing out of his water tank, onto the ramp that would take him up to the high dive again.

Out of the water will come your salvation.

Mikey McGill made a sharp turn, pushing his way through the angry mob, and toward the horse.

Allie once more had to get used to the soft, sucking nature of living ground. The Atlantic City boardwalk kept drawing her feet into it, and she had to stay on the move to keep from sinking. She could walk the sixty miles home. She could even make a fresh pair of road-shoes to make the journey easier, but she didn't even know which roads to take.

"Excuse me," she said to a passing couple, "could you please tell me how to—"

But the couple walked by as if they didn't see her.

Well, duh, of *course* they didn't see her. Had she forgotten the simple fact that she was a ghost? Yes. She could admit it now. "Afterlight," and all the other nice words for it, didn't change the fact. She was dead. She was a ghost. But she was also a ghost with powers. . . .

As she considered her options, she heard a sound that made her look back toward the two dead piers. It was the sound of hoofbeats on wood. She waited for the telltale splash of the diving horse, but this time there was none.

Instead she saw the horse—now with a rider—race out from behind the giant zeppelin. Following the horse was a mob of kids in pursuit, but the horse was too fast. The moment the horse hit the living-world boardwalk, the sound of its hoofbeats stopped, but its momentum barely slowed. It turned toward her, surging forward—and in a moment it was close enough for her to see the rider. Mikey McGill. He saw her at the same moment she saw him, and she could see the anger in his eyes.

Allie was terrified. To her, the eyes of this angry boy were even more frightening than the eyes of the monster.

She tried to run, but it was useless, the horse was too fast. Mikey was bearing down on her, and there was nothing she could do. He would trample her, he would capture her. He would punish her for betraying him. She looked back again; his eyes were still on her. Those eyes said, *"You will suffer for what you did to me."* Those eyes said, *"You can't hide from me!"*

And then Allie realized that maybe she could.

In front of her was a girl in sweats, jogging down the boardwalk. She was nineteen or so, her hair pulled back in a ponytail.

Allie turned to look behind her once more. Mikey McGill was only a few yards away. The horse was in a full gallop, and he was already leaning to the side, reaching for her. With no time to lose, Allie leaped into the girl, catching the wave of her body, and surfing it for all she was worth.

In the hiccup of an instant, Mikey McGill and his horse vanished. The piers and the *Hindenburg* vanished. All she could see was the misty morning of the living world through this living girl's eyes. Allie felt the full chill of the day and goose bumps on her skin. She felt the pounding of a heart. She felt the exhaustion of a body that had jogged up and down the boardwalk for at least an hour.

Mikey McGill and the mob of kids that chased him were still there, but they were invisible, and she was untouchable. Nothing and no one in Everlost could get to her now, for she had hitched herself a ride into the living world.

What's going on? said the confused soul who owned the body Allie had skinjacked. *Why can't I move my arms and legs? What's wrong with me?*

"Shhhh . . . ," Allie told her. *"It's going to be all right."* Then Allie turned and jogged away.

CHAPTER 27

All Souls Day

Mikey had gotten away, and although Mary accepted that the monster known as the McGill deserved the mob's wrath, she was secretly relieved that her brother was not sent back to the center of the Earth. Whatever had happened to make him such a monster, she would never know. But now the monster was gone—at least on the outside. What Mikey made of himself now would be entirely up to him.

The crowd had returned from their fruitless chase of her brother, and now looked to her for guidance.

Beside her, Nick surveyed the sheer mass of the crowd. "There didn't seem to be this many when we were hanging upside down."

Mary looked at the airship. It was only designed to carry about a hundred passengers. It would be crowded but it could be done. The passenger compartment was only a small portion of the ship. Most of it was catwalks and girders, holding the massive hydrogen bladders that gave the airship lift. There was room up inside for a thousand Afterlights, and Speedo assured her that weight wouldn't be a problem since, technically, Afterlights had no actual *weight*, only the memory of it—memory enough to sink the unwary to the center of the Earth, but not enough to ground an airship determined to fly.

"What time is it?" asked a boy who looked curiously like a shark.

"Time to go home," she told him, then she called out to the crowd. "Listen to me, everyone. We have much to do. I know some of you have been imprisoned for a very long time, but now you're free—and I have a wonderful place for you! There's room for everyone, and you'll never have to suffer again!"

"Are you the Sky Witch?" asked a small girl, no older than five.

Mary smiled, and knelt down to her. "Of course not," she said. "There's no such thing."

"All right," said Nick, "let's form a single line right here—and line up by the numbers on your chest, so we know we're not missing anyone!" The kids began to rearrange themselves, like it was a game. "No pushing—there's room for everyone!"

Mary smiled. She and Nick were a team now. She could get used to this.

"Hey!" someone called. "Look what I got!"

They both turned to see Lief struggling with a heavy bucket. While the others went off chasing Mikey, Lief had gone back on board the *Sulphur Queen*. "The McGill left his safe open! I got the McGill's treasure!"

Mary took the bucket from Lief. It was full of old, faceless coins.

"Some treasure," mumbled Nick.

"It's a wonderful treasure," Mary said, and gave Nick a wink. "There's enough here for everyone to get a wish at the fountain." A few kids tried to look inside, but Mary held the bucket away from them.

They returned to the job at hand. The kids were still rearranging themselves into a line, trying to read their numbers, which were all written upside down. Some kids stood back, not getting in line, not certain if they should—and so those were the kids Mary went to.

She handed Nick the bucket. "Hold this," she said. "Make sure you keep it away from them until we're at the fountain." Then she went off to talk to the kids who were reluctant to get in line. In the end, with Mary's kindness and charm, there wasn't a single Afterlight who didn't want to come.

So concerned was Mary with making sure that every Afterlight was accounted for, that there was one she forgot. It wasn't until they were airborne and gently gliding north, thousands of feet above the shoreline, that Mary realized it.

"Where's Vari?"

She turned to Nick, who just shrugged. "I haven't seen him at all."

Mary searched the airship—the cabins, corridors, and the catwalks up in the ship's infrastructure. Vari was nowhere on board. Somehow they had left him behind.

In spite of 146 years in Everlost, some things about a small boy never change. A penchant toward moodiness. A limited attention span. And, of course, curiosity.

While Mary had loaded the thousand souls aboard the airship, Vari had boarded the deserted *Sulphur Queen*, along with Lief. While Lief might have been satisfied with a bucket of coins, Vari explored deeper until he found the treasure holds. The moment he saw them, Vari was in heaven, and he lost himself in the search and discovery of it all. Toys and jewels, and things he couldn't identify. It was a wonderland of riches and mysteries.

By the time he emerged back on the deck with as much booty as his small arms could carry, the great zeppelin was gone, and his worst nightmare had finally come true. Mary had forgotten him. He dropped his plunder to the deck with a clatter.

"Who are you!"

Vari spun at the sound of the voice.

"Who are you, and why didn't you leave with the others?"

It was a tall boy with a crooked smile, and a head that was just a little too small for his body. Although Vari was on the verge of tears, he sucked in his emotions, determined to show no weakness to this single straggler from the monster's crew.

"Maybe I didn't want to go," said Vari. Although Vari couldn't be sure, the small-headed boy seemed somewhat abandoned himself. "This is a good ship," Vari said. "I like all the stuff below."

"It served us for twenty years," the boy said, and then he introduced himself as Pinhead. Vari could have laughed, but he didn't. The name fit, as did all names in Everlost. Pinhead was waiting for the crew to return, but no one had. Vari suspected no one would.

Vari looked out to the Steel Pier to the right and the Steeplechase Pier to the left. He supposed he could make a home for himself on these piers—but then he spotted a huge jewel-covered chair sitting on a platform on the open deck of the *Sulphur Queen*. The chair was both beautiful and ugly. Vari found himself drawn to it.

"What is that?"

"The McGill's throne," Pinhead answered. Vari got closer. It was, in its own strange and horrible way, very impressive. Vari climbed into it and sat down. He was so small, he practically disappeared into it, and yet it made him feel big. It made him feel larger than life. Larger than death. Larger than anything.

Pinhead looked at him for a long time, as if preparing to snap a picture with his eyes. "You never told me your name," Pinhead said.

"My name is Va—" but he cut himself short. Mary had left him. Which meant he no longer had to be her obedient servant. He could be anyone he wanted—any*thing* he wanted.

Vari leaned back in the throne and stretched out his hands, caressing the jewels on the armrests. "I am the McGill," Vari said. "Hear my name and tremble."

Pinhead gave him a great slanted mudslide of a smile. "Very good, sir," he said. Then, with an understanding that required no words, Pinhead went to the bridge, started the engine, and manned the tiller. Together they headed east out of Atlantic City and across the ocean in search of a new crew. And a violin.

CHAPTER 28

Skinjacker

This jogger girl was a pain. At first Allie thought it was going to be okay, but as soon as the girl realized what was happening to her, she started fighting back. She was much harder to control than the ferry pilot had been.

"Can't you just take it easy?" Allie yelled to her, in her mind. *"It's not like I'm going to hurt you. I just need to* borrow *you a little."*

—Steal me, you mean.—

"Stealing," said Allie, *"means that I'm not giving it back."*

—No, stealing is taking something that doesn't belong to you without permission, and you don't have my permission!—

Their body limped and jerked along the Atlantic City boardwalk as the two willful spirits fought for dominance. Allie really didn't have the time or patience for this.

"We could do this the easy way," said Allie, *"or we could do this the hard way."* But, like Allie, this girl was a fighter. *"All right then, you asked for it!"*

Allie forced her eyes closed, and concentrated all her will on the task of usurping . . . possessing . . . controlling.

Allie imagined her spirit like a hammer pounding, pounding, pounding until the jogger girl was no more than a tremor in the tips of her fingers.

When she opened her eyes, her body was no longer jerking around. It was Allie's to use as she pleased—and although she didn't particularly like the idea of being a skinjacker, it was a means to an end. Allie had to admit that being in this girl's body was tempting. She was attractive, and in good shape, even if she was a few years older. It would be easy to stay here, and make this body home. Were Allie a different kind of person, she might have done it, but Allie's strength of will also gave her plenty of resistence to temptation. This girl was merely a vessel to transport her home, nothing more. The jogger girl was wrong—Allie was not stealing her body, she wasn't even borrowing it—she was *renting* it—because the girl would get paid for her trouble. Her payment would be the absolute knowledge that there was more to the universe than living eyes could see.

Allie found a set of keys in her pocket, and the key chain said "Porsche."

"Where's your car?" Allie asked the girl, but she was still being uncooperative, responding in a whole slew of foul thoughts. *"Fine,"* said Allie. *"I'll find it myself."* Allie began searching one hotel parking structure after another, hitting the alarm button every few seconds. It took a while, but finally she heard the car alarm going off.

The biggest problem now was that Allie did not know how to drive.

Had she lived, she most certainly would have had her learner's permit by now, but things being what they were, when she started the Porsche, it was the first time she had ever turned a key in a car ignition. It was also a stick shift, and although Allie knew something about gears and the working of a clutch, she had no practical experience. Just pulling out of the parking lot became a nerve-racking experience of sudden starts, stops, and loudly grinding gears.

—My car! My car!— cried the jogger girl from deep inside. *—What are you doing to my car?—*

Allie ignored her, determined to tool around side streets until she got a hang of it.

Driving, however, was not as easy as she thought, and "getting a hang of it," was going to take much longer than Allie realized. It was past noon now, and Allie felt no closer to being capable of driving the Porsche than when she started. Allie supposed she could ditch the car, and find other transportation—a bus maybe, but then, all the buses from Atlantic City went to New York or Philly. None went down to Cape May.

*—Please—*said the jogger girl, much calmer now. *—I've heard your thoughts and I know where you want to go. Let me have control of my arms and legs so I can drive—*

Distracted, Allie ran a red light, and slammed on the brakes, coming to a stop right in the middle of the intersection. Angry horns blared, and cars swerved around her.

—Please— said the jogger girl again. *—Before you get us both killed—*

Since Allie had no desire to experience death again, she relented, and backed off—not entirely, but enough to let the girl control her arms and legs, so she could drive. To Allie's relief the girl didn't fight. She simply pulled the car out of the intersection, and headed back to the main road that would take them out of Atlantic City.

Allie relaxed, like the captain of a ship letting the first mate navigate. "Thank you," she told the jogger girl. The jogger girl said nothing.

All was fine until they reached the bridge that connected Atlantic City with the mainland. Halfway across the bridge, the first mate mutinied. The jogger girl launched a sudden mental offensive that caught Allie completely off-guard.

—Steal my body, will you? Invade my space? I DON'T THINK SO!— Then the jogger girl began to push—but she wasn't pushing down, she was pushing *out*! Allie felt herself being hurled out of the girl's body like a bad buffet lunch. She couldn't feel a heartbeat anymore, or air moving in and out of her lungs. She was disconnected, and losing her grip.

Allie fought back, hoping it wasn't too late, trying to dig her spirit in like a grappling hook, refusing to be cast off. She pulled herself back inside, and as they fought for control, the car began to swerve wildly on the bridge.

They sideswiped a car to the left, bounced off of it, and headed for the guard rail above the bay.

Do you see what you did? screamed the jogger girl.

"*What* I *did?*"

They smashed into the guard rail, and Allie had a horrifying moment of déjà vu. The sound of crashing glass and metal. She was flying forward, she hit the windshield, and in an instant the windshield was behind her. . . .

. . . and yet this wasn't the same as her fatal crash, for when she looked back she saw the jogger girl still in the driver's seat, behind an inflated air bag. The girl got out of the car, frightened, bruised, but very much alive.

Only then did Allie realize what had happened. The crash had thrown Allie clear out of the girl's body. Now Allie was a spirit again, and on the hood of the Porsche, sinking right through it.

Desperately she tried to find something to grab on to, but everything here was living world—there was nothing she could grasp. She felt the heat of the engine inside her as her body passed through it, and in a second she plunged through the car, which hung out over the edge of the bridge, and then she was falling through the air.

"Oh no! Oh no!"

She didn't even feel the difference as the air became water—only the light around her changed. She was falling just as fast, and the dimming blue light of the bay became the charcoal darkness of the earth as she hit bottom. She could feel the mud of the bay inside her, and then solid bedrock. The density of the earth slowed her, but not enough. Not enough. She was going down, and nothing could stop it now.

Stone in her heart, stone in her gut. Soon it would get hot. Soon it would be magma, and still she would fall until years from now she would find herself trapped in the center of gravity waiting for the end of the world. Allie was doomed.

Then she felt something grab her arm. What was that? She couldn't see a thing in the solid stone darkness, but a voice, faint and muffled said, "Hold on to me, and don't let go."

And then she heard, of all things, the whinny of a horse.

On Everlost coins, Mary Hightower's books have only this to say: "They do not sparkle, they do not shine, and they contain no precious metals. These so-called 'coins' are nothing more than useless, leaden slugs, and are best discarded along with one's pocket lint, or better yet, tossed into a fountain for luck."

CHAPTER 29

The Great Beyond

At Mary's insistence they had returned to Atlantic City to search for Vari, but he was nowhere to be found. In the end, Mary had to accept that something horrible had befallen him. Either he had slipped off the pier, or he had been captured by the McGill's returning crew, and taken out to sea aboard the *Sulphur Queen*, which was also gone.

She could have gone after the ship, but it wasn't even on the horizon anymore, and there was no telling in what direction it had gone. As it had been when Nick and Lief were captured by the Haunter, Mary had to put her children ahead of her own desires. She had a thousand refugee Afterlights aboard the airship, and her first responsibility was to them. Vari was lost, and it weighed heavily on her, for, it had been her fault and her fault alone.

With mournful resignation, she ordered Speedo to take the *Hindenburg* aloft, and the ship of refugees resumed its journey north. Once they were airborne, Mary took to the stateroom she had claimed for herself, closed the door, lay down on the bed, and cried. Then she did something she hadn't allowed herself to do for many years. She closed her eyes and slept.

Nick, however, did not sleep. He was emotionally exhausted, and should have, at the very least, taken some time to rest, but there was too much on his mind. There were things that simply weren't sitting right, and he knew he wouldn't be able to relax until he figured them out.

High up in the girders of the airship, Nick sat on a catwalk, in front of the bucket of coins that Mary had left in his care.

Lief found him up there, and sat across from him.

"They're mine, you know," Lief said. "I found them."

"I thought you didn't care about things like that anymore."

"I don't," said Lief, "I'm just saying."

Nick pulled out one of the coins. It was so worn there was no way of telling what kind of coin it was, what country it had come from, or what year it was made. They were all like that—even the one he had found in his pocket way back when—the one he had used to make a wish in Mary's fountain. Funny how both the McGill and Mary had a collection of these coins.

As he held the coin, cool in his palm, Nick could have sworn it felt a little different. It felt almost . . . electrified . . . like a fuse completing a circuit.

That's when an understanding began to come to Nick—an understanding that Nick instinctively knew was the tip of something very big and very important. He took the coin from his palm, and held it between thumb and forefinger.

"Did you know," Nick told Lief, "that they used to put coins on dead people's eyes?"

"Why?" asked Lief. "To keep their eyelids from opening and making people scream?"

"No—it was this old superstition. People used to think that the dead had to pay their way into the afterlife. The ancient Greeks even believed there was this ferryman you had to pay to take you across the river of death."

Lief shrugged, unimpressed. "I don't remember any ferry."

Neither did Nick. But then, maybe people saw what they expected to see. Maybe the ancient Greeks saw a river instead of a tunnel. Maybe they saw a ferry instead of a light.

"I have an idea," Nick said. "Give me your hand."

Lief held out his hand. "Are you going to do a magic trick? Are you going to make the coin disappear?"

"I don't know," said Nick. "Maybe." He put the coin in Lief's palm, then folded Lief's fingers around it until the coin was firmly in his closed fist. "How does it feel?"

"It's warm," said Lief. "It's *really* warm."

Nick waited and watched. A moment passed, then another, and then Lief suddenly looked up and gasped. Nick followed his gaze, but saw nothing—just the girders and hydrogen bladders of the airship.

"What is it? What do you see?"

Whatever it was, Lief was too enthralled to answer. Then, when Nick looked at Lief's eyes, he saw something reflected in his pupils. It was a spot of bright light, growing larger and brighter.

Lief's expression of wonder mellowed into a joyous smile, and he said, ". . . I remember now!"

"Lief?!"

"No," said Lief. "My real name is Travis."

Then, in the blink of an eye, and in a rainbow twinkling of light, Travis, also known as Lief of the Dead Forest, finally got where he was going.

Mary called the coins worthless, but Nick now knew the truth. He also knew that Mary wasn't stupid. She must have known the coins' true value—their true *purpose*—and it troubled Nick that she would hide something so important.

Lief was gone. Gone forever to some great beyond. The air where Lief had been just a second before now shimmered with color, but in a moment the shimmering faded.

Nick no longer had his own coin—he had hurled it into Mary's wishing well, just as every single kid in her care had done. It was a requirement of admission. But now Nick had an entire bucket of them in front of him.

He reached in and pulled out another coin, placing it in his own palm, feeling that odd current again. The coin was still cold in his hand though, and Nick instinctively knew that while Lief had been ready for his final journey, Nick wasn't. Nick still had work to do here in Everlost, and he had a sneaking suspicion he knew what that work would be.

Hammerhead was happily, if somewhat unsuccessfully, gnawing at a girder when he saw Nick approaching. "What time is it?" he asked.

"I don't know. Noon maybe. Hey, Hammerhead, could you do something for me?"

"Sure. What?"

"Could you hold this for a few seconds?" And he put a

coin into Hammerhead's hand. "Tell me, is it warm, or is it cold?"

"Wow," said Hammerhead. "It's hot!"

"Good," said Nick. "Would you like to see a magic trick?"

It was late in the afternoon when Mary awoke. When she looked out of her cabin window, she saw the asphalt of the airfield tarmac. They had returned to Lakehurst. Speedo had told her he didn't feel comfortable landing the airship anywhere else. It was hard enough to get him to land on the Steel Pier. She supposed convincing him to take them all the way back to Manhattan was out of the question.

If they were lucky, the train would still be there waiting for them. If not, they would have to walk, following the dead tracks all the way home. At worst it would take them a few days to get there. Then she could begin the task of processing this large group of children, and integrating them into her society. In one fell swoop, the population of her little community had quadrupled—but as she had told them, there was more than enough room. She would convert more floors into living space. She would work with Finders to furnish them in comfort. And in the meantime she would give each of these children her personal attention, helping them, one by one, to find their perfect niche. It was a monumental, yet noble task—and with Nick's help she'd be able to do it.

When she left her cabin, she was surprised to find the hallways and salons of the airship empty. There were no voices coming from the higher reaches of the ship either.

Nick must have already roused them and gotten them off the ship. He was very efficient, and it was good of him to let her sleep, although it wasn't exactly her plan to sleep the entire day.

She descended the gangway expecting to find kids clustered around, but there were none. There was only one figure out there. Someone sitting on the ground a hundred yards away.

As she approached she could see that it was Nick. He sat cross-legged, staring at the *Hindenburg*. She realized he was waiting there for her. Beside him sat the bucket of coins.

Only now did Mary begin to get worried.

"This is a pretty big dead-spot," Nick said.

"The entire tarmac," Mary answered. "The death of the *Hindenburg* was a large-scale event. The ground here will remember it forever." She waited for Nick to say something more, but he didn't.

"So," Mary said, "where is everyone?"

"Gone," said Nick.

"Gone," echoed Mary, still not sure she had heard him correctly. "Gone where, exactly?"

Nick stood up. "Don't know. Not my business."

Mary looked into the bucket at his feet. To her horror the bucket was empty. She couldn't believe what she was seeing—what he was telling her.

"All of them?" She looked around the tarmac hoping for a sign that this wasn't true, but there was not a soul in sight.

"What can I say?" said Nick. "They were all ready to go."

For the first time in her memory, Mary was speechless.

This was a betrayal of such magnitude there were no words to express it. It was as awful, and as evil as anything Mikey had done in all his years as a monster. It was worse!

"Do you have any idea what you've done?" Mary knew she was screaming, but she didn't care. How dare he! How dare he do this to her!

"I know exactly what I've done," said Nick with all the calm in his voice that Mary had lost. "I let them go to where they should have gone in the first place."

"How dare you presume to know where they should have gone. They were *here*, which means *this* is where they were meant to be!"

"I don't believe that!"

"Who cares what you believe!" It was as if she was looking at a different boy. She had taken him into her confidence—she had trusted him. They were going to be a team, benevolently leading the Afterlights of Everlost forever and ever. This wasn't supposed to happen!

Then Nick's expression changed, and for the first time his calm took a turn toward anger, and accusation.

"How long have you known?" Nick demanded.

Mary refused to answer him.

"Did you know about the coins from the beginning? How long have you been robbing them from the children who come to you for help?"

She found she couldn't face the accusation, and couldn't meet his eye. "Not from the beginning," she grumbled. "And I'm not a thief—they throw their coins into the fountain by *choice*. They can take them out any time they want—but no one does—and do you know why? *Because they don't want to.*"

"No! They don't take back their coins because it's *your* fountain, and they wouldn't dream of going against Miss Mary. But if they knew the truth about what those coins did—what they were *really* for—they'd take them in a second!"

"My children are happy!" insisted Mary.

"They're lost! And you're no better than your brother!"

Before Mary even knew what she was doing, she brought back her hand and slapped him across the face with the full force of her fury. For a moment she wanted to take it back, and tell him that she was sorry, but then she realized she wasn't sorry at all. She wanted to slap him again and again and again until she slapped some sense into him. What had she done to deserve this treachery? She had cared about him—more than that, she had loved him. She loved him still, and now she hated the fact that she loved him.

Nick recovered from the slap, then picked up the bucket and tilted it toward her. "Strange," he said, "but there were exactly enough coins in there for every Afterlight."

"So what!" said Mary. "A thousand Afterlights, a thousand coins. Nothing strange about that."

"Look again."

Mary looked into the bucket to see that it wasn't entirely empty. Two coins remained.

"Two coins," said Nick. "Two of us."

"Coincidence!" insisted Mary. She would not be swayed by it. This was *not* the universe trying to tell her something. This was *not* the hand of God reaching out to them. Mary didn't need a bucket to tell her what God's purpose for her was.

She reached in, picked up a coin and prepared to throw

it as far from her sight as possible. . . . But then Nick said—

"—Is it warm or is it cold?"

Mary felt the coin in her hand. "It's cold," she told him. "Cold as death."

Nick sighed. "Mine's cold, too. So I guess neither of us are going anywhere for a while. And then he added, "All these years here, and you're still not ready."

"I'll never be ready!" said Mary. "I'll never leave Everlost, because *this* world is the eternal one, and it's my job to find lost souls to fill it. It's my job to find them and take care of them. Why can't you understand that?"

"I do understand it," Nick said. "And maybe you're right—maybe that is your job. . . . But now I think I have a job, too. And my job is to help those same lost souls get where they're going."

Mary looked at the ugly coin in her hand. What was so wonderful about the end of the tunnel? How did anyone know if that bright light was a light of love, or of flames?

If there was one thing Mary knew it was the simple rule that every mother tells her child: If you're lost, stay put. Don't walk away, don't wander off, don't talk to strangers, and just because you see a light, it doesn't give you permission to cross the street. Lost children stay put! How could Nick not see the sense in that?

At the sound of a car engine, Mary looked up to see Speedo drive up in the Jaguar she had given him. At least *he* was smart enough not to hurl himself down a dark tunnel.

"The train's waiting," Speedo said.

Nick turned to Mary. "I'm going back to the Twin Towers," he said. "And I'm going to tell all those kids what I know."

"They won't listen to you!" Mary told him.

"I think they will."

There was certainty in Nick's voice, and Mary knew why. It was because he was right, and they both knew it. As much as Mary wanted to believe otherwise, she knew her children would take their coins back. They would not be able to resist the temptation. That's why the temptation had to be taken away.

"Why don't you come with me," Nick said. "We can do it together."

But Mary already knew what she had to do. Remove the temptation. And so without even dignifying Nick with a response, she turned and ran back toward the giant zeppelin alone.

"Mary! Wait!"

She didn't want to hear anything he had to say. She climbed into the piloting gondola of the airship. If Speedo could pilot this thing, then so could she—and she would get back to her children before Nick did. He would never get the chance to poison their minds, because she would get there first, and save them all.

CHAPTER 30

Leaving Everlost

Although Allie had no way of knowing it while she was encased in the jogger girl's body, Mikey McGill had never let her out of his sight. After what she had done to him, he wasn't letting her go, and even though she was hiding inside a living girl, eventually she would have to come out, and he'd have her! Vengeance drove him at first, but after a few hours, the feeling began to fade. The truth was, he admired Allie. She had been a worthy opponent. She had successfully outsmarted him, playing him for a fool—and he was a fool, wasn't he? How could he despise her for being more clever than him?

Although Mikey had no skill at skinjacking, he did have another useful skill. He could rise from the depths. It was a skill he had never seen in anyone else. He only hoped it was powerful enough to do the job this time.

Shiloh the Famous Diving Horse had no problem leaping into the bay and following Allie as she fell—after all, diving from a frighteningly high place was exactly what it was trained to do. Like Allie, the horse and its rider passed through the air, through the water, and found themselves plunging through the darkness of the Earth. The horse, not expecting this, began a panicked gallop through the stone. Locking his legs around the horse, Mikey spread his arms out wide, fishing with his fingertips for a sign of Allie, until he finally found her, grabbed her, and pulled her onto the horse with him. Then he dug his heels in, and the horse worked harder against the stone. Mikey tried to imagine them all filled with hydrogen, like the airship. Lighter than air, and most definitely lighter than stone. His powerful will battled the will of gravity, and soon they stopped sinking and began to rise.

The forward momentum of the ghost horse trying to gallop through stone was greater than their upward momentum, but that was fine. Even if they were only moving up inch by inch, they'd get to the surface eventually.

At last they surfaced in a New Jersey wood. It was dusk now, and they were a few miles inland from where they had begun.

The second they were on the surface, Allie leaped off the horse, fully prepared to run if she had to. As far as she was concerned, Mikey McGill was not to be trusted—even if he did just rescue her.

"I should have let you sink," Mikey said.

"Why didn't you?"

Mikey didn't answer. Instead he said, "Where were you trying to go? Maybe I can help you get there."

She hesitated, expecting to see some sort of deceit in him, but found none. "If you must know, I'm going home."

Mikey nodded. "And then?"

Allie opened her mouth to answer, and found that nothing came out. Allie was a goal-oriented girl. The problem was she rarely thought beyond the goal.

What was her plan, really? She would get home, but then what? She would see if her father survived the car accident. She would spend a little time watching her family's comings and goings. She would try to communicate with them—maybe she would even find a neighbor willing to be skinjacked, and then talk to her family, convincing them it was her by telling them things that only she could know. Allie would tell them she was all right, not to worry and not to mourn. But then what?

It was now that Allie figured out something she should have figured out a long time ago: Home was no longer home. She had denied it, refused to think about it, pretended it didn't matter, but she couldn't pretend anymore. If her great victory was going home, then her victory was an empty one.

"I asked you a question," said Mikey. "What will you do after you go home?"

Since Allie had no answer, she threw it back in his face. "That's my business," she said. "What about you? Are you going to make yourself into the One True Monster of Everlost again?"

Mikey gently kicked his heels into Shiloh's side to remind the horse to keep pulling his hooves out of the ground, so they didn't sink again. "I'm done with being a monster," he said. Then he reached into his pocket and threw something to Allie, and she caught it. It was a coin.

"What's this for?"

"You can use it to get you where you're going."

Allie looked at the coin, so similar to the one she had tossed into Mary's fountain. Did he mean what she thought he meant? To get where she was going—it was terrifying yet enticing. Electrifying. She stared at the coin, then looked back up at Mikey. "Is that what you're doing, then? 'Getting where you're going'?"

Allie thought she read some fear in his face at the suggestion. "No," he said. "I don't think I'm going anywhere good. I'm in no hurry to get there."

"Well," said Allie, "you can probably change where you're going, don't you think?"

Mikey didn't seem too convinced. "I was a pretty nasty monster," he said.

"Were," reminded Allie. "That was then, this is now."

Mikey seemed to appreciate her practical, logical view of things. "So then, how long do you think it would take to make up for being a monster?"

Allie thought about the question. "I have no idea. But some people believe that all it takes is a sincere decision to change, and you're saved."

"Maybe," said Mikey. "But I'd rather play it safe. I was a monster for thirty years, so I'd say I need thirty years of good deeds to wipe the slate clean."

Allie smirked. "Is Mikey McGill even capable of good deeds?"

Mikey frowned. "Okay, then. Sixty years of halfway-decent deeds."

"Fair enough," said Allie. She looked at the coin in her hand. It was lukewarm. She suspected if she held it long enough it would get her where she was going, but just because she was ready to go, it didn't mean she had to just yet. It was a matter of choice.

What was it her fortune had said? *"Linger or light. The choice is yours."*

Allie chose to put the coin in her hip pocket for now. She always had been good at saving her money.

Mikey held out his hand to her, ready to lift her up on the horse.

"Home?" he asked.

But suddenly it didn't seem all that urgent. There were still plenty of unknowns to explore here in Everlost. She could squeeze a lot of them in between here and home. "There's no hurry," she told him, but Mikey wasn't pleased.

"Taking you home," he said, "was going to be my first halfway-decent deed."

"I'm sure you'll find another one."

Mikey sighed in frustration. "This is not going to be easy. I'm good at being bad, but I'm bad at being good. I don't know the first thing about good deeds."

"Well," Allie said, with a grin, "I *do* know a twelve-step program." Then she grabbed Mikey's hand, climbed on the horse with him, and they rode off together toward all things unknown.

Nick had to win this race, even if the odds were against him, and so when the ghost train dropped him off at old Penn Station, he wasted no time. It was dusk now. The train had been fast, but an airship didn't have to worry about tracks. His only hope was that Mary's learning curve when it came to flying the thing had slowed her down. When she had first taken to the air, the airship was erratic, turning this way and that, unable to set a course. With any luck, she was still zigzagging across New Jersey, trying to get the hang of it.

He ran at full speed from the station all the way down to the plaza at the base of the towers. The same kids were there playing kickball, jumping rope and playing tag.

"Is Mary here?" he called out. He expected them to rush him and capture him. What was Mary's version of chiming? Nick had a suspicion that he was about to find out.

But they didn't rush him. Instead, one of the kickball kids playing the outfield turned to him and said, "Meadow says she went away for a while, but she'll be back real soon."

Good, thought Nick, he had beaten her here—and now, when he looked west, he could see that he hadn't beaten her by much. Between the buildings to the west, Nick could see the zeppelin in the sky across the Hudson River, still high, but dropping toward them. It couldn't be any more than five miles away. Nick knew he didn't have much time.

"Go get Meadow," he told the kickball kid. "Tell her to gather everyone at the fountain." Then the kickball kid ran off, confounding the daily pattern of his game.

Nick went over to the fountain himself, and stood on its lip, calling out to all the kids in the plaza.

"Everyone! Everyone listen to me! I have a message from Mary!"

That got their attention. Jump ropes stopped spinning, balls stopped bouncing. Kids began to converge on the fountain.

Nick looked to the west again: The airship was there, halfway across the river. It was still too high, but that didn't matter—as soon as the kids saw it, the game would be over. He would lose their attention. He had to keep everyone focused on him.

Meadow began to arrive with kids from the higher floors. "Mary wants me to tell you that you no longer have to fear the McGill. She's cut him down to size!"

A cheer from the kids.

"And," said Nick, "I have something very exciting to tell you!" Okay, thought Nick. Here it goes. . . . "How many of you threw your wishes into the fountain?"

Every hand went up.

"And how many of your wishes came true?"

One by one the hands went down, until not a single one of them was left.

"Well," said Nick, "it's time for all your wishes to come true." And with that he jumped into the fountain, reached into the water, and started pulling up coins. "C'mon," he said. "Everyone gets their coin back!"

At first they were reluctant . . . until the first girl came forward, all pigtails and big eyes. She stepped into the fountain, and Nick took a coin, pressing it into her palm. The entire crowd watched and saw with their own eyes what happened next.

The girl got where she was going.

There was a long moment of silence as it hit home for these kids exactly what this meant for each of them . . . and then they all began climbing into the fountain themselves, lining up, and accepting the coins from Nick. In less than a minute their excitement reached critical mass, all sense of order broke down, and it became a wild rush of kids leaping, splashing, grabbing coins, and disappearing in rainbow sprays of light. Nick left the fountain, and stood back to watch.

To the west, the zeppelin was growing larger as it neared, eclipsing the setting sun, but if the kids crowding the fountain noticed, they didn't care. By the time Mary arrived, she would be too late; they'd be gone. Perhaps not every single one of them, but most of them. All the ones who were ready. As it should be.

Nick looked up to the peaks of the Twin Towers, converging as they scraped the sky. He marveled at their majesty the way tourists had during the Towers' twenty-nine years of life. It was a comfort to know that they would never be gone completely, because they were here, a timeless part of Everlost. They were great monuments of memory, and although Mary had, for a time, turned them into her own personal orphanage, that was over now. They had a greater place in the scheme of things.

By now more than half the children were gone, and the rest were well on the way. Meadow came up to Nick, and together they watched the joyful vanishings.

"Mary's going to have a fit when she sees this," Meadow said. "It'll totally trip her out." Then she smiled. "Good thing I won't be here to see it."

Then Meadow ran toward the fountain, jumped in, and a moment later she was gone.

Nick pulled his own coin from his pocket—the one he had salvaged from the empty bucket. It was still cold as cold could be, but that was all right. He realized now that while his arrival had tied him to Allie, his departure was tied to Mary. As long as she was fighting to keep children here, he would be fighting to free them.

He supposed that made them enemies. It almost made him laugh. How strange it was to be in love with your enemy.

With the zeppelin coming in for a landing, and the last of the children vanishing from the fountain, Nick put his hands in his pockets and left, strolling leisurely uptown.

Perhaps Mary was right about Everlost being an eternal world: a place where all things and places that have earned immortality remain forever in glory. If that were the case, then Everlost was like the grand museum of the universe, a heavenly and priceless gallery. As Mary once said, they were blessed to be able to see it—but a museum was to be visited, and appreciated, not to be lived in. That was Mary's mistake. Afterlights were merely visitors passing through.

Nick knew there were more lost souls in lost places to free. There were more fountains and more buckets of coins to be found—and although he didn't know when he would ever get where he was going, he knew that when the time was right he would get there.

In the meantime, he had work to do.

EPILOGUE

The Sky Witch

The little girl sat knees to chest on the playground sand, not knowing what to do. The last she remembered, she was at the very tippy top of the jungle gym, above all the other kids. Then she had lost her balance, and fallen. For the strangest moment, she had found herself running down a tunnel toward a distant light . . . if only she had listened to her mother, and tied her shoelaces, she might not have tripped over her own feet on the way.

And now she was here, still in the park, sitting on a small patch of sand beneath the jungle gym. Her parents were gone, and she instinctively knew they weren't coming back, but she didn't know how she knew it. When she had fallen, the park had been full of children, and the day had been hot. Now it was empty and cold. Even the trees, which had been lush and green, were now yellowing and losing their leaves—and the worst thing about it was that she couldn't move, because the rest of the playground had turned to quicksand.

There was a sound far off in the sky, but getting closer: a mechanical groan that didn't quite sound like a plane, or helicopter, and when she turned toward the sound, she saw something amazing. A big, silver . . . thing . . . came over the trees, and lowered into an empty soccer field. It was like a blimp she had seen hovering above baseball games, but much, much bigger. Still, she held her knees to her chest, excited, terrified as the giant blimp-thing dropped down, hovering just a few feet above the soccer field. Then some sort of hatch opened, a ramp came down, and a creature all slender and green came out.

No, not a creature at all. This was an angel. An angel in a green dress. She was coming right toward the girl, and the closer she got, the more of the girl's fear melted away.

Finally the angel reached the playground, and looked at the girl through the wide cagelike bars of the jungle gym.

"Don't be afraid," the angel said. "Everything's going to be all right. I promise."

The girl looked toward the blimp-thing, and the angel smiled. "Would you like a ride on my airship?"

The girl nodded.

Then the angel said, "It only costs a nickel."

The girl looked down sadly. "I don't have any money."

But the angel only smiled. "I'll bet you do. Why don't you check."

The little girl reached into her pockets, and to her surprise she found a nickel in there. Or at least she thought it was a nickel—it was too worn to tell. She held it out to the green angel, but then hesitated. After all, this nickel was all that she had. Something told her she might not want to part with it so easily.

The angel's smile faded, but only slightly.

"I'm sure you don't want to stay here alone," she said. "If you do, the Chocolate Ogre might find you."

"The Chocolate Ogre?"

"A monster," said the angel. "He lures you with the smell of chocolate, and then he captures you, and sends you away."

"Where?"

The angel shook her head. "That's the scary part. No one knows." For a moment the girl thought she saw a wave of sorrow wash across the angel's face, but it passed. "Now, wouldn't you rather come with me?"

And so the girl gave her the coin, and the angel gently took her hand. "Now, let's find out what you like to do, and let you do it!" The girl rose, and holding the angel's hand, she walked right through the bars of the jungle gym like magic!

"Welcome to Everlost," the angel said as they crossed the field toward the silver blimp-thing. "My name is Mary."

"Are there other kids like me in your balloon?" the girl asked.

"Just a couple," said Mary, "but there are lots more out there—and we'll find them all, won't we!"

The girl nodded. "Yes—before the Chocolate Ogre does."

Together they climbed into the silver airship, and rose into the Everlost sky.

ACKNOWLEDGMENTS

Everlost would have been ever lost, had it not been for the tireless efforts of those who helped me find my way to the light.

First and foremost, my deepest thanks to David Gale and Alexandra Cooper for their insightful editorial work, and everyone else at Simon & Schuster for being so supportive every step of the way.

Many thanks, the Fictionaires: the writing group from heaven, who continue to hold me up and keep me from sinking to the center of the Earth. Thanks to Barbara Rattigan, for her research on ghost ships, razed hotels, demolished piers, and other such oddities. Thanks to my parents for their unending support, and for always being there whenever I need them, as well as Patricia McFall, my "big sis" in every way that matters.

Thanks to Andrea Brown, agent/goddess, as well as Danny Greenberg, Shep Rosenman, Steve Katz, Trevor Engelson, Nick Osborn, and Will Lowery, all of whom have given a career to a guy who just thinks weird stuff and writes it down.

My gratitude, also, to kids in schools across the country who listened to bits and pieces of the story, and voted on the title. Your enthusiasm gives me the motivation I need to write every book! And finally, a very special thanks to my children—Joelle and Erin, who are my muses, and Brendan and Jarrod, whose thoughtful comments on early drafts of *Everlost* were crucial to shaping the book.

Everlost has been a labor of love, and without all of you, I would have never have gotten where I was going!

Turn the page for a sneak peek at

Everwild

Fresh Havoc

There were rumors.

Of terrible things, of wonderful things, of events too immense to keep to oneself, and so they were quietly shared from soul to soul, one Afterlight to another, until every Afterlight in Everlost had heard them.

There was the rumor of a beautiful sky witch, who soared across the heavens in a great silver balloon. And there were whispers of a terrible ogre made entirely of chocolate, who lured unsuspecting souls with that rich promising smell, only to cast them down a bottomless pit from which there was no return.

In a world where memories bleach clean from the fabric of time, rumors become more important than that which is actually known. They are the life's blood of the bloodless world that lies between life and death.

On a day much like any other in Everlost, one boy was about to find out if those rumors were true.

His name is unimportant—so unimportant that he himself had forgotten it—and less important still, because in a brief time he will be gone forever.

He had died about two years earlier, and, having lost his way to the light, he slept for nine months, then had woken up in Everlost. The boy was a wanderer, solitary and silent, hiding from others who crossed his path, for fear of what they might do to him. Without camaraderie and friendship to remind him who he was, he forgot his identity more quickly than most.

On the occasions that he did come across packs of other Afterlight kids, he would listen to them from his hiding spot as they shared with each other the rumors of monsters, so he knew as well as any other Afterlight what lay in store for the unwary.

When the boy had first crossed into Everlost, his wanderings had a purpose. He had begun in search of answers, but now he had even forgotten the questions. All that remained was an urge to keep moving, resting only when he came across a deadspot—a solid, bright patch of earth that had, like him, crossed into Everlost. He had learned very quickly that deadspots were unlike the faded, unfocused world of the living, where every footfall pulled you ankle-deep, and threatened to take you all the way down to the center of the earth if you stood still for too long.

On this day, his wanderings had brought him to a field full of deadspots—he had never seen so many in one place . . . but what really caught his attention was the bucket of popcorn. It just sat there on a deadspot, beside a huge Everlost tree, like it had no better place to be.

Somehow, the popcorn had crossed over!

The dead boy had not had the luxury of food since

arriving in Everlost—and just because he didn't need to eat anymore, it didn't mean the cravings ended—so how could he resist that popcorn? It was the largest size, too—the kind you order with big eyes in the movie theater, but can never finish. Even now the corn inside glistened with butter. It seemed too good to be true!

Turns out, it was.

As he stepped onto the deadspot and reached for the tub, he felt a trip wire against his ankle, and in an instant a net pulled up around him, lifting him off the ground. Only after he was fully snared within the net did he realize his mistake.

He had heard of the monster that called itself the McGill, and his soul traps—but he had also heard that the McGill had traveled far away, and was now wreaking fresh havoc across the Atlantic Ocean. So then, who had set this trap? And why?

He struggled to free himself, but it was no use—his only consolation was that the bucket of popcorn was trapped in the net with him, and although half of its contents had spilled onto the ground, half still remained. He savored every single kernel, and when he was done, he waited, and he waited. Day became night, became day over and over, until he lost track of time, and he began to fear that his eternity would be spent strung up in this net. . . . Until he finally heard a faint droning sound—some sort of engine approaching from the north. The sound was echoed from the south—but then, as both sounds grew louder, he realized it wasn't an echo at all. The sounds were different. He was being approached on two sides.

Were these other Afterlights coming for him, or were they monsters? Would he be freed, or would he become the victim of fresh havoc himself? The faint memory of a heart pounded in his ghostly chest, and as the whine of engines grew louder, he waited to see who would reach him first.

The View on High

"Miss Mary, one of our lookouts spotted a trap that's sprung."

"Excellent news! Tell Speedo to bring us down close, but not too close—we don't want to frighten our new friend."

Mary Hightower was in her element this far from the ground. Not so high as the living flew, where even the clouds were so far below, they seemed painted on the earth, but here, in that gap between earth and the heavens, is where she felt at home. She was queen of the *Hindenburg*, and she liked that just fine. The massive silver airship—the largest zeppelin ever built—had gone up in a ball of flames way back in 1937, leaving the living world and crossing into Everlost. Mary, who believed all things happened for a reason, knew why it had exploded: It had crossed into Everlost for her.

The Starboard Promenade, which ran the full length of the passenger compartment, was her plush personal retreat, and her center of operations. Its downward-slanted windows gave her a dramatic view of the ground below: the washed-out hues of the living world, speckled with features both man-made and natural that stood out more boldly than the rest. Those were the places that had crossed into Everlost. Trees and fields, buildings and roads. While Afterlights could still see the living world, it was blurred and faded. Only things and places that had crossed into Everlost appeared bright and in sharp focus. Mary estimated that one in a hundred things that died or were destroyed crossed into Everlost. The universe was very selective in what it chose to keep.

Only now, as she spent her days riding the skies, did she realize she had stayed put for way too long. She had missed so much up in her towers—but then the towers were a citadel against her brother, Mikey—the monster who called himself the McGill. Mikey had been defeated. He was harmless now. And now Mary no longer had to wait for Afterlights to find her. She could go out and find them herself.

"Why are you always looking out of those windows?" Speedo would ask her, when he took a break from piloting the airship. "What do you see?"

"A world of ghosts," she would tell him. Speedo had no idea that the ghosts she spoke of were the so-called living. How insubstantial that world was. Nothing in it lasted, not places, not people. It was a world full of pointless pursuits that always ended the same way. A tunnel, and surrender. *Well, not always,* she thought happily. *Not for everyone.*

"I'd still rather be alive," Speedo would say whenever she spoke of how blessed they were to be here in Everlost.

"If I had lived," Mary would remind him, "I'd be long dead by now . . . and you'd probably be a fat, bald accountant."

Then Speedo would look at his slight physique, dripping wet—always dripping wet in the bathing suit he died in—to reassure himself that he'd never have grown fat and bald, had he lived. But Mary knew better. Adulthood can do the most horrific things to the best of people. Mary much preferred being fifteen forever.

Mary took a moment to gather herself and prepare to greet the new arrival. She would do it personally. It was her way, and it was the least she could do. She would be the first out of the ship—a slender figure in a plush green velvet dress, and with a perfect fall of copper hair, descending the ramp from the impossibly huge hydrogen airship. This is how it was done. With class, with style. The personal touch. All new arrivals would know from the first moment they met her that she loved each and every child in her care and they were safe under her capable protection.

As she left the Starboard Promenade, she passed other children in the common areas of the ship. She had collected forty-seven of them. In her days at the towers, there had been many, many more—but Nick had taken them from her. He had betrayed her, handing each of her children the key to their own undoing. He had placed a coin in each of their hands. The coins! Those horrid little reminders that a true death did await all of them if they were foolish enough to seek it—and just because there was a light at the end of the tunnel, it didn't mean it was something to be desired. Not the way Mary saw it. Heaven might shine bright, but so do flames.

As the ship descended, Mary went to the control car—the ship's bridge which hung from the belly of the giant craft. From there she would have the best view as they descended.

"We should touch down in a few minutes," Speedo told her, as he intently piloted the sleek silver beast. He was one of the few Afterlights to refuse to take a coin on the day Nick betrayed her. That had earned him a special place. A position of trust and responsibility.

"Look at that field." Speedo pointed it out. "Do you see all those deadspots?"

From the air it looked like a hundred random polka dots on the ground.

"There must have been a battle here once," Mary suggested. "Perhaps the Revolutionary War."

There was one Everlost tree, standing on its own deadspot. "The trap is in that tree," Speedo told her as they neared the ground.

It was a grand tree, its leaves full of rich reds and yellows, set apart from the greener summertime trees of the living world. For this tree it would always be the early days of fall, but the leaves would never drop from its branches. Mary wondered what had caused it to cross over. Perhaps lovers had carved their initials in it, and then it was struck by lightning. Perhaps it was planted in someone's memory, but was then cut down. Or maybe it simply soaked up the blood of a fallen soldier, and died years later in a drought. For whatever reason, the tree didn't die entirely. Instead it crossed into Everlost, like so many things that the universe saw fit to preserve.

The foliage of the tree was so dense, they couldn't see the trap, even after they had touched down.

"I'll go first," Mary said. "But I'd like you to come too. I'll need you to free our new friend from the net."

"Of course, Miss Mary." Speedo smiled a smile that was slightly too large for his face.

The ramp was lowered, and Mary stepped from the airship to the earth, keeping the grace of her stride even as her feet sank almost to her ankles in the living world with each step.

But as she got closer to the tree, she saw that something was terribly, terribly wrong. The net had been taken down, and there was no Afterlight inside. All that remained was the empty popcorn tub on the ground—the bait she had left, just as her brother used to—but while the McGill offered his captives slavery, Mary offered them freedom. Or at least her definition of it. But there was no Afterlight in the net to receive her gift today.

"Musta gotten out," Speedo said as he came up behind her.

Mary shook her head. "No one gets out of these nets."

And then a scent came to her from the tree. It was a sweet, heady aroma that filled her with a rich blend of love, swirled with loathing.

The aroma was coming from a brown handprint on the trunk of the tree. A handprint left there to mock her.

"Is that dried blood?" Speedo asked.

"No," she told him, maintaining her poise in spite of the fury that raged within her. "It's chocolate."